CAPTIVE
HEART

CAPTIVE SERIES BOOK THREE

paige press

CAPTIVE HEART

CAPTIVE SERIES BOOK THREE

STELLA GRAY

Paige Press
Leander, TX 78641

Ebook:
ISBN: 978-1-957647-40-1

Paperback:
ISBN: 978-1-957647-47-0

Editing: Erica Russikoff at Erica Edits
Proofing: Michele Ficht

ALSO BY STELLA GRAY

The Zoric Series

Arranged Series

The Deal

The Secret

The Choice

The Arranged Series: Books 1-3

Convenience Series

The Sham

The Contract

The Ruin

The Convenience Series: Books 1-3

Charade Series

The Lie

The Act

The Truth

The Charade Series: Books 1-3

ABOUT THIS BOOK

Nothing lasts forever... except the Bellanti's hatred for the Bruno family.

My family prepared me to fight.
My best friend taught me loyalty.
My husband showed me who I am.

And now I'm caught between them all.

The thing about secrets is that they always come out.
The past is never gone.
No one expected it to explode.

I finally understand why my life led me here.
I was the only one who could uncover the truth.
And I'm damn sure I'm the only one who can prevent a war.

Men have pushed me around my whole life.

But I was built for this... I am Mrs. Armani Bellanti.

CANDI

THE PHOTO OF LILIANA BELLANTI—AKA Juliana Guerra, aka my best friend—trembles in my hand. I'm still reeling. It feels like the floor just dropped out from under my feet.

Liliana didn't drown in a boating accident all those years ago. She's alive and well.

And she's been raised by...the Brunos. The Bellanti family's archenemies.

How the hell did this happen?

I had no idea that such an earth-shattering revelation would come to me when I showed up at my sister-in-law's house today to help her put together a christening scrapbook for her baby. But here we are. Our little crafting session has turned up quite a bit more than a dusty old box of Bellanti family photos.

Yet even as I'm shocked into a stupor, I realize that I can't go around making wild accusations without any proof. I can't let on that anything is amiss until I fit all the pieces together and make a legitimate case. I have to be absolutely certain, beyond a shadow of a doubt, that the Liliana Bellanti in this photo really is Juliana.

The very same woman who has spent her life plotting to get revenge on the Bellantis for killing her parents. The woman who's about to marry into the Russian *mob* to seal a Bratva-Bruno alliance that will enable the Brunos to take the Bellantis down for good. Juliana just might be working to annihilate her own flesh and blood, and she doesn't even know it. Does she?

"Candi, are you okay?"

"What?" I snap my gaze to Frankie.

"You're a million miles away," she says.

I force a sheepish smile. "Yeah, sorry. I totally zoned out for a second there."

Still in a daze, I set the photo back on the pile. That's when a wave of dizziness suddenly washes over me. Gripping the edge of the table, I press the back of my hand to my forehead and silently remind myself to keep my shit together.

"Let me get you some water," Frankie says, sliding her chair back.

"No! I mean, thank you, but I'm fine. I just...haven't been sleeping well lately."

It sounds weak even to my ears, but Frankie just eyes me with concern.

Is it possible I'm wrong about this? Maybe it's just a coincidence that Jules looks like Liliana. In fact, I don't even know when Juliana's parents were killed. Maybe she was eight or ten or twelve; older than the girl in this photo who allegedly died the same day as her mother.

Dammit, none of this makes sense. Dante admitted that Enzo Bellanti could have been responsible for the death of Juliana's parents, and Juliana says that the Bellantis killed her parents...but if Juliana was the Bellantis' sister, then... does that mean Enzo murdered his own wife and attempted to take out his daughter as well? Why would he do that? What could make him lash out at his own family so horribly?

One scenario instantly comes to mind. Did Enzo maybe suspect—or find out—that Juliana wasn't his biological child, and then order a hit on his allegedly adulterous wife and her daughter? It makes sense, but then...how did Juliana survive the boating accident? And how did she end up getting raised by the Brunos?

I need more information. I need to talk to Juliana. As soon as possible.

God, and I need to talk to Armani, too. But will he even take my suspicions seriously?

"I'm actually feeling a little nauseous," I tell Frankie, hoping it's enough of an excuse for my odd behavior. "Maybe that water is a good idea."

"Of course. Just sit tight. I'll be right back."

She quickly checks on Lili in the bassinet—still sleeping like a baby, of course—and then glides out of the room, returning moments later with a full carafe and two glasses, pouring a cup for each of us. I down half of mine in a rush and then lower the glass, slightly out of breath.

"Ah. Better already!" I say. "I just got dizzy."

Frankie just rolls her glass slowly between her hands, assessing me.

"Are you...sure you're not pregnant?" she asks. "I mean the nausea, the not sleeping..."

I nearly drop my water. "No! God, no. Ha. I'm fine now. Really. It was probably just low blood sugar or something."

She nods slowly, but she looks skeptical.

"We still have a long way to go on the scrapbook," I point out. "Let's do this."

Feeling more composed, I reach for the bin of stickers and notions and begin sorting through it with a smile plastered on my face. Inside, though? My stomach is churning, my mind racing. If my theory about Juliana/Liliana is correct, it'll blow up the Bellanti family's whole world. And what about Juliana? Will she still align herself with the Bruno clan? Or will she have a sudden change of heart? If I'm right about this, she'll be forced to reevaluate her entire identity. Her entire life. But that doesn't mean she'll automatically consider herself a Bellanti.

And who's to say the Bellantis would even welcome her back? She's been conspiring against them for years; working with their enemies to take the Bellanti empire down. Blood is supposed to be thicker than water, but maybe the Bellantis won't feel that way.

The only thing that's certain is that I have to investigate. And quickly. Right now, I'm the only one who knows about this, so I have to use that to my advantage while I still can.

"Are there any other pictures of their sister?" I ask as casually as possible.

Frankie sets down the length of lace she's cutting and rifles through the stack of old photos. "Only one. It's in here somewhere. Um...here."

She passes it over to me. In this one, each of the Bellanti children is reaching up to place an ornament on the Christmas tree. The girl's back is to the camera, but her face is turned to reveal her profile. Her nose and the tip of her chin are prominent, while the rest of her features are hidden by her thick tumble of hair. But it's enough. I don't need to see her entire face to recognize the slight upturn of her nose and the shape of her chin. It's Juliana all the way.

"These pictures are flooring me," I say sincerely. "Armani never talks about his past. This is probably the closest I'll get to catching a glimpse of his childhood."

"Yeah." Frankie sighs. "I just wish I could believe this was a happier time for them. And in a lot of ways, I'm sure it was. But I also see that perpetual frown on Armani's face, the way Dante's body language is always tense or protective. And Marco's always smiling or covered in mud, but who's to say how much their mother was able to shield them from their dad?"

I nod. "The few times Armani has mentioned his father, he's made it pretty obvious that they all had a really hard time growing up." Lowering my voice to a whisper, I add, "Who wouldn't, when your dad is a mafia boss?"

"Honestly," Frankie whispers back, "I think their dad's funeral was the first time those boys felt truly free."

Her words chill me. As rough as my own childhood was, I never worried that either of my parents would physically hurt me. Or that my dad's day job involved ordering executions. I didn't have to grow up surrounded by crime and armed men and violence and blood. My heart aches for Dante, Armani, and Marco. Their loss, their grief, their fear. All those lost years.

"I'm so glad they had each other," I murmur, my eyes tearing up.

"Me too," Frankie says, reaching across the table to give my hand a gentle pat.

As I put together a photo collage of the christening reception, the wheels in my head keep right on turning. Juliana is stubborn, strong-willed, and honestly dangerous. How am I supposed to tell her that I think she's the Bellantis' dead sister? That she's currently doing everything in her power to destroy *her own brothers*? It's not too much of a stretch to suggest that she doesn't know the full story of her family, but it's news that she will not receive well.

What if she doesn't believe me? I doubt her ego will let her accept the possibility that her uncle Sergio brainwashed her when she was young and impressionable and spent the rest of her formative years twisting her for his own gain. Hell, he still is. Right down to her impending marriage to that Russian mobster.

Oh God.

I need to speak to her. *Now*. But I also need to figure out exactly how I'm going to approach her with this. Because I know Juliana, and I know how quickly she freezes people out when she feels threatened, insulted, or misunderstood. I have to play my cards just right or else she'll kick me to the curb before I have the chance to explain everything I know.

The urgency of the situation makes me restless, but I don't have a plan of attack figured out yet. I'm also reluctant to cut the scrapbooking session short. Frankie had been so angry when she found out I was a spy for the Bruno family, and it killed our relationship. Once I declared my allegiance to the Bellantis, she'd finally started to thaw a little. And then today, she'd offered an olive branch by asking for my help with the baby's scrapbook. I'm desperate to stay on the right foot with her.

"What do you think? I didn't glue anything yet," I say, sliding the collage toward her.

"It's perfect. The courtyard was so pretty. And there are so many good candids in here of all the guests."

"Your sister did an amazing job decorating. As usual."

"She really did," Frankie agreed. "I'll start gluing this together."

I take a fresh piece of scrapbook paper and begin picking satin rosettes out of the notions box. As innocently as possible, I ask, "Did Dante ever tell you what happened to their sister?"

I've heard the story, but I'm hoping to learn something new that I can use when I approach Juliana.

Frankie shrugs. "He said she died in a boating accident. I'm not sure if he said it was a drowning or if I just assumed that part myself. I don't have the details, of course. I never pry."

"Right. Me neither. Armani's also barely said two words about it. Which, I get it. That kind of thing scars you forever. I wouldn't want to talk about it either."

But maybe the Bellanti brothers never got the full details. Why would they? They were kids when it happened. And it's unlikely their father would have filled them in on the horrible details of their mother and sister's deaths.

Baby Lili begins to fuss in her bassinet. Frankie leans over and picks her up, gently lays her against her shoulder and begins to pat her on the back. I watch the tender moment and smile when I catch Frankie's eye.

"I need to feed her. Maybe we should call it? We got a lot done so far, but we can finish up another time."

"Yes, of course. This was so fun," I gush. "Thank you for inviting me."

"Oh gosh, thank *you*. I couldn't have done this without your help," she insists.

Frankie shifts the baby as she begins to cry. Standing, I begin to gather the photographs and crafting papers.

"You go ahead and I'll clean this up. I'll just leave everything in a neat little pile."

Frankie's eyes light up with gratitude. "That would be great. And I'm really glad we did this. I've—missed having you around."

I nod, but I don't respond because the lump in my throat prevents words from forming.

Once they're gone, I stare down at the scattered photographs again. I know I shouldn't do it, but when I spy the picture of Liliana Bellanti standing with Armani, Dante, and Marco by the Christmas tree, I slide it into my back pocket.

Frankie will notice, of course. Eventually. And I'll have to admit what I did, explain why I took it...and I will. But first, I need to dig into this with both hands.

I think about Armani again as I head outside and text Donovan for a ride back to the Bellanti estate. I know I need to bring this information to my husband soon, but I'm not sure that he can be objective right now. The Bellantis are hard at work pulling together a plan to prevent Juliana's wedding, and they've all got more than enough on their plates at the moment. Suggesting that Juliana is their sister might push Armani over the edge.

But if I'm right...if Juliana truly is a link in the broken chain of this family...how can I prevent her from destroying her own brothers?

2

ARMANI

I HATE POKER.

And yet here I am, once again, playing it with my associates. I just can't escape it.

Why the disdain? Because it's a vile game that requires little cunning and no skill to win. Luck of the draw and knowing how to keep your mouth shut and your expression blank are the only components needed to walk away with someone else's cash. Obviously, I'm good at it. But personally, I'd much rather immerse myself in a game of chess with a worthy opponent.

Unfortunately, that's literally not on the table tonight. The men I've come to see are elbow deep in their cards with the spoils creating a volcano of coins, bills, a watch, and other assorted valuables heaped on the table between them. The sight brings me right back to my childhood, walking in on my father and his colleagues playing the same game, Dad sending me on errands so he didn't have to leave the table. The man loved poker.

No wonder I despise it.

Antonio Bakka is expecting me, and he nods in curt greeting as I enter the private card room in the basement of the Andaz Napa hotel. The five other players turn hastily to look at me, likely to ascertain if the newcomer is friend or foe. But they all know me, and they know I'm not a threat... unless I have to be.

Bakka gestures for me to pull up a chair. The deep scar running down his cheek and temple almost looks purple in the overhead lights. I give each of the other men a nod in turn.

Every one of them was on the yacht during my honeymoon trip with Candi, save for one. I recognize him as one of the Colosimos, who I consider more or less trustworthy since the family basically acts as an extended branch of the Bakkas. Besides Colosimo and Bakka, it's Clio Romo, the Marzello brothers, and Nicolo Riggante.

I know that this is more than just a card game we're playing here. Everything I'm about to say and do during this meeting counts. These men and I had discussed stopping the Bruno-Bratva alliance on the yacht, but now it's time to take action.

A cocktail waitress arrives to freshen everyone's drinks, and I order a top shelf whiskey. Then I settle into my chair. Cards are set face down in front of me as I'm dealt into the game.

"It's 500 bucks to get in," Bakka says.

Unblinking, I pull out a thousand in one-hundred-dollar bills and throw them into the pile. No one raises a brow, and the game continues.

I play a hand. Lose. Hold back my irritation at how long it's taking for the cocktail waitress to bring me my damn drink. She finally does, and I toss it back in one hard swallow, then hand the glass back and indicate that I want another.

"Are you sure that's all you want?" Bakka asks suggestively, making a show of eyeing the waitress's ass cheeks that spill out the bottom of her black spandex shorts.

"I'm not here for a fuck." I pull a card.

He scoffs and low laughter comes around from the table.

"That wife of yours must be keeping you on a short leash."

I don't respond. He can bait me all he wants, but he won't get a rise out of me.

"The offer I made at the island still stands, Bellanti," he says. "I'm happy to take her off your hands when you're ready. She'll learn her place with me. Who knows? Maybe I'll gift her back to you after I've trained her up right."

Without a single hint of emotion in my voice, I reply, "I'm here to talk business. My wife isn't part of the deal."

Slamming my gaze into his, I hold it for a length of time that becomes uncomfortable for everyone but me. I can see the sweat beading on Bakka's balding scalp. Colosimo nudges him to take his turn and only then does Bakka look away from me.

"To what do we owe the pleasure of your company today, Armani?" he says as he calls.

"I'm here on business. Some new information about our mutual enemy has come to light," I tell him, glancing around at the rest of the men to be sure they're all taking this in. "Turns out Sergio Bruno is marrying off one of his own to the Bratva to seal their alliance."

That gets their attention. The game stops as a stalled hush claims the room.

"Where did this information come from?"

Incidentally, my wife, I think, but I don't want to bring her into this.

"A reliable source close to my family who knows the bride. The wedding is happening in a few weeks."

Pausing, I let that sink in before I move on to my request.

"Let me get to the point. This wedding cannot happen. So. How much to enlist your collective resources to come together and stop it?"

The cocktail waitress reappears with another round for the table before anyone can reply. They're all looking at their cards as if they didn't hear my question, save for Bakka, who entertains himself by squeezing the server's ass. Taking his time, he fondles her while she stands there obediently until he finally gives her a pat and sends her on her way.

"This is quite the...exceptional request, Armani," he says carefully, nodding at my cards.

It's my play. Considering my move, I pick a card and drag it out just for the hell of it. I could be strategic, but this game is an insult to my brain, so I don't bother.

"I entertained you on my yacht. Fed you very well. Provided you with all the Bellanti Vineyards wine you could drink as well as a generous quantity of exquisite scotch and some very, very attractive company with whom to enjoy it," I remind him.

He inclines his head, waiting for me to go on.

"You accepted my hospitality and agreed that we had to

14

stop the Bratva at all costs when I laid it all out for you," I continue, addressing the entire table. "We discussed how it would affect *all of us* if Sergio Bruno makes this alliance, so let's quit fucking around. It's time to act."

Dead silence falls.

"No groom, no wedding." Nicolo Riggante tosses out the words casually as he rearranges his cards.

He's the oldest one here by a few decades, and even though Bakka acts like he's the alpha dog, there's no question that Riggante has the most experience and the most seniority. Not to mention the most notoriety—this guy's one of the OGs. He's not a man to be crossed.

"Seems to me that's the easiest solution to our problem," Riggante adds. "One and done."

I subtly arch a brow at his use of "our" which indicates he considers the Bratva a mutual issue. Excellent. It's just what I was hoping for. Riggante is the man the rest of these mafiosos will take their cue from, even if they play lip service to Bakka.

"What do you have in mind?" I ask. "It needs to look like an accident. Or a frame job that would have to be flawless, maybe a robbery gone wrong or—"

"Whoa, whoa, whoa. Slow down. Let's discuss terms first," Bakka cuts in.

I've considered what the price will be for their help. It will be high, of course, and likely something that I don't want to give. But well-to-do mob families rarely ask for money in exchange for manpower. It's always much more personal than that.

Riggante outlines what he's asking for. Then Romo. The others chime in along the way. Clenching my jaw, I force myself to relax my shoulders and keep the tension off my face. Bakka is the last to name his price, and I know before he speaks that it will involve Candi. He became infatuated with her on the yacht, and despite the array of women at his disposal, he continues to focus on her.

Making eye contact with him, I hold up a hand to stop whatever he's about to say.

"As I said, my wife is not part of this deal. Before you ask, the answer is no, and it will always be no."

A smirk slowly spreads across his face and crinkles the corners of his beady eyes, making them even smaller.

"Then I'm afraid I have nothing to offer you," he says.

Addressing the table, I ask, "Would any of you hand over your women to this man? Wives, daughters, sisters?"

Riggante flicks a finger toward Bakka. "Forget about it. You don't need him."

"You do need me," Bakka retorts. "The amount of manpower I have is too valuable to walk away from."

I catch the threat in his tone. So does everyone else.

"Are you implying you might offer your assistance elsewhere?" Riggante asks, setting his cards down coolly and shifting his hard gaze to Bakka.

Bakka immediately shrinks back. "I didn't say that."

"Then kindly offer your assistance to the Bellantis without chasing Armani's goddamn wife. Show some honor," Riggante says harshly.

Everyone watches Bakka, the pressure of their scrutiny making him sweat even more. Finally, he throws down his cards and gestures wildly to them with his hands.

"Are we playing or not?" he says.

The game resumes for an agonizingly long time before someone finally speaks.

"Do we know where the Russian likes to hang out?"

"I have eyes on him. Orloff is being monitored 24/7," I say.

Somehow, amazingly, Clayton got a bug inside Orloff's SUV. It was a crapshoot considering the Russian has three vehicles he likes to rotate, but the black Cadillac seemed to be his favorite. We reviewed the audio this afternoon and hit paydirt when Orloff discussed his schedule with someone on the phone.

"We got tabs on his movements over the next few days?" Romo asks.

"I'll do you one better," I tell him. "The Brunos own a few bakeries, one of which is located in downtown Napa. He'll be there with his fiancée at noon tomorrow."

Colosimo nods. "I know the place. Tomorrow at noon, though? That's a pretty narrow timeline to work with."

"The sooner the better," one of the Marzellos says. "I say we burn the place to the ground."

"And make sure he's incapacitated before the fire starts," his brother adds.

We discuss the finer details. A sniper will take out Orloff as strategically placed incendiaries ignite and light the place up. Since the plan is to ignite and not explode, the bride-to-be—Candi's friend—should have time to escape the burning building before it becomes an inferno. I've surveyed the place myself. It's old—historical and charming, but not up to code. The wood is dry and untreated, essentially creating a tinderbox for a stray flame. It will go up quickly, but if Orloff's woman is smart, she'll bail at the first scent of smoke.

If not, well, consider her a casualty of war. A sacrifice for the greater good. She's been working with the Brunos, so she knows what she's in for should things go south. Just like my wife did when she decided to work for Sergio.

Rationally, I know I'm right, but it doesn't stop the small pang in my gut when I think about how Candi will feel if her friend is killed.

The hand we're playing ends. I lost—hard. Not surprising. My head's not in the game.

Taking out another thousand, I toss it onto the pile. A new game begins.

Riggante takes out his cell phone, dials, and lights up a cigar. He talks around the fat Cuban, giving orders to one of his men to acquire, transport, and plant the incendiaries.

I'd like to be there and keep an eye on things myself, but that would be foolish. Of course, Bruno will know my family had a hand in the job regardless of how careful we are, but the bulk of this thing will bear someone else's stamp. He'll know that I didn't act alone, that I'm united with other families.

Ending the call, Riggante tosses his cards onto the table. They scatter and flip, some falling onto the floor. "Armani, gentlemen. I have work to attend to. Please excuse me."

One by one, the other men get up, too. They all have work to do. Soldiers to prepare, logistics to discuss, and other devious shit to plan to ensure that Maxim Orloff doesn't make it out of that bakery alive.

Alone with Bakka, I finish my drink and glance at my hand. He lays down his cards. I've trumped him and the pile of cash on the table, including my own bills, are mine. Gathering up the money, I work the bills into a neat stack. Then I slide the winnings to my counterpart. His eyes flash with greed and interest.

"What's this about? You won."

"A peace offering," I say. "Winnings between friends."

He takes the money. And smirks, which has become his default when interacting directly with me. Standing, Bakka stuffs the cash in the inside pocket of his jacket.

"Long-term relationships are often tested," he says. "Let's hope ours withstands the storm."

"Indeed," I say.

Lighting a cigarette, he walks out, leaving me alone. His passive threat means nothing to me. I only hope that he makes good on his part of this plan.

Taking my jacket from the back of the chair, I slip into it and spot something on the chair where Bakka had been sitting.

Three one-hundred-dollar bills, messy and crumpled, left behind.

He may have left a peace offering for me, too.

But I still don't trust him.

3

CANDI

Don't forget *it's cake tasting day! See you at noon,* the text from Juliana reads. *Oh, and wear something stretchy in the waist. We're going to have a LOT of options, lol.*

Then she sends me the address for the bakery—it's the same Bruno-owned bakery responsible for my and Armani's wedding cake fiasco, except this location isn't in Santa Rosa. It's right here in downtown Napa, a cute place with a store-front café that's open to the public, which the other location isn't. I'm glad it's a short drive, otherwise I'd probably talk myself out of meeting her before I even got there.

Chewing my thumbnail, I reread Juliana's messages and wait to see if she sends anything else. She doesn't.

Can't wait! I type back.

My stomach is in knots. The last time we spoke, we got in a huge fight over my refusal to hand over the names of the "associates" that Armani met with on the yacht during our honeymoon. Now, Jules is acting like our argument never even happened.

This isn't unusual behavior for her—deciding when or if

to forgive someone she believes has crossed her without any kind of discussion or input from the other person—but it's going to be hard to play along like everything's fine this time.

How am I supposed to pretend I'm having fun sampling options for her wedding cake when I know full well that my husband's family is actively plotting to sabotage that wedding? I'm not exactly a great actress. But there's no way I can beg off. I'm the matron of honor.

I just hope to God Juliana doesn't turn this tasting into a full-on interrogation. I've got an interrogation of my own to conduct.

Realizing that the morning has gotten away from me, I hurry to get ready. Dress, strappy sandals, minimal makeup, a braid in my hair. I'm going for an understated look; the last thing I want to do is upstage the bride-to-be. After I call Donovan to get my car brought up to the house from the main garage, I give Mr. Sprinkles a quick snuggle for good luck. Then I set him back on his favorite perch on the cat tree and head out.

My pulse is pounding with adrenaline as I slide into the driver's seat and buckle in. I plug the bakery address into my map app and send Juliana a quick text.

On my way. See you soon.

This is it. No turning back.

The whole drive over, all I can think about are the various ways things could go sideways with the Bellantis' secret plan to sabotage Juliana's wedding. And what if the plan fails, and the wedding does go on as planned? Juliana will have married into the Russian mob, unifying the Bruno clan and the Bratva. Effectively creating a villainous superpower that will threaten not only the Bellantis, but who knows how many other families? With the Bratva in his corner, Sergio Bruno will be free to act with impunity. Even the old guard Brunos over in Italy won't be able to keep him in check anymore.

I wish I could talk to Armani about all of this. I still don't know what he's plotting with his brothers. In fact, I don't even know where he is right now. He left yesterday to go meet up with some associates—a term I'm getting all too sick of hearing—and hasn't been home since.

The only thing keeping me from having a full-blown meltdown about his safety is the fact that he took a stealth security detail with him. I have to believe they're keeping him alive. That, and every time I've texted to ask when he'll be back, he responds with, "soon."

As I exit off the freeway, my insides are a mess. I was hoping the drive would calm me down a little, but fresh waves of nausea and heartburn wash over me in turns while I look for a parking spot. Hopefully I won't hurl all over the wedding cakes. That would definitely put a damper on my fact-finding mission.

The second I park the car, I take a deep breath. I need to focus. Part of me wants nothing more than to drive straight back to the Bellantis' and hide, but if I do that, Juliana will probably never speak to me again—no matter how good my excuse is—and I'll lose my chance to find out if she really is who I think she is.

The old photo of young Liliana is tucked away in my handbag. I study it again and then slip it into my hip pocket in between my phone and my credit card. I'm not sure I should have even brought it, but I figured it might help

23

convince Juliana that there's a chance she's the Bellantis' sister. Otherwise she might just dismiss me out of hand. Supposing our discussion even reaches the point where I reveal my suspicions out loud. I may not even get that far.

After I swipe my Visa at the parking meter, I head down the street to the bakery. As I approach, I can see Juliana through the large front windows, animatedly chatting with someone.

"Candi!" she squeals when I walk through the door, waving me over.

"Hello," I say, addressing Juliana and the older woman in an apron standing with her.

"This is my matron of honor, Candi," Jules says, introducing me to the woman, "and Candi, this is Regina. She and her husband own the bakery, but she does most of the dirty work."

"*Buongiorno*," Regina says.

"*Buongiorno*. So nice to meet you," I say as Juliana wraps me in a side hug, which is actually a whole lot of physical affection from her.

My body is so tense that I know she must be able to feel it, but she doesn't let on. Her lacy black designer dress fits her perfectly and she's glowing with genuine happiness.

Wait a second. Is it possible that she...has genuine feelings for this guy?

I hadn't considered it before—she'd framed it as nothing more than a marriage of convenience. But now I'm starting to wonder...

Suddenly, I take notice of the three bulky men in black suits and sunglasses who are standing around watching us. Bruno bodyguards, no doubt. One of them nods at me, and I nod back, trying to pretend that they don't make me nervous.

"Maxim's running late, so we're going to just go ahead and get started without him," Juliana says once Regina excuses herself.

My blood runs cold. "Maxim?"

"You know, Maxim? My fiancé?" Juliana says with a laugh.

"Right, I know, I just...you didn't mention he was going to be here today."

"He said he wanted to approve my final decision," Juliana says with a shrug. "But don't worry, the tasting is still on us. And there's no way I won't get what I want."

She gives me a smug little smile and I try to smile back, but my heart is pounding in my chest. This isn't exactly a welcome surprise. I wasn't prepared to meet a Russian mobster today.

Linking her arm through mine, Juliana leads me over to a long table in the corner that has been set with a linen tablecloth, carafes of coffee and water, and a variety of cake slices. Each one is accompanied by a card stating the flavors, and there's another card for Juliana to use to mark down her favorites.

I ease into a chair and pour cups of coffee for Juliana and myself. She's inspecting the samples that have been set out for us, her eyes narrowed judgmentally.

"Here, let's try this one first. It's lemon cake with lavender frosting."

Gross. Jules slides the slice over to me and I make a face at the gray-purple frosting dotted with dried lavender buds.

"Go on," she says.

I take a minuscule bite, but it's not to her satisfaction.

"Oh come on! You can't actually taste it like that."

"I'm not really fond of food that tastes like bath salts."

She laughs, pushing the plate away. "Me neither. Maybe I'll just skip this one."

"You wench!"

"Sorry! Don't want to traumatize my taste buds. You can pick the next slice," she offers.

We move on to a red velvet with bourbon cream cheese frosting next, a cake that's pure vanilla inside and out, and then an amazing chocolate with mocha caramel layers and dark chocolate ganache on top. Even though we're taking small bites, I'm feeling very sugared-out by the time we reach the middle of the table. And sipping coffee only makes my jitters worse.

She writes on her card. "Maybe *this* chocolate cake but with *that* bourbon frosting, oh, and a sprinkle of toasted brown sugar on top for extra caramelization!"

"I like it," I say. "Very non-traditional."

"Not everybody likes boring white cake with butter-cream," she says with a shrug. "Besides, I think something dark on the inside suits me."

Honestly, I can't argue that.

We continue down the table. Juliana hums as she samples a raspberry crème cake, scribbling on her card thoughtfully.

"Maybe chocolate and raspberry?" she murmurs. "But do bourbon and raspberry jive?"

"Gosh, I wish I'd been able to plan a wedding like this," I say quietly, finally feeling at ease enough to delve into my questioning. "It sounds so dumb now, but I used to daydream about you and my mom doing all the planning stuff with me."

Her brows draw together. "Seriously? Your mother is an asshole."

"I know. I guess I just always held out hope she'd... change. Eventually."

"You poor thing," Juliana says with a sigh.

I nod sadly, hoping I've planted a seed and opened the door a little. The truth is, I never gave much thought to getting married at all. But I've got to get Jules talking about her mom. And fast. Before Maxim Orloff arrives.

She moves to the next piece of cake, pokes at it, then glances at me.

"I hear you with the mom thing, you know. Every little girl probably has that bridal magazine fantasy at some point. With their mother and all their best friends in tow for every little thing along the way. The dress fitting, the bachelorette party, all of it. But that's not reality."

Silence. More cake. Then I push a little. "I mean, my mom is around and I'm not even sure she would have done any of the wedding stuff with me if I hadn't eloped. Maybe she would've. But you—losing your mom in an accident like that—it's different."

Her head snaps toward me. "Who said it was an accident?"

My hairline tingles. "Oh. I don't know. I guess I always just...assumed."

"She was murdered, Candi. *Murdered.* I've told you that. It wasn't an accident." Her voice goes tense. "And you know exactly who's responsible."

Shit. "I'm sorry. I shouldn't have brought it up."

But why is she *so sure* it was the Bellantis? And how can I ask without pissing her off?

"It's fine."

I bite my lip. I know I've riled her up, but I'm not done yet. "Do you...remember her?"

Bracing myself for another scathing reply, I'm relieved when she looks into the distance for a moment and the barest of smiles lifts her mouth.

"A little. I remember a birthday where my cake had these...sparklers on it, and decorating the tree at Christmas, riding a carousel somewhere. The 'Hallmark moments,' I guess," she says sardonically. "But nothing specific about her. It's like trying to remember a dream after you wake up. I *really* wish I could remember her face, but I was so young when she died..."

The photo is in my purse. Should I show her now, or try to draw her out some more? And if she sees it, will she even recognize herself?

"*Juliana.*"

A deep male voice echoes through the room, and my heart jumps into my throat. Turning in my chair, I do a double take at the dark, very well dressed, very imposing man coming toward us from the behind the bakery counter. He must have come in the back door.

Wearing all black, his scowl is as dark as his hair. Beneath heavy brows, his piercing blue eyes assess me with efficiency before landing on Juliana. His jawline is even more incredible than the photo Jules showed me, I can't help but notice.

This is the man she's about to marry? He's going to kill her. He's going to—

His hand is outstretched to me, and I have no choice but to take it, my face flaming.

"Candi. Nice to finally meet you." The words drip with a heavy Russian accent.

He slides his hand down Juliana's back, taking extra time to smooth his palm over her spine before it settles on the rise above her ass. She grins like they're being naughty, and it strikes me how easily she settles into him.

"Did you find one you like?" he asks, nodding at the demolished cake slices.

Juliana tilts her head. "I'm not sure yet. Candi? Which is your favorite so far?"

My brain isn't working properly. "The...the lavender. Delish."

Juliana draws back, looking at me like I'm nuts. "I thought—"

"I need to borrow you to the back," Orloff interrupts.

He doesn't wait for her to agree or not as he pulls out her chair, takes her hand, and tugs her along with him. She looks over her shoulder and gives me a little wave.

"Be right back. Keep on tasting."

Two of the three guards go with them, leaving one here with me.

So far, my fact-finding mission has been a failure. I didn't find out much about Juliana's childhood or her memories of her mother, nor what actually happened to her parents. I *did* confirm that she was young when they died—young enough to not remember them well—but that's about it. Thus, Plan B must be enacted, whereby I ply her with enough alcohol to get her talking without putting up all her walls. Should I propose a girls' night out?

Just then, a loud *click* goes through the room. The guard instantly goes tense and looks around to locate the source of the sound. That's when the light coming in from the large front window suddenly blacks out.

I do a double take, hardly believing what I'm seeing as something big and dark—fabric?—shifts over the window. More clicking. What the fuck?

The guard grabs the door handle, but it doesn't budge.

Loud, angry voices sound from the back of the bakery.

Heart pounding, I ask, "What's going on?" though I know I won't get an answer.

The door and window are barricaded. We're trapped inside.

I press a hand to my chest and go completely still as my senses detect something new.

Something dangerous.

The scent of wispy, acrid smoke.

4

ARMANI

I HAVE a bad feeling in my gut.

Considering how often things don't go to plan, it's no surprise that I'm uneasy about the takedown planned for the Bruno bakery. Particularly since I have far less control of the operation than usual. It's not my standard MO, of course, but because I approached my associates for help, setting aside my ego and letting them run point was necessary. Otherwise, I'd never let someone else run the show.

The whole drive back home from my meeting this morning with Nicolo Riggante, I try to convince myself to sit back and enjoy not having to be front and center for once. All I have to do is wait for the phone call that tells me it's done. Nothing could be easier.

And yet. This nervous energy just won't leave me. I've been on edge all day.

I haven't spoken to Candi about what's going to happen because I can't risk having her tipping off the Brunos by trying to warn her friend. It's no skin off my back if this Bruno "niece" gets hurt in the crossfire—it would serve her right for linking herself to the Bratva—but I know it will devastate my wife if something terrible happens to her best friend.

There's nothing I can do. I can't very well let Candi in on the plan. But...I suppose I could encourage her to inadvertently protect the woman by taking her out for lunch this afternoon. Or shopping. Or whatever it is that women do when they meet up. It's the closest I can get to telling Candi that Juliana is in danger without compromising the entire operation.

Frustrated with myself for not working this out earlier, I speed the rest of the way home and then burst into the house like the devil himself is chasing me. A few concerned security guards call after me as I take the stairs two at a time to the bedroom to find my wife.

"Everything's fine!" I shout over my shoulder.

Our room is empty. I call her cell and then her office number, but she doesn't pick up. She's not in any of her usual spots inside the house, either. The disconcerting feeling I've had all morning grows stronger. Where the hell is my wife?

I text her and stare at my phone, waiting for an immediate response. Then I call her again. When she doesn't pick up, I dial the office line of Bellanti security.

"Morelli," a voice answers.

"Tony. It's Armani. Did my wife leave the property this morning?"

He pauses. "Her vehicle was brought around to the main house just over an hour ago. She said she didn't want a driver."

My head starts to pound. "Where did she go?" I grind out.

There's another slight pause. "Donovan didn't question her, sir. You...haven't given new orders that she should be tracked again."

"Fuck."

He's right. Since giving Candi a little bit of freedom, I dissolved the order that security should monitor her at all times. Maybe it was a mistake to allow her to drive herself around. The saving grace is the tracking device hidden in the undercarriage of her vehicle. All Bellanti vehicles have them as a safety precaution.

Keeping security on the line, I open the tracking app on my phone. It's not perfect but the GPS can pinpoint a vehicle's location within a ten-meter radius. That's just over thirty feet. I find the device transmitting from Candi's sedan and all the breath goes out of me.

"Jesus Christ," I rasp. "I need eyes on everyone who's inside today's target."

"Today's target, sir?"

Then I remember that I don't have any of my men assigned to today's mission. They don't know anything about it.

"Fuck. Never mind." I hang up.

Riggante was adamant that he had everything under control. He'd said he didn't want any of my men involved, to keep them from being recognized by any of Bruno's security. I'd pushed to have at least two of my men in the wings, but he'd been firm, and I knew I wasn't in the position to argue with Riggante.

But my wife's location shows her car parked within thirty feet of the goddamn bakery.

She's there. Right fucking now.

I have no doubt that she's there with Juliana, probably ordering a cake for the upcoming wedding. Candi is the maid of honor, so of course she's there, playing along. She would have known it'd look bad if she suddenly opted out of helping her best friend plan her nuptials.

Once again, our epic lack of communication has tossed her right into the viper's pit.

I need to know if she's stepped foot inside that bakery yet.

Before I can call security back, my phone rings in my hand.

"What?"

"It's Morelli, sir. Rico's got eyes on the bakery. You sounded worried so I had him check. Your wife is inside with another woman...and apparently Maxim Orloff just arrived."

The hair on the back of my neck rises.

"How would you like us to proceed?" he asks.

"I'll handle it myself," I growl.

I can't have my men rushing in to save Candi and thwarting the entire operation. The other families would be irate, and I would lose their support going forward.

"And for the love of God, keep your man out of sight," I add, hanging up.

Dialing Riggante as fast as I can, I pace the length of the room as the phone rings and rings. He'd better answer or I'm going to put a stop to the operation myself.

I'm about to throw my phone against the wall when he finally answers.

"Riggante! You have to stop the mission. Call it off. My wife is inside."

He makes a smacking sound with his mouth as if to say, that's too bad. "Impossible, my friend. The package has already been delivered. I am truly sorry."

"The package? What the—Riggante!"

The line goes dead.

"Fuck!"

I can't let her die. My heart races as I bolt down the stairs, out the door, and into my black SUV. I throw the vehicle in reverse, kicking up gravel as I slam it to a stop and shift to drive. Then I speed down the driveway.

There's no time to lose.

I pull onto the main road, tires screeching as I take the corner too fast. The SUV fishtails before I get control of it and race to the highway. The reassuring weights of the guns strapped to my shoulder and hip calm me as I drive. I'm going to get my wife out of there. Alive.

Confidence has never been my problem. I am extremely secure in my ability to fight, strategize, and implement a deadly strike. Second-guessing myself is never an option. But this time, I don't have a plan. Bruno's men will shoot me if I'm spotted within ten feet of that building, and with Orloff inside, security is probably even higher than usual. I'm not sure how Riggante's men planted the incendiary devices without being noticed, but he said they'd been "delivered," and that means the fire could have already started by now.

Fuck, fuck, fuck.

I feel it, the lack of time. Every passing second ticking down to zero hour. What if I don't make it?

This mission was supposed to go off without a hitch, without my involvement. I'm supposed to be sitting back, waiting to hear that Orloff is dead. Instead I'm speeding down the freeway ready to blow the entire mission if it means getting my wife out alive.

My body is taut as a wire with adrenaline by the time I reach downtown. Parking in the rear alley that leads behind the bakery, I grab a pair of thick leather gloves from the glovebox and pull them on. Then I jam a ball cap on my head and throw on a pair of sunglasses. It'll have to do. Moving stealthily from my car, I creep along the back side of the building to reduce my chance of being seen, navigating toward the bakery.

Surveying my surroundings as I get closer, I catch the side profile of a man in black perched on top of a building to my left. Adjusting my line of sight, I find two more men, both of them holding machine guns aimed at the bakery's back door. These must be Riggante's guys. The first man probably has the detonation device. Problem is, they won't know which side I'm on if they see me. My chance of getting shot is high. New plan.

Detouring around the cinderblock dumpster enclosure between me and the bakery, I'm just coming around the corner when a blast shakes the ground beneath my feet.

"No!"

I'm too late.

The moderately quiet street suddenly becomes a flurry of activity. Gunshots sound from the rooftops. Shielding my face with my arms, I peer around the side of the building to see the bakery engulfed in flame, black smoke billowing from the ventilation ducts on the roof, blanketing the atmosphere around the street. I hear car tires skidding, horns honking, people screaming. And then a row of gunfire belts the air behind the bakery.

I can't see if there are any more gunmen. I can barely see anything in front of me as I race to the side of the bakery. Cutting through the smoke, I find a small window that has been blown out. Shards of glass dig into my leather gloves as I grip the pane and break them away so I can climb over and through without gutting myself.

Managing to land on my feet, I cover my nose and mouth with the collar of my jacket, hold my gun close and steady with my right hand, and get my bearings.

It's an odd mix of silence interspersed with bursts of frantic voices, but I can't tell where they are coming from. Men are shouting. In Russian. And a bit of Italian that I recognize.

"He's dead. Leave him! Leave him!"

The back of my neck prickles at a feminine tone—high pitched, shaking, familiar—seemingly close. Shuffling through the smoke, I use my free hand to feel my way through. A sweet scent catches my nose through the acrid air and my heart jolts.

She's close.

"Juliana!"

Candi's voice is small and husky. She coughs painfully and calls again for her friend, but there isn't another female response. The male voices sound farther away now, too.

Someone yells, and that's when I spy the flames above me. They appear in a rolling wave, slinking insidiously across the ceiling like a living, breathing animal. Muted booms sound from far away. More gunfire. Riggante's men are picking off Brunos as they exit the building.

Is Orloff dead?

The thought is fleeting as I follow the scent of Candi's perfume. The trail dies as flames begin to lick at every available surface.

"Candi!" My voice chokes. "Where are you?"

Something touches my leg. Aiming my gun, I rear back at the small, pale hand reaching toward me through the melee. Her wedding ring glints red and orange as her fingers close around mine. Pulling her up, I try to look her over, but my eyes are burning and it's too smoky to see.

"Are you okay?"

It takes her a second to answer. I'm already half carrying, half pulling her back the way that I came.

"I don't know."

"Can you walk?" I ask.

She coughs again, her entire body shaking with the force of it. Fuck! She's already taken in too much smoke. Picking her up, I navigate to the side window. Heat scorches my face. My eyebrows tug as if they're curling from the heat, but I don't stop.

"I'm putting you through this window feet first. You're going to have to land on your feet. Candi?"

She's coughing too hard. She'll never make the drop.

Fuck.

But a broken leg is worth her life.

Flames rush toward the window, sucking the oxygen and growing fatter as I slide an old chair over to the window and, praying it holds, stand on it with her limp body in my arms.

"Candi. You have to go through. Okay?"

The inside of my throat is drying out and I can barely drum up enough saliva to speak. My words come out in broken, dehydrated bursts. She helps a little as I get her feet through. There's just enough clearance for her to sit on the ledge, and then she jumps. Bracing myself for her scream of pain, I wonder that it doesn't come and slide out after her.

Sweet, cool air hits my face and I drink it up in hungry, greedy gulps.

Beside me, Candi is crumpled against the brick wall, coughing onto the ground. She spits up blood and my stomach bottoms out. Quickly checking her body, I feel her legs for any sign that she's broken them. She doesn't wince or pull away from my touch and I don't feel anything out of place. A good sign.

"Where's...Juliana?" she rasps.

The heat radiating from the building is growing too severe. I can't go back in there.

Gently scooping her up again, I hurry as fast as I can behind the cinderblock enclosure I used as a shield before.

"Juliana," she chokes out haltingly, tears streaming down her soot-streaked face. "Did she...get out?"

"I don't know," I tell her.

She puts her head to my shoulder and sobs.

5

ARMANI

IF THE NURSE tells me to leave the room one more time, I'm going to do something he'll regret.

Candi has barely moved since I rushed her to the emergency room. She coughed the entire way to the hospital, and her lips were a terrifying combination of sooty black and low-oxygen blue by the time we arrived. It looked like somebody had smacked her in the mouth.

She responded to me on the drive over, but she was listless and slow about it, as if she didn't have the strength to speak. Part of me worried she might stop breathing. But there was no time to wait for an ambulance, and I couldn't risk getting spotted by the Brunos or the Bratva at the scene. As far as I know, neither outfit was aware that I had shown up at the bakery fire.

Finding Candi inside that burning building was a ridiculous stroke of good luck. If I had been a few minutes later...but no. There's no sense in dwelling on it. I made it to her in time and got her here right away. Everything is going to be okay. It has to be.

I've been in this all-too-familiar place before. Standing in a hospital room, listening to the monitors beep, not knowing what the numbers flashing across their screens mean. But this time is different.

Candi dozes as an IV line drips hydration into her veins. She'd had a cannula in her nose initially, but the doctor said her blood oxygen levels are looking better and took her off it. She's breathing well on her own now, and the nurse just informed me that Candi's lungs sound good. They're keeping her here longer for observation, simply because they don't know how much smoke she inhaled. We're now into the early morning hours and I'm as restless as ever.

I texted Riggante a few times to inquire if our target was erased. The last I heard from him, he couldn't confirm. A few of Bruno's men had died in the explosion, but Orloff's body hasn't been found. With police and firefighters still swarming the scene of the crime, the status of the man we care the most about is yet to be determined. Will they find what remains of him in the charred wreckage of the bakery, or did Orloff escape? Only time will tell.

My brothers and their wives are on standby back at home, but I told them not to come to the hospital. I don't have the heart to face them just yet. First, I want a concrete answer on whether Maxim Orloff is alive or dead.

I stop my pacing and drop into the chair by the bed, studying Candi's prone form. I don't like seeing her this way, but I can't pinpoint exactly why it bothers me so much. It wasn't long ago that I had no problem sacrificing her for the greater good. Not having her best interest at heart was a price to be paid if it meant getting information that I needed from her.

But something changed along the way.

Dante and Marco must be rubbing off on me. Thanks to their wives, they've become malleable, but I can't afford to do the same. I don't have the luxury of going soft when every single person in this family relies on me to keep them safe. I need to pull myself together.

Candi's face is peaceful as she sleeps. The nurses helped her with a bath earlier so she could clean the soot from her skin. Without her hair and makeup done, she looks younger and more innocent somehow. The urge to protect her at all costs is overwhelming. How is it possible to see someone in such a different light simply because they're lying in a hospital bed?

Anxious, restless, and needing something to do, I take the water pitcher from her bedside table and go down the hall to the ice maker, fill it, then return to the room and fill it with filtered water. I wonder if I should wake her up and—

"Did you fill that up for me?"

I startle at the unfamiliar sound of her gruff, scratchy voice. She doesn't open her eyes as she tilts her head toward me. Licking her lips, Candi presses her fingers to her temple and then her throat as if checking herself over for injuries. Her eyelids flutter and my heart skips a beat as she looks at me.

"Am I burned?"

I set the pitcher down and move closer. "No."

She sighs. "My throat is killing me."

"You had a lot of smoke inhalation. Do you remember anything?"

"I don't know."

She struggles to sit up, and I hurry to help her. Her

43

spine seems so fragile where the thin hospital gown conforms to it. Holding the water for her, I'm strangely pleased as she takes a small sip. She swallows a few more and then leans back against the bed.

"Tell me what happened," she says with effort. "How did the fire start and how did you know about it? How did you find me?"

"Don't worry about that right now. The important thing is that you're safe now."

She blinks rapidly as tears fill her eyes. "Am I?"

Her hands tremble where they rest against the white hospital sheet. She looks at her hands, watching as she twines her fingers together. It's something she does when she's nervous, I've noticed. I softly lay my hand over hers to still the movements.

"*Yes*, you're safe. And the doctor said you'll make a full recovery. Pretty soon I'll be able to take you home."

"What about Juliana?" she croaks. "One minute we were talking, and the next, the entire building was on fire. The smoke got so bad so fast and I...I tried to find her, but I couldn't. I couldn't find anyone."

I ran the scenario over and over in my mind as I waited for Candi earlier during her examination with the doctor. Riggante's men had to have planted smoke bombs as well as incendiaries in order for the smoke to be that thick. It was an extra layer meant to disorient and trap Bruno's men. I'm not going to tell Candi any of this, of course. Not yet.

"We'll talk about it at home, after you've had some time to rest," I tell her.

She looks at me and the grief and desperation in her expression makes my chest tighten.

"Did she survive?" she asks. "Don't lie to me."

"Honestly, I don't know," I tell her.

Candi's chest hitches as a sob works its way out of her.

"Shh," I say, giving her hand a squeeze. "You need to not get worked up right now, okay? You have to heal."

Another sob lodges in her throat and then she gasps. "Wait. Armani. There's something I need to tell you." She looks around. "Where's my purse?"

"You didn't have it when I dragged you out of there."

She clenches her eyelids shut. "Shit."

Another sob threatens to break, so I help her take another sip of water, holding the cup steady until she's done. And then her face changes.

"My dress. Where's the dress I was wearing?" she says, sounding panicked. "I need it."

"I'll get it, I'll get it. Sit tight."

I go grab the plastic bag that they used to store her personal belongings and take out the folded dress, still completely saturated with the smell of smoke and soot and something chemical. I hand it over and Candi digs around inside the pocket, tugging out a small white card. She breathes a sigh of relief.

"Thank God. The photo. It's—"

Just then the nurse comes in, smiling and cheerful even though it's three in the morning.

"Oh, Mrs. Bellanti. You're awake now," he says. "How are you feeling?"

Candi looks annoyed that we've been interrupted. "Not great, but I'm sure that's to be expected."

The nurse nods and checks the monitors and IV. He taps on a small iPad and then asks Candi to lie back against the pillows for one more blood pressure reading.

"You have a couple blood tests first thing in the morning —well, later this morning. And if everything checks out okay, you should be able to go home," he says.

As soon as he leaves, Candi turns back to me. I can't quite read this new expression on her face. Rubbing her eyes, she looks at me and quickly inhales.

"I don't know how to tell you this except to just say it and, well, to show you."

She pats the bed and it takes me a second to realize she wants me to sit. That's not going to happen. Whatever she's about to tell me doesn't seem like it's going to be good, and I'm not the kind of man who likes to take bad news sitting down.

"Armani, please. Sit by me."

I do as she asks. She slides the picture she's holding into my hands and I realize it's a photo I've seen before. A memory comes to me, from the day when it was taken. Christmas. Us kids were hanging ornaments on the tree. My mom had told us to smile, but I didn't feel like smiling because my dad was drunk and screaming obscenities at her from his armchair across the room. My sister Liliana is there, and it looks like she's up to no good. Per usual. Even with her being photographed in profile, I recognize that sassy little smirk of hers. Was that look a reaction to our father's tirade?

"Where did you get this?" I haven't seen this picture in years.

"I found it. When I was helping Frankie with the baby's

scrapbook. Look, it doesn't matter where I found it. What matters is that..."

A surge of anger goes through me, making my hairline itch. What is she trying to do? Why is she resurfacing these memories? Remembering that she's injured, I will myself to calm down. I'm not really mad at her, anyway. It was a knee-jerk reaction to seeing my sister's face. My memories of her are long buried, but with this photo in my hand, it's almost like I can hear the sound of her voice and her laughter again.

Candi takes a deep breath. She looks at me with concern, her brows knit. "Armani, just listen and...please don't overreact, okay?"

I nod, finding myself waiting expectantly, curiously, for her to speak.

"Armani, this little girl, your sister? It's Juliana. My *friend* Juliana, the one who's marrying that Russian mobster."

"What?" My brain does not compute.

"Juliana is...she's Liliana. She's your sister."

6

ARMANI

I DROP the photo like it stung me, staring at Candi as it falls to the floor.

What kind of trick is this?

"My sister is dead," I tell her coldly.

She searches my face, but all I offer her is a hard glare.

"Armani, look at the picture," she pleads.

"I already did."

Even that brief glance was enough to resurrect memories I'd long ago walled up inside. I was a child when my mother and sister died, and I didn't have resources to learn how to deal with that properly. So I did what anyone who grows up with the overwhelming weight of grief does. I constructed walls inside walls inside walls to hold the pain back. I'm not letting that out, not ever. How could Candi do this to me? *Why* would she do this to me?

Candi throws off the blankets and swivels, so her feet hang over the side of the bed. I try to stop her, but she pushes back at me with one hand as she slides to the floor.

She retrieves the photo and then sits back on the bed, holding it out toward me. I have no choice but to look.

"I'm telling you, this child, this young girl, is Juliana," she insists. "I can prove it to you. Just listen—"

"Stop! You have no idea what you're talking about. What kind of nonsense has Sergio planted in your head?"

"He didn't plant anything."

"This is another Bruno trick, then. You're trying to play me."

"I swear I'm not. Armani, please. I'm telling you the truth."

"Enough."

I rip the picture out of her hand and shove it in my back pocket. It crinkles as I force it down, but I don't care. At the first available opportunity, I'm burning the hell out of the damn thing. I never want to see it again.

"Armani—" Candi begins coughing, her slender body rocking violently.

I pour her some more water and rub her back as she sips it. It's hard to be angry at her, and I know I shouldn't be, considering what she's been through, but I am. Or maybe I'm just pissed that someone would plant this idea in her head—maybe even Juliana herself—and persuade Candi to believe that it's true. Because now she thinks she's helping me, when really, she's just playing another one of Sergio Bruno's wicked hands.

"Get some rest. I have to make a call. I'll be back in a few minutes."

She doesn't try to stop me but I pause at the door, uncertain if I should leave her alone. Her monitors are beeping softly and steadily, which I take as a good sign. If something were wrong, the beeps would be more chaotic, I suppose. Plus, the nurses' station is right down the hall, so Candi is in good hands.

I head down the hall, take the elevator to the ground floor, and find a coffee vending machine. It's almost four in the morning, so I'm awake for the day. The machine hisses and spurts and fills the paper cup with what looks like muddy water. It smells terrible, but I need the caffeine and the hospital cafeteria is still closed for another few hours.

Just up ahead, I see a sign for the public chapel. It's empty when I step inside, which is its own kind of blessing. Ignoring the sign that says no food and drink, I make a silent promise to God not to spill my terrible coffee in His house, walk to the front, and take a seat.

I start mentally ticking off the list of things I need to do. It's how I keep myself calm and focused. I need to follow up with Riggante again. There's got to be something he's not telling me. He's too deep in this not to know anything.

Setting the coffee on the pew, I take out my phone and dial his number.

He answers on the third ring. "What now, Bellanti?"

I switch to Italian just in case someone walks into the chapel. Riggante easily switches to Italian as well.

"Did you find Orloff's woman dead or alive?" I ask.

"We can't confirm the body count yet. Just the three Bruno men dead outside."

"What about the Russian?"

"Are you listening to what I'm telling you? Cops are still sifting through the wreckage. They might have to identify these people with dental records, for all we know. You need to be patient, my son. It will take days to sort out the IDs on the bodies."

I close my eyes and take a breath. "So we have no idea if the mission was a success?"

"Everything I do is a success. You'd better remember that. *Stammi bene.*" Take care.

He clicks off and I listen to dead air for a few seconds before hanging up. Then I find a photo of Juliana that I forwarded to myself from Candi's phone last week and text it over to Clayton with a message, *Find out everything you can on this woman.*

He texts back immediately. *Is that Orloff's fiancée?*
Yes.

Do we have a last name?

Guerra, though that may be an alias. Get on it.

I let out a long breath, taking comfort in the fact that Clayton will work his magic. He'll have an entire dossier on this woman in a couple of days. She might be a lot more dangerous than my brothers and I realized.

Against my better judgment, I take the crumpled picture out of my back pocket and smooth the edges carefully. The photo paper is decades old and brittle; I could've destroyed it just by crushing it in my hand. Despite the creases, the scene is easy to remember.

Liliana. Occasionally Lili, but never Lil. She was always adamant about that.

Dante and Frankie named their daughter after her. Liliana Grace. Now Candi wants me to believe that the original Liliana isn't dead? That she's been alive and well all these years?

I study the face of the young girl in the photo, then look

at the picture of Juliana on my phone. Biting my lip hard, I fight back the emotions that try to rise up inside me. I can't deny that the similarity is striking. It's almost as if a small child morphed into a beautiful, adult woman, one who bears more than a passing resemblance to our mother. It's the eyes, the chin, the mouth.

If I were one to take information at face value, I could easily entertain the possibility that this Juliana Guerra is indeed our lost sister.

But I'm not so easily persuaded. I'm not that naïve. After all, people look alike. And if the Brunos are taking advantage of the visual similarity between Guerra and my mother, well, that sounds right in line with Sergio Bruno's tactics.

Or maybe this woman had plastic surgery to make her look like my mom. How sick is that? I wouldn't put it past Sergio to force someone—either in his family, or maybe a daughter or sister of one of his associates—to undergo identity falsification just to further his hand.

It makes me wonder, and not for the first time: how well does Candi really know this Juliana, anyway? She said they'd been friends since college, but that's only five or six years. And when Candi talks about her, I get the impression that there's a lot of information missing. From what I've gathered, Candi has bent over backwards to curry Juliana's favor—and that means she hasn't pressed too hard about this woman's history or background. Which means we have no idea who this woman really is.

Not that I blame Candi. I understand how my wife grew up, and I can sympathize with her need for acceptance. Look how easily she was goaded into becoming a spy for the Brunos. At the same time, they've manipulated her relentlessly to serve their own agenda—so Candi has no idea what's up and what's down. Even if she truly believes her friend is my sister, it doesn't mean the story has any veracity.

So no. I don't believe it. I can't let myself believe it. Wishing something is true doesn't make it so. It just makes you weak.

Sliding the photo back into my pocket, I text Dante to let him know that Candi is still stable and that we'll likely be home in a few hours. He's been relaying information about Candi's status to the rest of the family, particularly Frankie and Karina, who have been worried sick. The only reason they didn't all show up here at the hospital is because I convinced them it wouldn't be helpful. At this point, though, I'm starting to wonder if I made the right call.

It's not just that I'm physically exhausted. It's that I've been stressed, on high alert, and admittedly emotionally overwrought since I first heard the sound of Candi's weakened voice in that burning building. I was so scared that she'd be dead before I made it to the bakery, and once I had her in my arms, the fear didn't abate. It wasn't until she was wheeled away on a gurney at the hospital that I finally started to relax a little, because I knew she was in good hands.

I do care about her. There's no denying it. But how am I supposed to feel when she's suddenly telling me this crazy story about my dead sister? I can't ignore my gut instinct to suspect her motives, to question her loyalty all over again.

The other thing that's been bothering me is that I initially asked Candi to enter this relationship for a term of six months...and even though we ended up getting married somewhere along the way, the clock is still ticking on our original agreement. Candi has lived up to her role relatively well, and soon, it will be time for me to make a decision. Do I let her simply walk away? Or do I offer to extend the terms of our agreement to see if I can get a little more out of her where Bruno is concerned?

Sipping the disgusting coffee until the cup is half empty, I stand and leave the chapel.

Candi is asleep again when I enter her room. Taking my seat beside her bed, I look out the window into the pre-dawn darkness. I haven't slept all night, but I won't try to nap. I'm too paranoid that Sergio Bruno might realize that my family was involved in the fire and send some men to the hospital to find Candi and retaliate. Without a guard sitting outside the door, I can't be sure we won't be ambushed. So far, so good, but I can't get lax.

Would Bruno take Candi out so mercilessly? Does he suspect that she's switched sides? All I can do is hope that he wouldn't try to go after his best pawn in the middle of this thing.

A light rap on the doorframe precedes the doctor's entrance. Candi's eyelids flutter open.

"Good morning, Mr. Bellanti," the doctor says. "I'm going to assume you haven't slept?"

"No, ma'am."

She smiles kindly. "You'll both be out of here soon, home and in your own bed."

She glances at the monitors and then moves to Candi's bedside. After asking how Candi is feeling, the doctor listens to her lungs and then waves a small flashlight in front of her eyes. I watch this examination with a tightness in my chest that I can't banish.

"Well, good news. Everything's checking out great," the doctor tells us breezily. "Let's go over your labs."

She pulls up the info on her iPad and nods as she scrolls through the labs, muttering here and there as she reads over everything.

"Oxygen level in the blood looks good, arterial blood gas is good, carboxyhemoglobin and methemoglobin levels all looking great," she says.

Candi and I nod along. I'm not sure what all of that means, but I'm hanging onto the word *good* and the way the doctor is nodding to herself.

"And don't worry," she adds. "The baby's just fine."

My gaze snaps to Candi. Her eyes are wide, her face gone even paler.

"What?" I sputter.

The doctor smiles reassuringly.

"We ran a pregnancy test before we performed Mrs. Bellanti's chest x-ray to check her lungs for smoke inhalation," she says. "It's routine for women admitted to the ER. The test indicated elevated levels of hCG, consistent with pregnancy."

"I don't understand," Candi murmurs, sounding dazed.

The room suddenly tilts around me, spiraling into the narrow end of a funnel.

The doctor claps me on the shoulder. "Congratulations, Mr. Bellanti. You're going to be a father."

7

CANDI

My heart starts to race. I can't believe what I'm hearing.

"Are—are you sure?"

The doctor stares at me, her brows knitting together. "Yes. My apologies. I thought the nurse had informed you already."

"Maybe she did? I can't remember." I was so fuzzy when I got here.

"It's all right. You were having trouble staying awake when you arrived."

She gives my shoulder a light squeeze, but it does nothing to quell the panic I'm feeling.

"You've been through quite the trauma," she goes on. "Once we realized you were pregnant, we needed to do an ultrasound to double-check the health of the baby after what you'd been through. You're about seven weeks along."

I open my mouth but then close it again. My mind is blown. I don't know what to say. I don't know what to think. One minute I'm helping Juliana taste cakes for her wedding and the next I'm being told that I'm pregnant with Armani's baby.

Oh God. Armani.

My stomach drops when I look at him. He's...glaring at me. As if I've done something wrong. As if I'm not just as shocked as he is right now.

If the doctor senses the tension in the room, she doesn't acknowledge it. She pulls a card holder from the pocket of her long white coat, flips through it, and hands me a small card.

"Here's the number to our maternity center," she says. "All the information you need will be provided to you upon your discharge, as well. A nurse will be in contact to help you schedule your first obstetric appointment, though of course you're welcome to seek care elsewhere if you choose. In the meantime, if you have any questions, please do give the center a call."

I don't quite grip the card, and it flutters onto my lap.

"I'll get started on your discharge paperwork," the doctor says. She looks between Armani and me, seeming to finally realize that something is amiss. "And Mrs. Bellanti, I'll send a nurse in to do your final checks and get you ready to go. Mr. Bellanti, it would be best to give her some privacy while she's getting dressed."

She leaves, and the tension in the room grows by the thousands.

The first thing Armani says is, "I assumed you were using contraception."

His words are stilted, empty, and emotionless.

"I never said that. We never discussed it."

"So you had unprotected sex with me knowing full well

that you weren't using contraception? What did you think would happen?"

I narrow my eyes. "And *you* had unprotected sex with *me* without ever inquiring about my birth control status, and rarely bothering to use a condom. How is this all my fault?"

He shakes his head and digs a hand through his hair. "You did this on purpose."

I glance down at the card the doctor gave me, but the words go blurry as tears sting my eyes and I quickly look away. After everything I've been through, combined with the shock of finding out that I'm about to be a mother, how can Armani act so cruelly right now?

"Why would I do this on purpose?" I choke out.

"Why do women ever get pregnant on purpose? To trap the man they're with. You knew our agreement was up in a few more months, so you tried to trick me—"

"*Trick you?*" I sputter. "Are you serious?"

I'm suddenly exhausted, as if his anger has taken every last bit of strength I had. Shaking my head, I settle against the pillow and cross my arms.

"I'm not trying to trap you, Armani. I had no idea. I guess with everything going on, I wasn't really paying attention to my cycles and..."

I mentally think back over the last few months and try to remember the last time I had my period. It's just been so chaotic and so stressful lately, I never gave it a second thought. I honestly can't remember when it last was. Maybe two months ago?

"This arrangement still expires in three months," Armani says.

Disgust fills me at his cruel reminder. I'm still so shell-shocked that I don't even know how I feel about the pregnancy, but apparently my fake husband does.

"Asshole!" The words burst out of me. "I was almost blown up today, with a baby inside me. I could've died and I never would've known...but now that I *do* know, now that we both know, all you can think of is covering your own ass?"

There's no discernible reaction in his Resting Bellanti Face.

"Or perhaps you'd rather I 'take care' of the problem as quickly as possible," I hiss, even though there is no way in hell I'd consider ending this pregnancy. At least, not for him.

"That's not what I said," he growls. "I'm simply reiterating the fact that our timeline is in no way affected by this...situation."

An indignant huff comes out of my mouth. "Wow, Armani. Just...wow. I knew you were a cold bastard, but this is just beyond."

He spreads his arms wide. "Why should this change anything between us? I married you for a very specific reason. Because it was in the best interest of my family, and our business. I sure as hell never asked for a baby."

Turning my face away, I swallow hard. I'm two seconds away from falling apart. I don't look at him, nor do I expect a response to what I'm about to say.

"I don't want to argue about this," I manage. "As far as I'm concerned, *we're done*. All you have to do is let me go so I can handle this on my own. I don't need you in my life."

"I'm not done with you, Candi. You still owe me," he says. "And I intend to collect."

Whipping my head in his direction, I grip the thin hospital sheet with both hands as I yell, "Get out! Now! Get. Out!"

He stands his ground and I yell louder, rage and adrenaline pumping through me.

I can hear footsteps rushing down the hall. Nurses, probably.

Armani spins and storms to the door, looking back over his shoulder to add, "I meant what I said. You'll complete your term of six months, and then we're through."

He doesn't quite slam the door, but he definitely shuts it harder than necessary. Point taken. Guess I'm about to become a single mother.

"Mrs. Bellanti, are you okay?" one of the nurses asks as she rushes into the room, a male nurse right on her heels. "What happened?"

"Nothing," I lie, tears rolling down my cheeks.

One of my monitors is beeping like crazy. I must have disconnected a wire. My heart rate is also through the roof, according to the numbers on the screen.

As the nurses fuss and coo over me, checking my vitals and getting the machines back in order, I settle back against the pillow and cry it out, my hands shaking as I clench the bedsheet in my fists. My chest aches and burns as my breaths hitch in my throat. This can't be good for me. The doctor said it would take time for the tissues in my throat to recover. What about the baby? The thought instantly calms me down to sniffles.

"There you go, that's better," the female nurse soothes

me, rubbing circles over my back as she helps me take small sips of water. "It's okay. You're okay."

I nod. I am okay. Or at least, I will be. I know I will.

Because suddenly, there's something inside me that feels stronger. Harder. More fierce.

How is it possible that I feel so different already? Different than I did even an hour ago? I never could have guessed there was life inside of me, that my screwed-up relationship with Armani had created something unexpected.

But now that I know about the baby...everything has changed.

The funny thing is, I never thought about being a mother. Not really. Sure, I had passing thoughts about having a family someday, but nothing concrete. Nothing so soon. And yet the second the doctor said I was pregnant, I knew I wanted this baby. More than anything.

"I'm going to disconnect your IV and then Ebba will help you get ready to go, okay? The doctor said you're ready to be discharged," the male nurse is saying.

I sit completely still as he stops the IV pump and removes the catheter from my hand. Then the female nurse shoos him away so I can get dressed in the clean underwear, sweatpants, and T-shirt that Donovan dropped off at the hospital earlier per Armani's request.

"You weren't expecting to be pregnant, I gather?" Her voice is soft and nonjudgmental as she sits facing the wall, allowing me some privacy. "You might be surprised how often that happens. You're not alone."

I will not cry. I will not cry. "It is a bit of a shock," I admit.

I wonder if she overheard me and Armani yelling at each other? Or if the entire floor did? How mortifying.

She puts things away on a cart with rolling drawers, keeping herself busy as she waits for me to finish. "You know, there are resources if you decide that, you know, this isn't what you want. The prenatal nurse can talk you through your options when she calls."

"Thanks," I say softly. But my mind is already made up. "I'm ready now."

"I also have to ask..." She hesitates as she turns toward me. "Is it safe for you to go home?"

"Yes," I answer immediately. I know exactly what she's fishing for.

Her eyes search mine, and then she asks, "Have you ever experienced any form of physical or emotional abuse by your partner, or by anyone else close to you?"

It almost draws a laugh out of me. How can these questions even apply when you're married to someone in the mafia?

"It's not what it sounded like," I tell her. "This news is just—I mean finding out about the baby, right after the stress of the fire, and then all this other family stuff we've been dealing with the last few months—the whole thing kind of blindsided us both. We're in a bit of a freefall right now. But everything is okay. Really. I'm safe. Baby is safe. It's all going to be okay."

The corners of her eyes crinkle as she smiles. "That's good to hear. I brought you a prenatal vitamin to take before you go. I'll just leave it here and meet you down the hallway."

She walks out, closing the door gently behind her, and I

stare at the vitamin in the paper cup she set on the tray table. Everything I do from here on out is going to matter tenfold. Everything I eat, every activity I engage in, how much sleep I get, how much stress I have on a daily basis. All of it is going to impact the tiny life growing inside me.

The tiny life that Armani doesn't want. The child he's accusing me of tricking him into.

For a short, stupid while I actually thought he was beginning to care for me. He rescued me from that fire when I could've easily died. He stayed by my side in the hospital, watching over me. And then one little word—*baby* —made him show his true colors.

I'm not done with you. You still owe me.

Taking the vitamin from the cup, I swallow it down with half a glass of water.

Screw Armani.

He might not be done with me.

But I'm sure as hell done with him.

8

ARMANI

"BEFORE WE DISCUSS the Bruno situation, I have some... other news to relay first," I say, gravely meeting each of my family members' expectant gazes in turn.

The gang's all here. Dante and Frankie, Marco and Karina, Clayton. Charlie had a meeting with a client for an event she's planning, so Clayton will have to debrief her later.

"Just spit it out," Dante says, sounding exhausted. "Whatever it is, we'll handle it."

"Yeah. When it comes to the Brunos, we know shit can always get worse," Marco adds.

I called this meeting in the first-floor library to talk about the fire at the Bruno bakery and relay the outcome. Which, of course, I still don't know myself. But I figured I'd better let them in on Candi's little ploy right away, because there's no sense in keeping it a secret. Candi begrudgingly accepted the ride home from Donovan a few hours ago, but we haven't spoken since our fight in her hospital room. She's sleeping now. I still haven't gone to bed.

"This isn't about the Brunos," I say. "Candi is...she's pregnant."

For one tense, silent beat, everyone just stares at me like they're waiting for the punchline. But then, slowly, realization spreads across their faces as I stand there stoically and don't retract my statement.

"Seriously, bro?" Marco blurts.

"Would I lie about something like this?" I say coldly.

"Oh my God!" Frankie almost squeals. "Oh my God, Armani, wow! You're going to be a daddy!"

"That's one unavoidable outcome, yes," I say dryly.

I'm still pissed at Candi for trapping me into being the one thing I swore I'd never be: a father. I don't know how to raise a child. A man like me should never have children.

"Uh, congratulations?" Dante says tentatively.

"Not really."

Marco chuckles. "It's a surprise baby, then?"

"Big fucking surprise," I grumble. "She tricked me into it."

Frankie whips her head toward me, glaring daggers. "Excuse me?"

Ah, fuck. I didn't realize this would turn into a huge conversation. "What? She never said she wasn't on contraception, so—"

"Did you *ask* if she was?" Frankie hisses, rising from her chair. "Did you even have a single adult conversation about it before you started sticking your dick—"

"Enough," Dante interrupts, gently tugging her back to sitting.

Her frown deepens as her gaze jumps between me and Dante. "Enough *what*? I'm not shutting up. This is bullshit.

Discussing contraception is something that adults do, Armani. Apparently you never thought about it because you figured it was the woman's job to handle it. So, guess what? This is what happens. Sounds like you've just learned a very valuable lesson."

"This wasn't an accident," I insist.

"You're wrong," Frankie snaps.

"Please. If we can just stay on topic here," Dante says.

But Frankie's not having it. "Besides, I teased her about being pregnant the other day and her eyes practically bugged out of her head. She laughed at me for even mentioning it."

This catches my attention. "What made you mention it?"

My sister-in-law is clearly annoyed with me. Her voice is tinged with disapproval. "She wasn't feeling well, and I noticed. Dizzy, nauseous, spacy. All things I've personally experienced during my early pregnancy. All things I assume you never bothered to notice."

I'm pretty sure she finishes her rant by calling me a "dick" under her breath. My God, how she's changed. When Frankie first married Dante and moved in here, she was timid. Shy. Sweet. But at some point over the last year or so, she's turned into a goddamn tiger. I'm not sure if becoming a mother is what made her so fierce, or if it started even before that due to Dante's influence, but one thing is certain: Francesca Bellanti is not a woman to be trifled with.

Mulling over her words, a sliver of a doubt starts to wedge itself into my brain.

Is it possible that Candi *didn't* get pregnant on purpose?

"I've had a lot on my mind lately," I say, and although it's a weak defense, it's true.

"*All of us* have. It's no excuse," Frankie says. "And honestly, she seemed pretty freaked out at my suggestion. Not exactly the reaction of a woman who was planning to get pregnant all along. You know, Armani, it sounds to me like maybe you need to start paying more attention to your wife. Unless your head's too far up your own ass to—"

"I have other news," I interrupt, knowing that Frankie could go on like this all day.

Marco and Dante try to hide their smiles, but not well enough to keep me from seeing.

"Ding dong, the Russian is dead?" Marco throws out.

I hate to disappoint him.

"That's still unconfirmed. The building collapsed and was a total loss, not to mention the site is now crawling with law enforcement, the fire department, and a cleanup crew. It's going to take some time to comb through the debris and determine the identities of anyone inside. Three of Bruno's men were identified immediately afterward, but they died outside the building."

A low murmur of disappointment goes around the room.

"If Orloff survived, they're doing a great job of hiding him so far," Clayton says. "Meanwhile, the woman you asked me about is MIA. If she survived, it's going to be—"

Putting up a hand to stop him, I pull out the crumpled photo of myself and my siblings and hand it to Dante. His eyes go wide.

"Where the hell did you get this?"

I don't miss Frankie ducking her head guiltily, but I choose not to call her out.

"That's not important. What matters is the young girl looking at you." I hand him a printout of the recent picture of Juliana I got from Candi. "What do you see?"

He studies the pictures for a moment and then shrugs. "I guess I see an uncanny resemblance."

"Marco?" I say, motioning him closer.

Marco leans in, and so do Frankie, Karina, and Clayton.

"Holy shit!" Marco's voice trails off, stunned. "Is that...is it possible...?"

"No, it's not," I scoff. "It's a trick, courtesy of Sergio Bruno, and one that you all need to be aware of. It's the only reason I'm even telling you at all."

But they're not listening. The pictures are passed around, but as soon as Dante gets them back, his eyes stay transfixed on the image of us as children. Is he remembering her the same way I did when I first saw the old photo?

"Explain," Dante says gruffly, gripping the pictures tightly.

"Candi found this in a pile of old photos that were being used for Liliana's baby book," I say, careful not to implicate Frankie even though it's obvious who must have dug up the old pictures. "She thought the resemblance to her friend Juliana was too striking to ignore. She's basically convinced that her friend is...our sister. And look, I don't believe it myself, but if this is some sick strategy the Brunos plan to use against us, we need to be prepared."

"She looks like Mom," Marco says wistfully. He runs a finger over the photo of Juliana, then pulls back, shaking his head. "Really, she looks just like Mom did around the same age."

"How the hell would you know that?" I ask. "You were still sucking your thumb when they died."

He looks at me defiantly, as if what he's about to reveal might result in some sort of punishment, or anger. But whatever it is, he's not about to apologize.

"Because I had Mom's photo album from when she was young. I hid it behind the baseboard in my bedroom for years."

Dante's mouth drops. "*You* took it from my room? I figured it was Dad."

Marco looks down at his hands. "No. You didn't hide it well enough. But Dad *would* have found it if I hadn't taken it first. He'd never think to start prying off the woodwork in our rooms, but he would go through your closet."

They look at each other with mutual understanding.

Dante nods. "Yeah, you're right. And you're also right that Juliana looks a lot like Mom, but so what? I have to agree with Armani on this one. It could be a trick. Or just a coincidence."

"Seriously? Shouldn't we at least check it out?" Marco prods.

"Clayton is on it," I say. "Whatever we need to know about this woman, he'll find it."

All eyes turn to the Irishman. He shrugs. "Like I said, I haven't been able to uncover anything yet. Graduated from UC San Francisco, works as a consultant for a reputable company—owned by the Brunos, sure, but the business seem fairly above-board. She pays her taxes on time, has lived at the same address for half a decade. I dunno. So far, she's clean."

Half rolling my eyes, I move behind the desk and sit. "It's only been a matter of hours since I put you on it. It's going to take time."

Marco stands from the couch. "What do you mean when you say this might be a trick?"

"We know this woman is in Sergio Bruno's inner circle and that she intended to marry into the Bratva to seal the alliance. Obviously, her loyalty lies with Bruno. He could have found her anywhere. Maybe she already looked like a ringer for Mom. Or maybe he had her doctored up. Either way, there's no telling how he might be planning to use her against us."

Marco visibly slumps. Of course my baby brother was holding out hope.

There's a long beat of silence before Frankie speaks up. "But what if she *is* Liliana? You're telling me there's not even the smallest chance she's alive? When her body was never recovered?"

"No. It's not possible." It can't be, and I won't believe otherwise.

"It is possible." Marco runs a hand over his mouth and looks over at Dante.

Slowly, our oldest brother nods. "It's unlikely. It's implausible. But...there is a possibility."

Silence falls again as the revelation hangs heavy in the air. Truthfully, there's a part of me that has already been trying to piece together a history that could sensibly explain Juliana Guerra being our sister. But so many things would have had to fall into place to make that happen. I just don't see it.

"You guys have to meet her. Talk to her." Frankie looks at Dante. "You deserve a chance to know the truth."

"She's a *Bruno*," I remind them. "Even if she's one of us by blood, she's *not* one of us in practice. Okay? Besides, she was inside the bakery when it went up in flames."

All eyes are on me now.

"You're saying she's dead?" Marco sputters. "Did you kill our sister?"

I give him a hard stare. "We're not jumping to conclusions here."

Bursting from the couch, Marco strides angrily over to me. "This is unbelievable! Fucking unbelievable. You bring us this load of crap, setting us up with the possibility that this woman might be our sister, and then you say she's also probably dead thanks to the pyrotechnics you pulled with that old ghoul Riggante?"

Dante stands, instantly commanding the room. "Let's just try to stay calm. First things first, we need to know if she survived the fire. Then we can figure out what to do next."

"Agreed. And Clayton—I need you to investigate the accident that killed our mother and sister," I say. "I want to know who did it, who saw it, who heard about it later over a beer. Figure out if by some miracle a kid could have walked away from it alive. Track down every last detail, even the insignificant stuff. Rumors, gossip, leads that were dead ends. All of it."

"It was a bomb, right?" Clayton asks. "An explosion? Only one victim recovered?"

"Yes sir. This is your top priority now. Dig deep. And don't stop digging until you find something that we haven't. Police reports, eyewitness accounts from the search and rescue team, the Coast Guard...maybe you can talk to someone who remembers when it happened. Older mob guys, maybe retired now. Or their wives."

Clayton nods. He's already tapping notes into his phone. The conversation picks up around the room and it gives me a moment to think. If Juliana did survive, the only way to know for sure whether or not she's our sister is genetic testing. My phone vibrates in my pocket. I read the text beneath the desktop.

Orloff survived.

Fuck.

Hiding my reaction, I put my phone away. The fire was all for nothing. I made promises to the other families, stuck my neck out, and for what? This war is far from over, and who the hell knows what I'll have to do to rally the families again. If we even get that chance. Because now, Bruno knows we're on to his plan to ally with the Russians. This attempt to take out Orloff and stop the wedding has outed us, and we've lost the element of surprise.

If we get a chance to strike again, it's going to have to be from the inside.

"What is it?" Dante is standing next to me. I hadn't even heard him approach.

"Nothing."

"Bullshit. You got a message."

Clearing my throat, I drop my feet from the desk and sit tall. "Orloff survived."

Dante turns away. Marco looks at the ceiling and

73

curses. Karina rests her head on his shoulder, her expression fearful.

"So what happens now?" Frankie says.

I don't have an answer to that. "I'll meet with the other families again. We'll figure something out. Make a new plan."

Marco looks over at me. "What about Juliana? Did she make it out, too?"

"No word on her yet."

He looks between Dante and me. "I know you assholes don't think it's her, but my gut is telling me we need to look into this more. Dad lied about everything. Maybe they didn't die. Maybe he put them away somewhere or...who the hell knows what? Or maybe he really did believe they died, but they didn't. If there's even the smallest chance that this woman is our sister, we need to follow up on it. I mean, what's the last thing you remember Dad telling you that turned out to be true?"

I don't want to agree with him, but he's got me there. Our father never told the truth about anything.

Maybe our sister is alive, after all.

9

CANDI

"WHAT DO YOU WANT?" I say coldly.

I'm instantly on edge as Armani walks into our room and quietly closes the door behind him. But instead of answering, he breezes past me and Mr. Sprinkles—dozing through a National Geographic series on the sitting area's cushy sofa—and goes into the bedroom's en suite.

Seconds later, I hear the shower turn on in the bathroom. I turn up the volume on the TV and try to ignore the fact that my very hot, very asshole husband is stripping naked in the next room. Who cares? The only reason I'm even here at the Bellantis' house is because I haven't figured out my next steps yet. And if I'm honest, it's probably safer for me to be here than anywhere else. Maybe I can move into one of the guest rooms temporarily, just until I come up with a more long-term living situation for my tiny little family—myself, my cat, and my baby.

I snuggle deeper under the throw blanket and close my eyes again. My body aches, and my chest feels bruised from all the smoke I inhaled. My throat is less scratchy thanks to the tea I've been sipping, but my anxiety is causing more of my current discomfort than the trauma of the fire. At least I know what's causing my nausea now.

It still doesn't feel real. The baby. I just can't wrap my head around the fact that I'm going to have a child. My emotions are all over the place, and the way Armani reacted to the news only makes me feel worse. And on top of that, I can't stop worrying about Juliana.

She had to have made it out alive. She's too smart and too stubborn and too...too *Juliana* to be gone. She would have fought tooth and nail to get out of that bakery. I'm sure she managed to escape. But why haven't I heard anything from her yet?

Is she in a hospital somewhere, healing from her injuries? Or is she hiding out, lying low somewhere to avoid any further assassination attempts? That would explain the lack of contact. There's no way she'd use her phone if she was holed up in some safe house. Orloff could have even smashed it so she couldn't be tracked, wherever she is.

Or maybe her phone died, or got destroyed in the fire. I don't know. All I know is that as long as Juliana's fate remains uncertain, my mind won't stop overthinking this. I just can't understand why she hasn't reached out. She could have called me from another phone, or found a way to send a text or an email. Something. But she hasn't. Isn't she just as worried about me as I am about her? Or does she somehow blame me for the fire?

And what about Orloff? Did he make it out with her, or was he killed in the fire?

Something else strikes me then: maybe he died, and Jules is in mourning.

I pick up my new phone and navigate to her contact (my old phone wouldn't turn back on after the heat damage it suffered, but one of the Bellantis' staff got me a new phone and transferred my latest iPhone backup to it, so I haven't lost any of my data). But when I try to call her, it goes straight to voicemail. Just like the last three times I called. *Juliana, where are you?*

With a heavy heart, I drop the phone back on the coffee table. I don't know what to do with all my sadness and anxiety. The chaos of everything going on right now is almost too much for me to handle, and Armani's presence definitely isn't helping.

As if he somehow senses that I'm thinking about him, the bathroom door suddenly swings open and Armani saunters out with a towel around his waist. I pretend not to notice him, but he walks straight from the bedroom into the sitting room and stops right in front of me, so I have no choice but to look him in the eye.

"How are you feeling?" he asks.

I direct my gaze toward the TV screen. I'm not feeling any grace toward my husband, that's for sure.

"Not good. But I'd be feeling a lot better if I had any idea what happened to my best friend. Are you going to tell me what you know?"

He folds his arms across his chest. "I don't know anything yet."

"Right," I say sarcastically.

"We've got eyes and ears everywhere. We're trying to find her."

Finally, I look at him again, studying his eyes for signs of deceit. I think he's telling the truth. But I can't be certain.

"You'll let me know as soon as you hear something," I say. It's not a request.

He nods curtly and then goes back into the bedroom. I can feel myself relax as I watch him walk away. Not because I'm afraid of him...but because I'm afraid of what I'll do if he keeps parading around in front of me half naked with those delicious drops of water rolling down his chest and that tantalizing bulge under the front of his towel.

Down, girl.

Annoyed at myself for still being attracted to someone so grossly unworthy, I grab the remote and click the volume up a few more notches on this old house renovation show. I won't let Armani get to me. He doesn't deserve my attention.

But through the bedroom doorway, I can see him pacing back and forth like he does when he's agitated or thinking through a problem. First he goes into the closet, then seems to change his mind and goes back into the bathroom. A few seconds later he comes out dressed in a pair of low-slung sweatpants, the ones that make his ass look temptingly grab-bable. Of course.

He paces around the bedroom a few more times, driving me absolutely batshit. I wish he'd chosen to sleep somewhere else tonight. He's usually so good at not coming to bed, and then the one night that I *don't* want to see him, he decides to appear.

"How long will it take to know for sure if she survived?" I ask through the doorway.

Armani pulls up short, directly in my eyeline. "I can't predict that, Candi."

"A day? A week? Next month?" I prod. "You can't even

give me a ballpark guess?"

He spreads his arms wide. "It's not up to me. What do you want me to say?"

"I don't know. You sure had a hell of a lot to say when you found out I was pregnant, didn't you?" I shout. It's enough to send Mr. Sprinkles running for the closet, his hiding spot.

Anger flashes across Armani's face. This is probably the worst possible time to push his buttons, but I don't care.

"How did you expect me to react?" he says. "I was in shock. I still am."

"So was I, but I didn't react like a complete asshole on instinct."

"You're right. I should have kept my mouth shut until I had more time to think."

For a second, I'm too stunned to speak. Did he just say... that *I'm right*? Did the great and powerful never-admits-he's-wrong Armani Bellanti just concede for once in his life?

I open my mouth to give him another round of tongue-lashing, but as he walks toward me, the words dry up in my throat. It's almost hypnotic, the way his tattoos shift as his muscles flex under his taut, golden skin. His abs are practically begging for my fingertips to run over them, that waistband primed for tugging down. He watches me watching him and a smirk pulls at the corner of his lips.

"See something you like?" he says, his voice low.

"No," I lie, fighting the urge to reach for him.

Still looking smug, he stops next to the coffee table and drops his pants. Shamefully, my eyes go straight to his dick, which is hard enough to send a needy tremor through my core. This is torture. I want nothing more than to pull him onto the couch with me, straddle him and ride that cock until I'm coming fast and hard around him. Instead, I clench my jaw and look up.

Our eyes catch as I coldly say, "Not. Interested."

He actually has the nerve to laugh out loud at my lie. "I'll go easy on you."

"I said I didn't want to."

Leaning closer, he takes my chin in his hand. I do nothing to resist his touch.

"I can see it on your face that you do. Don't lie to me."

Narrowing my eyes, I say, "You're seeing what you want to see."

Without another word, he tugs the blanket off me and takes in the white T-shirt and plain cotton underwear I'm wearing, his jaw working to the side as he homes in on the peaks of my nipples beaded under the fabric. They're so hard, they're aching and tingling. I don't have to look down to know what he's eyeing.

"The fuck I am," he murmurs.

He drops his hand to pinch my left nipple and my body immediately responds. Arching my back, I let out a gasp, pushing my chest toward him. When he pulls my shirt up over my head, I don't stop him. I'm not wearing a bra, and his hands take advantage of my bare breasts, stroking softly as his thumbs rub electric circles over my nipples. My breathing picks up, soft little moans spilling uncontrollably out of me, and I make eye contact with him again.

I'm tempted to push him away and watch the excited expectation dissipate from his gaze, but I'm suddenly on fire for him and I don't want to stop this. It doesn't matter how pissed off I am or what he does to me—I always want him, and he knows it. I'm ashamed at how helpless I am, how badly I want him, despite everything he's said and done. But there's no holding back.

Before I even realize I'm doing it, I'm wiggling out of my underwear, hurrying to flaunt my naked body in front of my infuriatingly hot husband. Armani is on top of me instantly. He turns me so I'm kneeling on the couch, facing the back cushions, my elbows resting on the back of the sofa. He pulls my hips back so my ass is pushed out toward him and then covers me with his warmth, lining his cock up against my opening. Fisting my hair harshly enough to make me cry out in pain, he thrusts into me from behind in one perfect glide.

"Yes," I moan, leaning forward to rest my head on my forearms.

As he pumps into me, I close my eyes, relishing the feel of his lips and tongue cruising the side of my neck. His mouth trails down to my shoulder, drawing little shivers over my skin. But as gentle as his kisses are, each of his thrusts gets harder and deeper, as if he's working through whatever is going on in his head.

That's when I realize: he came up here to use me. Typical Armani, feeling pissed and confused and pushing it all so far back that what he's left with is nothing but adrenaline and testosterone and overwhelming horniness. And yet it doesn't temper the desire coursing through me, or how my body responds so easily to him. Bracing myself against the back of the couch, I flex my hips to meet him stroke for stroke, imagining that he wants me for me, and not as a vessel for pounding out his emotional tension.

Fuck it. Like I care. It feels too good for me to care.

"Mm," I sigh. "That's it."

His hand slides from my hair and covers my throat, not squeezing but gripping firmly. My mind replays the other times he's grabbed my throat—hard—and how it feels, what it does to me. But this time, he's being careful. Going easy on me, just like he said he would.

"Turn around," he growls, pulling out of me.

I do, and he's on me in a second, lifting me into his arms. I wrap my legs tight around him and he starts pumping into me again, even as he carries me into the bedroom. Arms around his neck, I moan in his ear with each thrust, trying not to come before we make it to the bed.

I'm tossed onto my back on the mattress, and then he climbs on top of me and rams inside me for the third time. Like a hand in a glove, a key in a lock, he fits me fucking perfectly. Every single time.

"Yes," I gasp.

Letting myself get carried away, I start moaning louder and longer, reveling in the sound. I'm high on his cock right now, my heart racing, my whole body strung tight as flames of ecstasy lap at my center. He hitches my legs around him and then looks down into my eyes while he fucks me. But even though he's looking at me, I can tell he doesn't see me. He's somewhere else, lost in his head. I'm not sure he recognizes my pleasure or cares if he gives it to me. He's too busy chasing release, relief, from something.

"Fuck me," I command. I want him to see me. Hear me. Acknowledge me. "Fuck me, Armani, fuck me, fuck me, fuck me."

I don't know if my words have any effect on him, but

suddenly he pulls out again and repositions me on my knees. I've barely gotten myself balanced when he's gripping my shoulders and pounding into me from behind. The bed rocks, the headboard tapping against the wall. Pushing back against him, I chase my own release and find it before him, shattering and crying out in a hot rush. He comes forcefully but quietly, choking back his grunts, as if keeping his orgasm completely for himself.

He immediately disengages and lies back against his pillows, throwing an arm over his eyes. Moving to my stomach, I turn my face away from him and catch my breath. I'm not surprised when his weight leaves the mattress and I hear fabric rustling as he gets dressed.

"The Russian survived the fire," he says, shocking me. "If he survived, maybe your friend did, too."

My heart flutters. Rolling over to look at him, I gape to find the bedroom door closing behind him. Where the fuck is he going? He can't drop a bomb like that and just leave.

But the important thing is, Juliana's fiancé is alive. Could he have gotten her out as well?

Pushing off the bed, I scramble for my phone. It's stupid, and I shouldn't get my hopes up, but I do. I dial her number one more time.

It rings. Anticipation flares in my chest. Maybe her phone is back on.

Click.

Voicemail.

I listen to Juliana's outgoing message, closing my eyes as I soak up the sound of her voice. And even though she didn't answer, I let myself believe that she will soon.

10

ARMANI

WE'RE BACK to business as usual around the Bellanti Vineyards, but everything feels wrong.

It's been two days now, and I haven't heard anything more about the fire, neither victims nor survivors. Nor has Sergio Bruno made contact to let us know that he's aware of our involvement. It's only a matter of time, however, and I need to be prepared.

To that end, I've increased security around our properties to ensure that the family and our winery employees are all safe. Additional guards are covertly watching every entry point, as well as the activity around the Bellanti offices and the winery buildings. I ran extensive background checks on everyone we hired, and had one of my hacker associates do an additional background check of her own. The way things are going, I can't be too paranoid.

It's unnerving to expect something to explode or gunfire to come from the shadows or some other act of violence to happen when I least expect it. Tit for tat, I know. It's all part of the game. But I hate it.

And my need to protect this place has compounded. I'm going to have a child, and that changes everything. The stakes are higher than they've ever been.

I'm in my office with the door locked and the blinds closed. It's gloomy and gray inside, but it suits me as I sit behind my desk and ponder my next move. Riggante isn't being forthcoming with information, and I'm sick of nagging him for intel five times a day. He was downright ornery during our last conversation, and my gut tells me it's because Orloff survived and Riggante isn't the type to take a failure in stride.

Normally, I would have insisted that I take over as the head of this (failed) operation already, but I can't risk causing offense when I know I'll need Riggante's cooperation again in the future. Because the fire didn't successfully neutralize our target, we'll have to come up with a new plan to erase the Bratva threat. Pissing off Riggante would be like shooting myself in the foot. The man holds a lot of sway with the other families, too.

My cell rings. It's Clayton. Adrenaline surges through me. Maybe he's dug up some news about the boat accident.

"Yes?" I answer gruffly.

"Maxim Orloff is here."

Well, shit. That's definitely not what I was expecting.

"Here *where*?" I ask, immediately on high alert. "On the property?"

"Security has him on camera in line for a wine tasting."

This gives me a serious pause. "A wine tasting? Is this a joke?"

"No, boss."

Just then, I hear a knock on my door, followed by the handle jiggling.

"Jesus, Armani, let me in!"

It's Dante. I get up to let my brother in while pondering what to do about the Russian.

"Let the man be, but keep a close eye on him. Dante just got here," I tell Clayton. Then I look over at Dante and tell him, "Orloff's at our wine tasting right now."

My brother's expression shifts to one of shock. "Are you insane? Go after him!"

"No."

"You don't want us to intercept?" Clayton asks incredulously over the phone.

"No," I repeat. "He came to us, and not in secret. He knows he's got a fuck ton of security on him. I don't think he's here to cause trouble. He wants something else."

"Copy that," Clayton says, hanging up.

"You're seriously going to just sit back and let that... ticking fucking time bomb strut around the property?" Dante says. "I don't trust him. You shouldn't, either."

"I didn't say I did."

Dante shakes his head and goes to my desktop computer. He pulls up the security camera footage, and waves me over to watch it with him. Sure enough, the video shows Maxim Orloff and his right-hand man standing in line at the entrance to the tasting room in all their stoic-faced, tattooed glory, waiting to be escorted inside.

Unbelievable.

Wanting to hasten this along, I call the number for the tasting room and tell the employee who answers to let everyone in the next group in right away. Then Dante and I watch the livestream as the guests filter into the tasting room, settling around tables and at the bar.

"Stay here," I tell my brother, already knowing he's going to argue.

"I'm going with you."

He follows as I head to the door but I stop him with a glare.

"I need to confront him alone. Man to man." I gesture at the computer. "Watch the livestream. If anything looks off, you can come to my rescue."

Dante searches my eyes with his own hard gaze, but doesn't give me any more grief.

"There are too many civilians in the group," I add. "He won't try anything and risk so much bloodshed, especially not with all the security cameras around. Trust me. The last thing Orloff wants to do is jeopardize his citizenship status by making himself a known terrorist. He's getting married for a green card, remember?"

What I don't add is that Orloff will likely be taking his revenge on us in a much more covert and individual way.

Without another word, I leave my office and head across the property to the tasting room. The sommelier is just beginning the tasting at the bar as I step into the bright, modern, high-ceilinged space that Frankie redesigned last year. The guests who aren't at the bar yet are looking over the menus at their tables, chatting with their dates or the waitstaff. All is calm.

Staying in the shadows, I observe Orloff and his companion as they speak over their wine glasses with an air of overconfidence. I'm too far away to make out their words, but the unfamiliar rhythm of their voices tells me they're speaking their native tongue.

A quick sweep of Orloff's body gives me an idea of where he's most likely hiding his weapons. He will be carrying several, as will his colleague. More than enough to do significant damage to these guests if provoked. Despite my dismissal to Dante, the truth is, I don't know the way the Russians work like I do with the Italian families. Everything I know about the Bratva leans toward unnecessary and unpredictable violence. Orloff could strike at any moment. But I'm not sure that's the hand he wants to play today. If it was, he would have struck already.

Unless my gut instinct is wrong.

Orloff and the other man receive their second pouring of wine, and then the sommelier begins describing the wine's features as he moves down the line of guests at the bar. Instead of staying with the group, Orloff picks up his glass and wanders around the room with his friend. He acts as though he's studying the vintages lined up on the shelves against the wall, but I know he's just killing time. He keeps scanning the room, clearly waiting for one of the Bellantis to arrive and confront him. So that's exactly what he's going to get.

What kind of host would I be to keep my guest waiting?

I casually approach Orloff and the other Russian, no urgency in my gait, keeping my eyes on both of them and assessing their every movement. Orloff is good at pretending to be relaxed and comfortable in enemy territory, though his friend looks tense and stiff. As if sensing me coming up behind him, Orloff spins slowly with a welcoming, friendly smile on his rugged face.

"Armani Bellanti. How nice of you to greet me. I was expecting your brother Dante. He is the one in charge, no?"

He looks healthy, clear-eyed, completely unaffected from the fire he was involved in only days ago. If he suffered any ill effects, I can't see them.

"I handle security concerns," I say. "Of which you are presently one, Mr. Orloff. Welcome to Bellanti Vineyards, by the way. Now tell me: what exactly do you want?"

His smile broadens. "You know my name."

"I like to know all of my enemies by name."

Orloff lets out a laugh. It's charming enough to make my stomach tie itself in knots. This man either has an abundance of natural charisma, or he's a sociopath. Possibly both.

He puts a hand on his chest to indicate a fake wound. "Who has said we are enemies? I have not declared my intentions. Have you?"

I don't respond.

Inclining his head at me, he wanders to an unoccupied four-top table in the corner of the room, and I follow behind him and his guard. We take our seats, and then a waiter comes over to drop off glasses of water. Before he can ask if we'd like to order anything, I shoo him away. It's just the three of us now, pretending to have an easy, amicable conversation by the windows.

"This wine?" Orloff says, lifting his glass to admire the ruby liquid. "It is very...palatable. Your family does good work here."

Again, I say nothing. He makes a show of drinking down the rest of the wine, then sets the empty glass on the table with a satisfied grin.

"Perhaps I will try another selection," he says.

I can't explain how or why, but this man is seriously getting under my skin.

"I'm giving you five more minutes inside my winery before I have security escort you out," I tell him. "What do you want, Orloff?"

He shakes his head. "This is not how honorable men treat each other, Armani Bellanti. But I have heard this about you, quick to anger. Even quicker to strike recklessly." His smile suddenly drops, replaced by a threatening sneer. "You are quick to strike, are you not?"

I give him a hard stare. "Get to the point."

"You might have heard about this...accident that my fiancée found herself in. Yes?"

"Word travels fast among the established families in the area," I say with a nod, ignoring the uptick of my heart rate at his mention of Candi's friend. "Though perhaps you're not aware of how tight we are here."

My implication is obvious. I've got friends, and Orloff's gang needs to watch their step.

Unperturbed, he goes on, "Lucky for you, she survived. Though she doesn't appreciate that you delayed her wedding plans."

A pang of relief goes through me to hear that she's alive, because Candi has been worried sick. Not because there's a chance that Juliana really might be my little sister.

"Please, give her my best. I hope she suffered no ill effects," I say.

"Oh, is that what you hope? That she suffered no ill effects. I'll keep that in mind when I come for you." His voice drops low and menacing. "This will not be our last meeting, Bellanti."

"I don't doubt that," I say, taking his threat in stride.

He nods to his heavyset associate, and they both stand from their chairs and leave. I watch them go, and I don't take my eyes off them until they've made it out the front doors. My phone vibrates immediately.

"I've got eyes on them." It's Clayton. "They're heading to the guest parking lot. Getting in the vehicle. Vehicle is moving down the driveway toward the main road."

"I don't need the play-by-play. Just make sure they go and they don't come back."

I hang up and stride back to the Bellanti offices.

My heart is racing, despite my best efforts to keep my cool. Dante rises from behind my desk the second I enter my office.

"What did Orloff say?" he asks.

I am reluctant to tell him. It's not good.

"In so many words, we're fucked," I answer. "He knows we were involved, and I didn't bother lying to him about it because it wouldn't have changed anything. It's war now with the Bratva *and* the Brunos. Also, Juliana survived."

Dante huffs out a breath and then looks to the ceiling. "Okay. Okay. We'll just have to try to take him out again. It's the only way."

He's not wrong. I need to come up with another plan—as soon as fucking possible.

"What are we doing about Guerra?" he asks. "We need to find out if she's our sister."

I shake my head, "Don't go there, Dante."

"Why not? What if Marco is right, and she is—"

"Stop it. You've already convinced yourself that she's Liliana, but we have no proof."

"So let's *get* proof," Dante pushes.

"Are you listening to yourself? Right now, it doesn't matter if she *is* our flesh and blood. We've got a war to fight. That's what we need to be focusing on."

And if I don't act fast, none of us might live long enough to find out the truth anyway.

11

CANDI

I CAN'T BELIEVE I'm doing this.

My hands are cold as ice as I pick at a piece of bread from the basket in the center of the café table. A glass of sparkling water collects condensation while the top erupts with tiny, fizzing bubbles. The waiter has come by three times now to see if my lunch date has arrived. He eyes me as he wanders past again, probably annoyed that I'm clogging up his afternoon flow.

Mom hasn't arrived, and I'm not so sure that she will. I've never invited her out to lunch before; maybe she's just as uncomfortable with the idea as I am. It's just not something that we've ever done together, and honestly, once I left home and started growing into my independence, the thought of spending time with her—with any of my family, really—made me feel...not good. Because whenever I'm around them, I somehow revert to my childhood self. It's like I'm a worthless little kid all over again, like I've taken a huge step backwards.

But for some reason, I want to tell her about the baby. I

don't know why. I just do.

I debated inviting her to the house, but ultimately figured neutral territory would be best. After all, Armani and I will be getting divorced in a few more months, right? I don't see the point in pretending I'm a happy little Bellanti wife, just for my mother's benefit.

When I tried to leave the house earlier, I found out that Armani had assigned me a driver-slash-bodyguard. Thanks to my near-death experience at the bakery, I'm apparently not allowed to go anywhere unaccompanied anymore. I didn't argue, for the baby's sake. The bodyguard brought me to downtown Napa, where I'd reserved a table at Julio's for lunch. There are people everywhere, and my guard is seated just a few tables away, not exactly blending in with his black suit and bulging muscles and oversized dark sunglasses. But I have to admit, I do feel safer.

When I check the time on my phone again, I realize my mom is half an hour late now. She's probably not coming. Her response to my text invite was, "I'll try," which wasn't exactly a yes. Maybe this was a bad idea. All I've done is set myself up for disappointment.

Speaking of disappointment, Armani told me that they finally confirmed Juliana survived the fire—and although I'm over the fucking moon that she's alive, her phone is still off and I still haven't heard from her.

Where is she? Why hasn't she reached out by now? Have I been officially cut off? Does she blame me for what happened at the bakery? All the worrying is making me sick.

Plus, I'm afraid Sergio Bruno is planning to retaliate against the Bellanti family—which includes me, at the moment—for the fire. I'm getting more anxious by the second as I sit here. My entire life is in shambles.

I push back from the table, but then hesitate as my chest wells with an inscrutable emotion.

It feels like regret, but I'm not sure if I'm regretting the fact that I got my hopes up about my mom showing up, or that I invited her to meet me in the first place. We don't have the kind of relationship where I tell her anything of importance, really. She's always kept me at arm's length, even when I was young. A therapist would probably say it was because she was in survival mode, dealing with years of my father's verbal abuse and the constant stress of caring for my four rambunctious brothers before I finally came along. And I can kind of understand that. But this baby news is important. I need her to show up for me.

Doesn't every daughter want her mom involved in her grandchild's life? And in my case, doesn't my mom deserve a chance to make up for lost time with me by showering her grandkid with all the love and attention I never got? And yes, I'm hoping she might want to be a part of my little family circle. Because once Armani and I are separated, it'll just be me and the baby. I'm sure I'll need all the support I can get, being a single parent.

Not that Armani won't support us financially—I'm sure he'll want to help with the money part of raising his kid, and I'm not going to turn that down—but I'm going to need emotional support as well. And my baby is going to need a lot more family than the mafia.

Then again, is it sheer wishful thinking to believe I can trust my mother to be a safe place for my child? She certainly wasn't a safe place for me. Staring at the fizz misting from my seltzer, I feel shame this time. Shame for thinking that things could be different. That she'd actually show up for me for once.

"Cassandra?"

My head snaps up at the sound of the familiar voice.

"Mom. You made it."

The hostess beside her smiles and hands my mother a menu after pulling out her chair across from me.

"Enjoy," the hostess says.

I nod. "Thank you."

The second the hostess leaves, my mother rolls her eyes. "What's with women pulling out chairs for other women these days? She think I can't seat myself?"

"Just a courtesy," I say neutrally, already shifting into diplomat mode.

Mom just hmmphs and lifts the menu to her eyes.

She made an effort; I can tell. The dark rinse jeans are probably the nicest ones she owns, with no hint of a hole or a stain anywhere, and she's wearing a burgundy cable knit sweater that's much too warm for the weather but which I'm almost certain I gave her for Christmas a few years ago. It looks lovely against her auburn hair. I'm inexplicably touched by her gesture.

"How is everyone?" I ask, trying to get her talking.

"Fine. They're all fine."

She lowers the menu and eyes me critically. "You gonna tell me about this secret wedding you and Armani had, or what?"

"What?" Heat rushes into my cheeks. "Who told you?"

"Sean heard something about it," she says with a shrug.

That...actually makes sense. My brother runs in some

shady circles, and I could easily see one of Sean's "associates" bringing up the fact that his baby sister married into the mob. Which, of course that kind of gossip would be way too juicy to keep to himself.

"It wasn't planned," I tell her. "We were in Vegas and we just...did it on a whim."

"Oh yeah? I figured it was a shotgun wedding. Minus the shotgun part, since you didn't bother to tell us about it. Did that Bellanti knock you up? I thought I liked him okay."

Fuck.

Before I can even begin to formulate an appropriate way to tell her the humiliating truth that yes, "that Bellanti" did knock me up, the waiter appears.

"Are we ready to order?" he asks, pouring fresh glasses of water for both of us.

Mom gets a torta sandwich with carnitas (I have no doubt she ordered it because it's the cheapest thing on the menu, not because it's what she really wants), and I get the filet mignon tacos—not because they're actually what I want, either, but because I know they'll be excellent and I want to send the leftovers home with her to enjoy later.

The second the waiter is gone, my mom looks me up and down and then nods to herself.

"So. You're pregnant," she states, as if I've copped to it already. "How far along?"

My jaw drops. There's no denying it now, but my God. I was not expecting this.

"Um. I guess it's almost ten weeks now," I say, quickly doing the mental math.

"And is this something you want?" she asks bluntly.

Once again, I'm astounded.

"Yes," I say.

She searches my eyes and then gives another nod. "Good. Is it something he wants?"

"I—I don't know," I blurt, still too disarmed to sidestep the question. "I'm not sure he knows what he wants."

"Men." She lets out a little annoyed sigh and then pats my hand. "You'll figure it out. With or without him. You always find a way to land on your feet."

All I can do is force a smile and try to not burst into tears. I'm not used to my mom offering words of comfort or kindness. This is the closest she's ever come to saying she's proud of me. Maybe she's softening up in her later years. Or maybe she sees something of her younger self in me now. I'm right around the age that she was when she married my dad. I wonder if she's saying the things that she wishes someone had said to her.

A basket of chips and salsa gets deposited on our table, and we both dig in.

"I was thinking maybe you could help me with the online baby registry?" I say. "Not the computer part, just the list of things I'll need to add to it. Obviously it's kind of early—I know you're not supposed to get too excited before the twelve-week mark—but I thought you might have some ideas. I don't even know where to start."

"Sure. I can do that. Been through it enough times myself."

"Thank you."

She takes a few chips and thinks as she eats them one at a time, and then says, "People are gonna bombard you with cutesie clothes and toys once the baby comes, and for every holiday after that, so don't ask for any of those things in advance. Ask for the stuff you really need. Diapers, mountains of 'em, plus wipes and burping cloths and onesies and socks. Those socks will be disappearing left and right, believe me. You can never have enough."

"This is great," I say, nodding as I hurriedly dig a pen out of my purse and start writing down notes on my napkin.

By the time the waiter drops off our food, we've made some really solid progress.

About two bites into the meal, Mom's phone rings. Her purse is hanging on the back of her chair and the ringing won't stop, so she fishes it out of her bag and winces before answering. It's probably my dad. I can't imagine any other name popping up on her screen would elicit that kind of reaction, and if it was a bill collector, she wouldn't feel the need to pick up.

"Hello?"

Even with all the ambient noise of the restaurant, I can hear the rumbling sound of my father's voice on the other end. She covers her other ear and tilts her head, squinting her eyes.

"Say that again," she says. "Sean what?"

I see it on her face the instant she comprehends whatever my dad is telling her. It's something bad. Something that has her turning white as a sheet.

"Mom? What's wrong?" I ask.

"He's...dead," she chokes out, her tear-filled eyes lifting to mine.

"*What?*"

The phone slips from her grasp, clanking onto the table. My mother just stares at it like it's a figment of her imagination. Somehow, I grab the phone. My hands are shaking.

My mouth is dry. My heart is slamming so hard in my chest, I can feel each thump like a hammer blow.

"Dad? What happened to Sean?"

My father sobs, then rambles on.

"He got shot by some fucking Russian. Shot him point blank, right in front of the house." His hoarse voice breaks off as another sob wracks him. "'God gave, God took back.' That's what he said when he killed my boy. I rode in the ambulance with him so he wasn't alone. All the way to the hospital, they tried to resuscitate him, but it was too late. There was so much blood."

There's a roaring in my ears, a numbness that has taken over my entire body. The restaurant goes blurry all around me. I can't process this. This can't be right.

My brother Sean. The only one of my brothers who ever let me walk to school with him. He was the youngest Gallagher before I came along, so he probably felt like he owed me one for taking his place as the family scapegoat. I remember when he was twelve or thirteen and joined the Boy Scouts, he started camping out in the backyard on Friday nights. Sometimes—not always, but sometimes—he'd let me drag my pillow and a flashlight into the tent and then he'd tell me scary stories until I got so scared I had to run back to the house to hide under the covers.

I just can't believe it. He's...gone. Dead. Sean is dead.

Murdered by a Russian.

Pain lances through my chest as the realization blooms. This wasn't some random hit. This was the Bratva's retaliation for the fire at the Bruno bakery.

My husband, the father of my child, started the fight that just killed my brother.

12

CANDI

My brother's funeral is a sparse affair. An overcast sky leaves the church interior dim and gloomy, and a mere handful of people are in attendance—including a few that I've never met. A group of young men who I assume are his friends take up the back row of seats, leaving the middle pews mostly bare and the front occupied by myself, my parents, and my three other brothers. Conor, Patrick, and Liam are red-eyed but their expressions are grim, not sorrowful.

I wonder if they're afraid of who might be next. I know I'm thinking about it.

I've heard a few coughs and sniffles, but I haven't seen a single guest shed a tear. Not my mother. Certainly not my dad; he's always been the stoic type. My brothers mostly stare at their feet during the service, while my mother fidgets with the strap of her black purse. The church is eerily silent during the pauses in Father Murphy's sermon, which has me feeling even more on edge. I've been to funerals before where emotions seem to drip from the walls and surround you with an almost palpable air of grief.

Not today. Not this funeral. There's something else brewing in this room.

This funeral is for a young man, barely more than a boy, who was gunned down in cold blood by someone he'd never met, someone who didn't know him. Someone whose boss sought revenge on Armani Bellanti, and wanted blood-for-blood.

Armani isn't here. I told him to stay at home. His face was the last thing anyone here needed or wanted to see, and for all I know, the Russians could be lying in wait for him and would open fire inside the church. I've barely spoken to my husband since my brother's murder.

Armani did try to comfort me when I told him the news, but he walked away after I rejected him and hasn't made another attempt since. Is it possible that he feels guilty about what happened? I nearly snort out loud at the thought. As if he'd feel guilty about anything, ever. He's an iceberg wrapped in steel. Probably the only thing he regrets is the fact that Orloff wasn't killed in the bakery fire.

As for my brother, I'm sure Armani considers him a casualty of war. Par for the course. Nothing more.

Picking anxiously at my fingernails, my stomach sinks with the sickly realization that it was probably only a matter of time before something like this happened to Sean. He played stupid games with dangerous men, regarding them like his frat buddies instead of the monsters they could be. Give him a few beers and a slap on the back and you could talk him into doing anything. He ran with a bad crowd and my family never discouraged it. In fact, I'm sure my other brothers have also been doing freelance jobs for the local mob families. They aren't the type to care which ones they work for, either. Their only loyalties lie in who pays the most.

My dad is already muttering about revenge, even though I know he won't act on it. He'd been griping all morning until Mom finally got him to shut up when the service started. I glance over at him and find his face schooled into a cold, emotionless façade. He may be silent now, but I can still feel his grief and angst. That's what's hanging in the air around us.

"Let us pray."

Father Murphy bows his head. The pianist plays a mournful song that I can't pinpoint. Someone shifts in the pew in the back, making the wood creak. My hairline starts to prickle.

Discreetly looking back, I reassure myself that it's not the Bratva here to finish us all off. Though it's some small relief to know that Armani has this place surrounded by a phalanx of security who will follow us to the gravesite and then back to my family's home. After that, my parents and brothers are on their own. How long before another of my siblings turns up dead?

Clenching my jaw, I push back my anger at Armani. He's responsible for this. If he hadn't gone head-to-head with the Russian, trying to take him out in that goddamn fire, none of this would have happened. A sob lodges in my chest.

I've never been close to my brothers, but out of all of

them, Sean was the most decent to me. We were the youngest Gallagher siblings, and the closest in age. Growing up, I never got bullied at school, because Sean was always one year ahead of me and his reputation as one of the Gallagher boys meant that nobody dared to mess with me. So in that respect, he sort of indirectly protected me. And yes, he was a braggart and a liar and a showoff...but he loved to have a good time and he always treated me like a human being.

Still, my sorrow is mostly for what our relationship could have been, not for what we did have. The connection we had was tenuous, I know that. But the loss is still hitting me hard. Maybe one day he could have turned his life around. Found love, built a family.

My mom lights a cigarette as soon as we leave the church and head to our vehicles to drive to the cemetery. This is hitting her hard, too. In fact, I'm sure she's carrying the weight of Sean's death more than any of us.

"Meet you guys there," I tell her, nodding to my car.

Though I drive myself, I'm tailed by Armani's men. My parents don't know about his involvement in Sean's murder. They don't know that my husband was the impetus for his death sentence, and I'm not about to tell them. I can barely bring myself to think about it. They'll find out in due time, I'm sure. Word gets around through these underground channels. Especially if my other brothers continue doing odd jobs for the local mafia clans.

It drizzles during the burial, which goes quickly. It seems we've no sooner gathered around the yawning hole in the ground than my brother's casket is lowered inside. Mom has a white rose in her hand, but she doesn't toss it on top of the casket. Instead, she holds it to her chest gently, like a child cradling a doll.

Father Murphy says a few more words. Then dirt hits the casket in thumping shovelfuls. Each one makes me jump a little until I'm desensitized to the sound.

We leave just as the rain starts to pour. I don't want to go to my parents' house for dinner now, but it's my duty. And even if I didn't feel obligated, I consider it a sign of respect to Sean.

Shockingly, the exterior of the house looks neat and clean when I get there. Even the yard is tidied up, which is really saying something. The fence still sags in places, but the grass has been mowed and the weeds are gone. The porch is swept and free of cigarette butts and beer cans, and when I step inside, I smell pine cleaner and something scented like....and then I see it. There's a candle burning in the center of the coffee table. Rosemary and maybe citrus.

"It looks great in here, Mom," I say.

She nods. "Your dad and brothers are getting changed. I need to get dinner ready. You can sit and watch TV or—"

"I can help," I say. The last thing I want to do is sit around.

She gestures for me to follow her into the kitchen, where she ties on an apron.

"Get the ham out of the oven, okay?"

"Sure."

Even though I have no appetite, I can see that it looks good, perfectly baked with a sheen of honey glaze over the top. That she knew how to time the baking of this while accounting for the funeral is a skill I certainly didn't inherit. I can barely boil pasta.

We don't speak as I help her finish preparing the meal—mashed potatoes, green bean casserole, buttery rolls. Comfort foods, though I'm not sure anyone is going to feel much like eating. Quiet conversation comes from the living room, which has filled with more people than were at the funeral. Some of them are neighbors, some are my parents' friends or coworkers. I see more young men that probably know my brothers.

"Should have made two hams," my mom sighs. "I'm not going to have enough food."

She darts across the kitchen and rummages through the pantry, pulling out three boxes of mac and cheese and a few cans of baked beans.

"Here, get started on these," she says. "And set the oven to 350. I think I've got a meatloaf in the freezer downstairs. We can bake that extra can of Pillsbury rolls, too."

The counters are already filled with bowls of potatoes, vegetables, bread, and salad, and two coffee pots plus a variety of generic sodas in two-liter bottles.

"Mom," I say gently. "I think there's more than enough. It's okay."

She frowns. "Better to have too much than not enough. Just do what I told you."

Less than an hour later, we've got macaroni and cheese, baked beans, and the reheated meatloaf ready to go, along with plates of crackers and cheese and cold cuts that Mom scrounged up while I was setting everything out on the table. Some of the guests have already left.

"What took you so long?" my dad snaps, coming into the room. "Everyone's gone already."

Her entire body melts, the energy draining right out of her. Something in my chest flares.

"There are still plenty of people here," I say pointedly. "Mom, I'll go tell them the food is ready. Why don't you sit down and rest? You haven't taken a break since we got home."

Soon, the mourners and my family are flooding into the dining room, heaping their plates and returning to sit in the living room around the television. My dad keeps the channel on sports, which at least seems to be distracting everybody. Once everyone is done serving themselves, I sit at the end of the dining room table and stare at the food, the smell turning my stomach.

It's not just the pregnancy hormones. My insides are in knots. I want to leave, but I feel guilty about my husband's part in Sean's death, so I don't. Glancing through the doorway into the living room, my eyes stray to the TV. The sound of everyone eating makes me even more nauseous. I'm about to call it and go when my brother Liam slams his fist on a folding tray.

"I'm going to make that Russian bastard pay."

The mouth sounds and clinking of silverware quiets down.

"Not now, Liam," Dad warns.

"If not now, when?" he insists. "If we sit around waiting, we'll be next."

Pretending not to listen, I stir the potatoes, glad my mother is in the kitchen and can't hear this crap.

"What do you have in mind, boy?"

109

"Easy. I find out where he lives, slip inside in the middle of the night, and take him out."

My God, does he really think it would be that simple? Pressing a hand to my forehead, I have to stop myself from interrupting. My husband, who is an experienced mafia insider, couldn't manage to pull off a well-organized attack and take Orloff down, but my brother...my inexperienced, hot-headed, ego-inflated brother, is going to do it. Sure.

Dad cracks open a beer. "Yeah. That could work."

That could work? Is he serious? He's actually *encouraging* this?

"Cassandra! Bring me a cold beer. This one's warm!" he bellows, making me jump.

It takes a second for me to realize that he's speaking to my mother and not me, because of course we share a name. But we don't have to share this dysfunctional trainwreck of a family. Touching my belly, I get up and slip the strap of my purse over my shoulder. Nothing in this house will ever change. One by one, my brothers will stupidly attempt to get revenge for Sean until they're all cold in the ground and the only one left is my father. Who will probably either die of a heart attack or hire a hitman who will eventually turn on him when he doesn't pay.

I don't want any part of this. And my baby sure as hell won't be part of this family either.

Without a word to anyone, I dart through the kitchen and leave, giving my mom a tiny wave as I silently close the back door behind me. I'm sure she'll understand my Irish goodbye, her more than anyone.

Digging my keys out of my bag as I make my way along the side of the house to the curb out front, I spy Armani's men parked down the street. Someone drives by the opposite way in a blacked-out SUV. When the driver's window rolls down, I gasp at the face staring back at me.

It's Maxim Orloff, dragging his eyes across my face until he suddenly speeds away, avoiding my guards and making his point very, very clear.

13

ARMANI

PULLING into the parking lot of the doctor's office, I take a deep breath and steel myself for what's about to happen. Candi seems to be doing the same. Once the car is off, I turn to her in the hope that I can say something soothing or encouraging, but she's already got her back to me, reaching for the door handle without so much as a glance in my direction.

We've hardly spoken since her brother's funeral. If I ask her a question, she answers in monosyllables. If I try to touch her, she jerks away like she's been burned. Sean's death is clearly weighing on her heavily. It weighs on me, too, more than she'll ever know. If it wasn't for me, her brother would still be alive. A fact that I am certain she is well aware of. I have no idea how I'm supposed to bridge this chasm between us. I don't even know where to start.

Jogging to catch up with her before she reaches the door of the clinic, I gently place my hand on the small of her back. She doesn't push me away, but she doesn't slow her pace either.

"How are you feeling?" I ask, pulling open the heavy glass door for her.

"Fine." Her voice is terse and clipped, which is nothing out of the ordinary.

"Is there anything I can do to...make you more comfortable while we're here?"

The words sound preposterous the second they're out of my mouth. I'm not sure what I'm even asking. I guess it sounded more solid in my head.

She whirls on me in the middle of the lobby. "I said I'm fine. Let's go, or we'll be late."

All I can do is nod and walk beside her to the OB-GYN's suite at the rear of the building.

After she checks in, I gently urge her to a seat near the waiting room exit. She doesn't put up a fight. One of my security guards, who has been trailing behind us, nonchalantly takes a seat behind us where he has a full view of the waiting room. No one seems to pay him any mind, but I can feel his presence like a weight on my back.

There was a short time when my family didn't have to be tailed by guards at every footstep, but here we are, back in that place where looking over your shoulder is a given. Candi buries her nose in a magazine while I sit and do nothing but think. That's all I seem to do lately.

My mind never turns off, never stops turning over and over.

Planning. Plotting. Worrying.

I can't stop wondering if it's really her. Liliana. Could Juliana Guerra be our sister? Dante is still on the fence, but Marco seems convinced, solely based on how similar she looks to our mother. And yes, the facial features are a dead ringer for our mother in her younger years. The only thing missing is the haunted shadow in her eyes and the lines around her mouth—being married to my father surely aged her more than we'll ever know.

The door to the back office swings open and a nurse checks her clipboard and calls Candi's name. I nod at the security guard to stay where he is and follow my wife to the back. After Candi's vitals are taken—blood pressure, weight, height—we're led to an exam room.

A different nurse comes in and asks Candi a bunch of health questions, tapping her answers on a tablet, and then tells us that the ultrasound tech will be in momentarily. My stomach drops when she says that. I knew the ultrasound was going to be part of the exam, but I still can't believe I'm about to see my child on a screen. I'm sure it's not much more than a clump of cells right now, barely big enough to be detectable, but seeing this confirmation of life is...it's a big deal. This image will shift the *idea* of this baby into the *reality* of this baby.

As for Candi, she doesn't look any different. No baby bump, no weight gain, none of that "glow" you always hear about. She looks completely normal. If it hadn't been for the fire, I—we?—wouldn't even know this baby existed yet, but here we are, waiting to see the evidence.

I'm still not sure I believe that Candi didn't plan this all along. As a form of insurance. Surely she would have considered the fact that once we got divorced, she'd have no financial safety net anymore. What better way to make that safety net permanent than to have a child with me, cementing my support for the next eighteen years?

Yet, as I side-eye my wife and spy her tired face, I start

to doubt my suspicions—and not for the first time. She definitely doesn't give off the self-satisfied vibe of someone who is successfully pulling off a con. I'm not even sure how she feels about being pregnant.

The door swings open and both our heads snap up, but it's just the nurse again.

"Mr. Bellanti, would you mind filling out this medical history form for yourself and your blood relatives, please?" she says. "We'll need it for the baby's health screenings in the future."

She hands me a six-page, double-sided packet that's attached to a clipboard. My eyes track to the nurse, and I swallow down an expletive and give her a tight smile.

"Of course."

"It'll just be a few more minutes," she adds.

Then she leaves me with this monstrosity of paperwork and a pen that won't fucking write. I grab my Montblanc PIX ballpoint from the inner pocket of my jacket.

"We're finding a new doctor," I inform Candi.

That gets her attention. "What? Why?"

"Why should I trust someone to deliver my child when they don't even have functioning writing implements in their office? And look at this floor. It's a disgrace."

The tiles haven't been polished recently, and dirty scrape marks are showing around the feet of the chairs. Hardly sanitary.

Candi scowls. "Dr. Perry is the highest rated obstetrician in Napa."

"I don't care. You'll go to the one Frankie went to," I tell her. "Dante vetted her already, so I'm sure she's the best—"

"This *is* the doctor Frankie went to," Candi interrupts.

116

"And excuse me, but since when do you give a shit about this baby? Because I didn't realize you cared."

"I'm sorry, are you referring to the fact that I've been less than enthusiastic about you tricking me into having a kid?"

"I didn't trick you!"

"So you've said. I'm still not sure I buy it."

Candi sighs with disgust, as if she's at the end of her patience with me, and turns away to stare out the window. I guess we're not going to be reconciling any time soon.

Focusing on the paperwork in front of me is difficult, mostly because I don't know if anyone in my family had any of this shit. My dad's health couldn't have been that great, considering the fact that he drank, smoked, ate a lot of red meat, and lived a contentious life, but I don't know if he was ever officially diagnosed with anything...and unfortunately, I don't see chronic asshole syndrome listed. I consider calling Dante, assuming he also had to fill this thing out, but don't get the chance before a young woman in hot pink scrubs walks in.

"Mrs. Bellanti? I'm the ultrasound tech. If you'll both come with me, please?"

She escorts us to another room. The lights are turned down, and there's a soft humming sound coming from a cart stacked with machines. The technician gives Candi a gown to change into, and then leaves the room. Keeping her back to me, Candi undresses and puts on the gown, tying it in the front. I scroll through some emails on my phone, giving her some privacy.

Candi gets on the padded exam table and lies down. A few moments later, there's a knock on the door, and then the tech comes back in. She has Candi open the gown and then squirts clear gel from a bottle onto Candi's belly.

"Ah, that's cold!" she yelps.

They share a small laugh, and then the tech picks up the long plastic wand, swirls it around in the gel, and begins to slowly move it side to side across Candi's stomach. The whole time, the tech watches the screen on top of the nurse cart, searching the gray and black patches of the dark image for...something.

Suddenly, a whoosh, whoosh, whoosh sound comes through. My eyes are immediately drawn to a small, light colored, oblong shape that's surrounded by a circle of black. Leaning over the technician's shoulder, I peer closer at the screen as the images becomes clearer. A wave of light-headedness hits me as my brain comprehends what I'm seeing.

"Is that...?" I trail off. I can't even say it.

"Yep. There's your baby," the tech says, pointing to the curved bean with a pounding little dot that I recognize as the heart, steadily beating.

"Wow," Candi whispers.

"Wow," I repeat.

Bracing myself on the exam table with one hand, I find that I can't pull my eyes away. My chest aches as if I've been punched.

"Baby is measuring at just about seven and a half weeks," the tech tells us. "The doctor will calculate your official due date when she comes in."

Due date. My baby is going to have a due date. He or she will be coming into the world at a moment in time I can circle on my calendar. This is really happening.

I'm going to be a father.

I look over at Candi and her eyes flick briefly to meet mine. There's the slightest hint of a smile on her face, as if she's afraid to let it out. The dim light from the monitor casts over her face, giving her a kind of glow, and something warm sparks inside me.

I might die on this hill. There's a very good chance of that happening. But I swear to God, I'm going to end this mob war for good.

For my family. For my wife. For my baby.

If it's the last thing I do.

14

CANDI

THE WHOLE DRIVE home from the appointment with the OB-GYN I can't stop looking at the ultrasound picture. Armani asked the technician to print out two, and he slipped a copy into his jacket pocket when he didn't think I was looking.

Just that small gesture gave me hope. It's not that I'm expecting some kind of fairy-tale ending, but knowing that he's invested in our child—again, not in terms of money, but him having an interest in helping me raise our kid—would be a huge relief. Plenty of kids grow up perfectly well-adjusted in nontraditional families, either with parents who are divorced or with a single parent or a grandparent caring for them. Armani and I can find a way to make it work.

And if not, well, I'll have to make up for it by loving this little bean as much as humanly possible.

Though I can't deny the fact that deep down, I'm still hoping that Armani might come around. That there's still a chance for us to make this marriage work. This *life* work.

Because even though things between us have been rocky lately, when we're good together, we're *so good*.

We've seen each other at our worst, and we can handle each other's darkness and light. We're a solid team. We just...fit.

I think back to that day at the waterfall on our fake honeymoon, but the connection we've shared isn't only about sex or physical attraction. There was that incredible day we helped harvest Bellanti grapes at the family vineyard, the day Frankie unexpectedly went into labor and we all had to pull together to make sure she got to the hospital in a hurry. Or even my and Armani's first real date, on the yacht, where I think we both surprised each other with our combination of teasing, personal confessions, and verbal sparring. There is something very real that exists between me and my husband. I know I'm not imagining it.

Heck, even when Armani is being a jerk, he still insists on protecting me, sending security to keep an eye on me, doing everything in his power to ensure I'm safe. He ran into a burning building to rescue me, didn't he? The man cares about me, even if he has trouble admitting it to himself. And it's no wonder, considering the fucked-up childhood he had and the fact that he lost the two females he cared most about in the whole world at such a young age.

Looking down at the picture in my hand again, I trace the shape of the little bean one more time. It's finally really dawning on me that I'm going to be a mom in less than seven months, and something is opening up inside of me. A deep well of acceptance and love that feels natural, as if it's been there all along. Just waiting for a minuscule human with a newly beating heart to reveal it. No matter what this baby's family looks like, or what kind of care their biological father can or cannot offer, I'm going to make it my mission to be sure that he or she feels cherished and wanted every single day. They'll never have to grow up feeling like I did.

After we get out of the car at home, I make my way to the stairs, figuring Armani will be rushing off to the Bellanti offices since he already missed a good chunk of his workday thanks to my appointment. But instead, he follows me up to the bedroom. Maybe he wants to talk.

Crossing my arms, I look at him and wait.

But instead of speaking, he locks the door behind him and strides purposefully toward me. I'm half expecting him to start a fight, half expecting him to rip my clothes off. What I'm not expecting at all is the way he lowers onto his knees before me.

Shocked, I stand there frozen as he takes my abdomen between his hands and stares at the space he cradles with his palms. My breath hitches. He leans closer and rests his forehead there and just...stays.

I gently lace my fingers against the back of his head, afraid he's going to pull away the second I do. But he doesn't. This big, imposing man simply remains on his knees in front of me, touching the space where his baby is growing. I don't know what it means, and I don't care. It's enough for me to close my eyes and appreciate this moment.

Armani exhales, his warm breath seeping through the fabric of my T-shirt.

"I...have to tell you something," I say hesitantly.

Armani doesn't move. "I'm listening."

I know it might not be the right time to tell him about

Orloff's appearance after my brother's funeral, but it's been nagging at me and I need to get it off my chest.

"At my Sean's funeral—well, afterward actually, at my parents' house—I saw Orloff."

Immediately he stands, tensing up. "Orloff showed up at your parents' place?"

"Yes. I mean, he wasn't inside the house. But when I left I saw him driving down the street in an SUV. He looked right at me. We made eye contact."

"How is that possible?" he says, clearly agitated. "I had security all over that neighborhood—"

"It was just a drive-by," I tell him. "I'm sure if he tried to get out of the car or go inside the house, your guards would have intervened. This was more like...a warning. A threat."

He starts pacing, pulling out his phone as he runs a hand through his hair.

"Fuck. Why didn't you tell me sooner? We're tracking his car, so it must have been a different car than what he usually drives. I need to get my men on this."

"Hey." I reach out and grab his arm, tugging until he stops pacing and faces me. "I didn't tell you because I knew you'd freak out like this. And I'm already under enough stress, and there's nothing you can do about it because it already happened."

"I can keep it from happening again," he insists. "No more going off property without a guard at your side. Two guards. And I'll tell security to treat every single unidentified vehicle as a potential threat. I'll send people to surveil Orloff and get a GPS on the new SUV, and—"

"Armani. Stop."

"No. I won't stop until Orloff is out of the picture. For

good. Even if I have to take him out myself. He's not going to hurt you or this baby, and he sure as hell isn't going to come creeping around you again."

He's gone full-on alpha male, the intensity rolling off him in waves. His fight-or-flight instincts are kicking, and he's ready to fight. But I don't want him to. Not right now. So I grab the phone out of his hand and set it on the dresser, then turn to face him again.

"Just be here with me, okay?" I plead. "That's what makes me feel safe. Even when you're being an asshole and I can't stand you, I still feel better knowing you're next to me."

Something in his expression shifts. And then, without a word, he shrugs out of his jacket and tosses it onto a chair. He unfastens his cuff links next and pulls his shirt hem free from the waist of his pants.

"If you're trying to seduce me now, it won't work," I bluff.

"Liar," he says, a smirk tugging at his lips.

He peels off his shirt, revealing those sexy tattoos hugging all that glorious muscle. Damn him. I can't tear my eyes away.

Dropping onto the bed as a hot ache blooms between my legs, I feel equally aroused and irritated at my own weakness when there's so much more we have to discuss, about the baby and everything. But I know what I need right now, and talking isn't it.

He unzips his pants and shoves his briefs down, revealing his thick, hard cock, and my mind narrows down to one thing only. Now it's my turn to drop to my knees, my mouth already opening as his hand slides to the back of my head.

Gripping my hair in his fist, he presses the tip of his cock against my lips. I quickly wet him with a circle of my tongue and then take him in deep, bracing myself with one hand on his hip. With the other, I hold his shaft tightly, moving him in and out of my mouth until he's breathing in quick little pants.

"Fuck yes..." he groans.

His pleasure quickens my pulse and spreads warmth through my limbs. Relaxing my jaw, I take him even deeper while tugging at his pants to lower them past his thighs. Armani grabs my head with both hands and starts moving his hips, trying to take control of the pace. Pushing against his hip, I hold him back and glance up at him, narrowing my eyes in rebuke. He eases up, but his gaze is so dark with passion that I can't help but moan as I run my tongue over the thick vein underneath his cock. God, I wanted this.

I work him until he begins to swell in my mouth. His eyes are closed now, and I'm certain he's completely lost in his own head, not that I mind. I love having that power over him. Knowing that I'm making him feel that way. Suddenly, his eyes open, and he pulls away and moves me so I'm lying on my back with my ass at the edge of the bed and my feet on the floor. Seconds later, my pants are down and he's slipping inside me.

"Armani," I pant helplessly as he pumps in and out. "Yes."

God, he feels good. Why does he feel so good? Every single time.

I wrap my arms around his neck and Armani lowers himself over me and kisses me with a searching, passionate hunger. Almost as if he wants me to lose myself the way he did.

Of course, it works. It always does with him. A few short breaths later and I'm drunk on his lips and the strokes of his tongue, nodding as he pulls my shirt up to my neck and pushes my bra up over my breasts. His hot mouth drops to my aching nipples, his thumb circling my clit as his thrusts get faster, harder, wetter.

Moaning, I arch my back as he works me to the brink of orgasm. His lips find mine again and as we kiss, as we fuck, as we hold each other tight, I'm utterly consumed by him. I feel something new beating between us, too. Something rich and full and promising.

It's...it's...

But whatever it is gets lost as my climax crests and crashes like a wave, hitting me hard and fast.

I cry out, barely aware of Armani finishing until he's bracing himself on one arm, his head resting against my shoulder. As we catch our breath, I absently run my fingers through his hair, becoming acutely aware of all the places our bodies touch. His cock still inside me. His thighs pressed against mine. His chest warming my side, his free arm casually draped over my breasts. Usually, he's quick to move away after sex, but this time he lingers and the tender feeling I had earlier returns.

He finally looks at me and runs a finger along my cheek. Hope flutters in my belly. Is he finally going to say he loves me? Or at least admit that he has feelings for me?

"I want you to know that I will always..." he begins.

My pulse is pounding. This is it.

"...take care of you," he finishes. "After everything is said and done, you and the baby will want for nothing, regard-less of any...ulterior motives."

Jerking my head back, I sputter, "Ulterior motives? What's that supposed to mean?"

Armani pulls away from me and gets up, leaving me disheveled and cold.

"It means that nothing changes the fact that you're going to be the mother of my child. Therefore, I'll always look out for your best interests. Make sure you have a nice home. A good vehicle. Credit card with a generous limit. Whatever you need."

The post-sex endorphins I was feeling explode and die. I'm caught between the joy of hearing that Armani will always be there for our child and the sick feeling in my gut at knowing that he's promised me nothing more than that.

Sitting up, I pull my shirt back down over my breasts and grab my underwear off the floor. As I slide them back on quickly, I feel my heart pounding, my stomach twisting sickly.

"What exactly are you saying? Just spit it out," I say, my tone harsh.

He's dressed again, his shirt still open, tending to his hair in the dresser mirror.

Without looking at me, he answers, "I'm saying that I still don't know if you did this on purpose, but that even if you did trick me into having this baby, it doesn't change the fact that I'm committed to taking care of my child and his or her mother." He finally turns to face me. "As for our arrangement, as I said before, it will still expire as agreed. I'm nothing if not a man of my word."

"Oh, I have no doubt of that," I say icily.

His cold words—and the detached efficiency with which he just delivered them—have left me with an ache in my chest that feels like a knife wound.

I'm hurt and furious and I don't try to hide it from him, not that it would bother him to see it on my face. I can't believe I was actually entertaining the thought that he might come around to the idea of being a family. Nothing could be further from the truth.

With one last glance in my direction, Armani finishes buttoning up his shirt and grabs his jacket on the way out the door.

I turn my back so I won't have to watch him leave.

Maybe it's a good thing that our marriage has an expiration date, after all. Because honestly? I'm not sure how much more of this I can take.

15

ARMANI

"Tell me again why we aren't just taking out Guerra," Clayton says, looking genuinely confused.

It's not the first time he's suggested killing Juliana, but removing her from the picture—permanently—to "solve" the Bruno War just isn't the quick-fix solution that my brother-in-law seems to think it is.

I've done a lot of questionable things, yes, but the thought of murdering a woman is inherently distasteful to me. Not only that, but murdering this particular woman would invite major backlash from the Russian mob as well, and it will be far worse than what we've come to expect from the Brunos, because Juliana is the fiancée of a Bratva kingpin.

Not to mention the fact that Marco is still convinced she's our dead sister. And she's Candi's best friend.

"We're not doing that," Marco says flatly, proving my point.

"In terms of expediency—" Clayton begins.

"No," I cut him off swiftly. "I'm with Marco. For once."

"So am I," Dante says. As the actual boss of this family, his word is law.

Clayton just shrugs, slumping in his chair and taking a hard swallow of his whiskey.

I've gathered my brothers and Clayton on our yacht in the Napa River harbor. Considering how frequently we've been infiltrated by moles in the past, I figured it was the safest place to discuss our next move. Which won't include killing Juliana Guerra.

But there's already tension in the air, and I have a feeling it's about to get much worse.

Usually, war room meetings like this are a flurry of opinions, one on top of the other. Not today. Ever since the bakery fire and the resulting revenge-murder of Candi's brother, my whole family has been laying low, everyone subdued but anxious.

Now, I know it's on me to figure out our next move, and the pressure has left me sleepless and irritable. In a word, I've been a real asshole lately. Though I generally like to be left alone to make big decisions, this feels too high-stakes to decide on my own. My ego isn't so big that I'm incapable of recognizing when I might be making a misstep.

I need my brothers' input. And Clayton's, too.

The other families in our circle don't know that I've called this meeting to arrange another offensive against the Brunos. This assault is too personal to involve anyone else. Besides, I suspect my colleagues will want to let the ashes cool a while longer before stirring things up again. They, like us, are bracing for the possibility of a major Bratva counterstrike.

Which is why the Bellantis need to strike first, and make it successful this time.

The clink of ice against glass tumblers is the only sound on the deck as my brothers silently sip their drinks.

"I know you said no," Clayton says, holding his palms up, "but I just want to reiterate one last time that getting rid of Guerra *would* remove the link between the Brunos and the Bratva. Sergio Bruno doesn't have another eligible bachelorette in his back pocket that he can marry off to seal the deal. He'll be forced to renegotiate with the Russians, but before they do, we can double-strike. Kick 'em while they're down and rip their balls off. That's all I'm saying."

"They're not 'down,'" I snap. "The fire killed a few of Bruno's men, but no one of importance. If anything, it's made him even more bloodthirsty than before. He's probably already got three soldiers in line to replace every one that he lost."

"My answer stands," Dante says. "Killing her will only bring violence back at us ten-fold, not to mention that we still haven't determined if she's related to us. And as a rule, I don't condone killing women."

Clayton nods and takes another long swallow of his drink.

"How's your work on the boating accident going?" I ask, eager to change the subject.

With a shrug, Clayton says, "I'm still going through the police reports, but there don't seem to be any answers there. As for the eyewitness who called in the Coast Guard—he only saw the smoke, that was it. Nothing but floating debris left when maritime response arrived."

"Dead ends," I say with disgust.

"Not all dead," he says. "I tracked down one of Bruno's old associates. A retiree, like you wanted. Not by choice, as it were. He's in the state prison over in Sacramento, locked up on racketeering charges. I was thinking I'd pay him a little visit."

"Do it," I say. "And if he won't talk, find out if he has friends who will."

"Don't worry. He'll talk," Clayton says darkly.

"That's all good and well," Dante cuts in, "but our priority right now isn't playing Nancy Drew. It's keeping the Bratva from making a pact with the Brunos. We're up against a wall, more than we ever have been in the past. We need a plan."

"I know that," I say irritably. "I'm working on it."

"Work faster," Dante says, his voice harsh.

What I don't want to tell anyone here is that I've been mulling an idea for the last few days, but it's not fully formed yet, which is why I've been keeping it to myself. If I make the wrong move, it'll push the Bratva to strike again, and there's no telling who they'll target next.

They could turn on our women.

Our children.

Setting down my drink, I walk away from it. The alcohol is sour in my gut. What if they came after *my* child? The possibility of a strike against Candi and our baby has been whispering in my head, getting louder each day. My brothers were the only ones I had to worry about for years, and then their wives, their children.

Now I have to worry about mine, too.

I still can't believe we failed so spectacularly at snuffing out Orloff. How the hell did he and Juliana escape that fire, when Candi barely made it out alive—and only thanks to me?

Could Juliana have been tipped off about the plan and invited Candi along on purpose? With the intent to leave her there to die? This is just speculation on my part, but considering all the double-crossing that's been going on lately, it's not out of the question that Candi's best friend might have stabbed her in the back. I know they haven't spoken since the day of the fire.

I glance over at Marco. He's rigid and has barely touched his drink. This meeting isn't sitting well with him, and his expression suggests he has something on his mind. Tapping a finger against his glass, he finally takes a sip.

"We could walk away," he says, mostly to himself. "Quit like we almost did last time. We were almost out for good. This could be our chance to wash our hands of the whole mess."

I let out a long breath. It's not the first time my little brother has brought this up. He's not wrong, either. We had the chance to leave the mob once, and we had every intention of doing so until Sergio Bruno pulled us back into the fray. We're in too deep now, though. Turning our backs on the mafia—and our allies—would have serious ramifications. We'd be considered traitors. We'd never be free and safe. Our friends could quickly become our enemies.

"We can't just walk away because we don't want to play anymore," Dante tells Marco.

Nodding, I add, "We'll get out someday—we will, Marco, don't look at me like that—but it'll only be possible after a lot of planning and preparation. Unfortunately, right now, the timing is shit. We can't lose our allies at the exact time we need them most. Because Bruno won't leave us alone until he's destroyed us."

"Bruno wouldn't be your biggest problem if the alliance with the Russians happens," Clayton points out. "The Bratva would kill you all, the minute you announced your departure. You'd be sitting ducks without the protection of the other mob families."

"There's no getting out," Dante says. "We have to play the game and we *must* win."

"Fine." Marco sits back. "But if Juliana is our sister, we have to get her out first."

I stroll over to the railing and look out at the river, sipping my whiskey. My idea begins to solidify.

"I agree." I turn back toward my brothers. "We do need to get her to safety. As soon as we possibly can."

All eyes are on me now.

"Which is why we're going to kidnap her," I say casually.

"We're *what*?" Marco says.

I shrug. "The only way to find out who she really is, is to get her on our turf. I can't do much without her physically here."

My little brother's expression darkens. "Why? So you can subject her to one of your little 'interrogation' sessions?"

I bypass the question, though interrogating Juliana is definitely on my to-do list.

"I need to get a sample of her DNA. To settle the question of her genealogy for good. Meanwhile, once she's with us, we'll have leverage to negotiate with Sergio Bruno and Orloff. Once they're assured that she's alive, they'll be much more cooperative. At least, temporarily. And it goes without saying that she won't be marrying Orloff if she's under lock and key."

"Only one problem," Clayton says. "She's been in hiding since the fire. Nobody's seen head nor tail of her. Her car is still parked at the bakery, her phone hasn't made any outgoing calls, her credit cards haven't been swiped. There's nothing to trace. Nothing but dead ends. God only knows where they're keeping her."

"I know how to get to her," I tell him.

"How?"

"My wife. Candi can do it."

Clayton scoffs. "You really think the Brunos are going to let a Bellanti wife within a mile of Orloff's fiancée? Not a chance. She'll be shot on sight."

"I doubt that. As far as Bruno knows, Candi is still his mole. And I'm sure Juliana will want to see her best friend. If anything, Candi is more at risk of being interrogated or detained. They're not going to kill a valuable operative. The fact that she almost died in the fire herself only cements her loyalty to them. Right now, they have no reason to be suspicious of her."

Dante frowns. "Do you honestly think Candi is going to *willingly* put herself in harm's way just so you can kidnap her friend?"

"She won't be in harm's way," I tell him. "I'll throw an entire security team at her if I have to, but I think we can be more subtle. All she has to do is invite Juliana out for lunch."

"You really think it's going to be that easy?" Marco scoffs.

I shoot him a death glare. He'll find out exactly how

easy this will be when Juliana Guerra is locked up on our property.

Because the one thing I know for certain is that my wife wants what's best for her friend. And that's a weakness I can use against her. All I have to do is convince Candi to lure Juliana out to a public place where they can talk, somewhere far from the eyes of Bruno and the Bratva guards, thus negating any risks to my wife and child. I'll have the perfect opportunity to pounce.

"You're delusional." Marco shakes his head. "Candi is not going to help you do this."

"Oh no?" Holding my brother's gaze, I take out my phone. "Dante, what's your wife doing right now?"

"Probably changing a diaper. Why?"

"Because she's going to help me."

I call Frankie. She answers on the second ring. "Armani? Is everything all right?"

"Everything is fine," I tell her. "I just need your help with something."

"Sure. What's up?"

"I need to seduce my wife."

16

CANDI

I'M EATING a light breakfast of fruit and toast, mindlessly scrolling through #nurseryinspo on Insta, when I hear the approach of Armani's familiarly assertive footsteps out in the hallway.

"There you are. I was thinking we could go look at paint swatches for the baby's room after I get done giving Mr. Sprinkles a bath," he says.

My head snaps up and the strawberry I'm holding drops out of my fingers and onto the floor. Armani stands in the doorway in his work attire, watching me intently as he loosens his tie.

"Um, are you okay?" I ask.

"I'm great. Why do you ask?"

I scrutinize his expression, trying to decide if he's messing with me or not. "Don't you have work today?"

He shrugs. "I clocked out early. This is more important."

For a moment, all I can do is stare at him.

"Sink or bathtub?" he asks.

"What?"

"For the cat," he clarifies.

"Oh, no. God, no. Don't do that. Mr. Sprinkles does *not* like water. And besides, cats bathe themselves. Why do you think he's always licking himself?"

Armani frowns. "So no bath?"

"No. But...you can brush him if you want," I say hesitantly, still wildly suspicious.

"Perfect. I'll do that while you get ready to go."

He spins on his heel and I practically have to chase after him as he jogs upstairs.

"Wait, are you serious? You really want to go look at paint colors?" I ask once we're in our room.

"Of course. I thought we'd redo the guest room next to ours. Maybe knock out part of the wall in the sitting room in here and add an adjoining door to the nursery. What do you think?"

"I think..." I think I'm floored. Practically speechless. This is not the Armani Bellanti I know. "I mean, are you sure? Isn't it a little soon?"

What I don't add is that Armani made it very clear that he intends to divorce me in a few months, so I don't see the point in setting up a nursery here at Casa Bellanti when the baby will be living with me at my new apartment, wherever that ends up being.

"Too soon? Come on, Candi, what kind of question is that? We have a baby on the way and they're going to need a room. Might as well get a head start on it," Armani says.

My heart flutters. *We have a baby on the way.* I think it's the first time he's brought up the pregnancy on his own.

"Then...I guess I think that sounds amazing," I say, still hardly believing my ears.

"Good. Just show me where the cat brush is and I'll be ready when you are."

After a brief search for Mr. Sprinkles, I leave Armani with the brush and then dig through the closet for something cute but not too fussy. As I hurry to switch out my sweatpants and T-shirt for dark jeans and a heather green cashmere sweater with short sleeves, I try to come up with explanations for Armani's bizarre behavior this morning. What is he playing at? And why?

Is it possible he's having second thoughts about the divorce? Did the ultrasound have a delayed effect on him, maybe triggering some hidden paternal instincts? Or did his brothers gang up on him and give him a good talking-to about what marriage and family are supposed to mean? But no...Marco and I get along well enough, but Dante has been wary of me ever since he first found out I was a Bruno spy. He wouldn't go to bat for me. Maybe Frankie or Karina intervened on my behalf? That seems more likely, but I doubt Armani would let himself be so easily swayed by his sisters-in-law. So then what the hell is going on?

I slip into a pair of leather sandals and then walk back out to the sitting room, only to do a double take at the scene before me. On the couch, Mr. Sprinkles is curled up on Armani's lap, purring like a little outboard motor as Armani slowly trails the brush from the cat's head all the way down to the tip of his tail. Over and over again, all the while telling Mr. Sprinkles that he's being a very good boy. All I can do is stand there with my jaw on the floor.

Did my husband slip and hit his head in the shower? In

what world is Armani cradling my emotionally needy white fluffball on his lap—while wearing a Tom Ford suit, no less—and whispering sweet nothings to him at the same time he's brushing him?

He's being so tender and sweet with my cat that I can't look away. Because, yes. I'm melting. Will he be this gentle and attentive with our baby? I imagine him cradling a swaddled infant in his arms, cooing softly, pacing back and forth like he always does—except this time, instead of pacing from anger or stress, Armani will be pacing to soothe our baby.

"Ready to go?" he asks, snapping me out of my daydream.

I nod.

He smiles—another shocker—and sets the brush down. Then he gathers Mr. Sprinkles against his chest, rises from the couch, and crosses the room to set the cat gently on the cat tree as if he's done it a hundred times. My chest is aching with warmth.

But as we make our way downstairs, I remind myself that Armani is very good at toying with my feelings. He's a master manipulator. So whatever this is that's gotten into him, genuine or not, I have to be on my guard. I have to remember who the real Armani is, and not just see the one I so desperately want to see.

Once we get into Armani's SUV, he starts the car and then looks over at me. My heart races at the hunger in his gaze. Leaning closer, he kisses me softly, searchingly, until I'm breathless...leaving me extremely turned on, and extremely confused.

"Thought we'd try Paint Works on Jefferson," he says as we pull out of the driveway. "They have the widest range of options and a full line of Benjamin Moore. Frankie said that's where they got their swatches for the nursery."

I shake my head. Who is this man?

My voice is a wisp as I say, "Sounds perfect."

Reaching into his jacket pocket, he digs out a folded piece of notebook paper and passes it over, prompting a curious side-eye from me.

"What is it?" I ask, almost afraid to find out.

"Look it over and let me know if you like any of them."

Holding my breath, I unfold the paper. My stomach fills with butterflies. Closing my eyes, I give myself a second. This was the last thing I ever expected him to do.

"You...*Armani*. You wrote down a list of baby names?"

His grin is full of pride.

"I'm pretty much sold on Marcello. Marcello Leonardo Bellanti. Has a nice ring, no?"

Looking at the paper again, I skim the list. He's written two columns. One for boy names and one for girls'. Marcello has a circle around it. So does Sofia.

Emotion jigs around inside my chest. I'm so torn. Is he serious, or is this just another game he's playing? But my heart is so hopeful that I decide to play along. Because it feels good.

And because I want more than anything for this to be real.

"Sofia is nice," I say carefully. "I haven't really thought about names yet, girls' or boys'. What about middle names, if it's a girl?"

"Don't know yet. But I'm open to your ideas."

Clearing my throat, I scan the list of female names. "Elisabetta is good, too. Elisabetta Bellanti. That's pretty."

"She'd need a proper middle name or two. What do you think? Irish names, maybe?"

"Sure, if you want Maeve or Saoirse in the middle of Elisabetta and Bellanti."

He nods. "I like that. Elisabetta Shur-sha Bellanti."

"Sur-sha," I say, hiding my grin as I gently correct his pronunciation.

We pull into the parking lot of a local French viennois-erie where Frankie gets all the baked goods for the Bellanti Vineyards tasting room. The people who run the place are brilliant. I've never tasted a less-than-perfect croissant or apple tart from them. They can do no wrong.

"What are we doing here?"

Armani grins. "Thought I'd pick up some pastries for dessert tonight, since we're in the neighborhood. I'll be cooking dinner, too, by the way. Going to try my hand at Chef Idris's secret risotto recipe and some seared scallops. Sound good?"

"Um, yes?"

Our next stop is The Paint Works, an unassuming white cinderblock building that's much more than meets the eye. Armani seems almost giddy as he leads me inside. The whole time we look at paint chips, my heart keeps telling me that maybe, just maybe, he *does* want this baby and our little family. That the reason he's kept on pushing me away is because of his past trauma, his fear that everything he loves will be taken away from him if he gets too attached.

We end up with five colors we like, so we get sample cans of each so that we can test them out on the wall at home. Most of the nursery décor I've been seeing on the internet leans toward neutrals—beige, cream, gray—but none of those trendy, minimalist, vaguely Scandinavian design schemes has resonated with me. I want my baby's room to be a soothing, happy place, but I also want color. Pale cornflower blue, ballet pink, seafoam green. Maybe wallpaper with fresh, botanical elements or a fun pattern. Armani seemed open to my ideas, and he even ordered a few wallpaper samples from the paint store that will be mailed to the house in a few days. I'm excited to start narrowing down our options soon.

Back in the car, Armani slides his hand over mine across the center console, and when he squeezes, a warm and reassuring feeling floods my veins. I shouldn't let him affect me, but this feels so nice. Like we're a real family. My eyes start to get misty, so I quickly pull my hand away and look out the window.

"Is this too overwhelming?" Armani asks, sounding concerned. "We can just head home if you need to decompress."

"No, no. This has been perfect," I tell him. "But...where else did you want to go?"

"Just a few more stops," he says mysteriously.

I'm on cloud nine as he takes me to an upscale shop for maternity clothes, and then out to lunch at Celadon, a fancy restaurant next to the Napa River that serves comfort food amidst an exquisite, sprawling courtyard. The food, the setting, the company...all of it is heaven.

By the time we wrap up at the baby furniture store in the late afternoon, I'm pretty sure I've fallen head over heels in love with my husband.

All over again.

17

CANDI

Two days have passed, and Armani's care and attention toward me continue on unabated.

He wakes me in the morning whispering sweet Italian endearments in my ear and kisses me from cheek to belly before he gets out of bed. He checks in throughout the day —via actual phone calls—to be sure I'm feeling well, that I've eaten, that I'm not stressed out now that I'm back to working from home. After dinner, instead of going back to the Bellanti offices to sneak a few extra emails in, he follows me upstairs to watch TV or snuggle.

He's a completely different person.

I still don't know what's up with him, and I'm still suspicious of his motives. But I'm not looking this gift horse in the mouth. I'm relishing every second of it.

At the moment, I'm sitting in the guest room adjacent to our bedroom. Half of the old furniture has been moved out so far, but we've still got a long way to go before the space looks anything like a nursery. A pile of shopping bags sits on the armchair next to me—the result of my impromptu outing with Armani the other day. Colorful squares of the sample paints we picked are painted on the wall opposite the windows, and I'm halfway done sorting through the haul of baby books and toys, maternity clothes, and a few other items I had to have.

Then I pull out a pair of adorable footie pajamas with knitted lamb's ears attached to the hood and a puffy little tail sewn onto the butt. I can't fight back a grin. I hadn't wanted to buy any baby clothes until I'm safely past the first trimester, but I'd held this pair of pajamas in my hand for a few moments, almost melting as I thought about my baby wearing it. And then I'd put it back on the rack. But somehow, here it is, in this bag. Armani.

We chose a crib, too—ridiculously expensive but solid and very high quality, the kind that converts to a twin-size bed once the baby is old enough—and a changing table, but I didn't want to pick out any more furniture before we figure out the layout of the nursery.

Just then, a knock on the doorframe has me looking over my shoulder. It's Armani.

"Hey," I say, unable to keep the smile off my face.

"Hey yourself," he says, pulling a couple of crinkling paper bags from behind his back.

"That better not be more baby stuff," I tease.

"Nope. It's lunch."

As he comes closer, I catch a delicious smell wafting from the bags.

"Where'd you go?"

"I sent Donovan to pick it up from this great Italian place called Antonio's," he says.

The name makes my stomach drop. It's one of Juliana's

favorite restaurants. Thinking of her hiding out somewhere, possibly still healing from the fire, is almost enough to ruin my appetite. She still hasn't called me.

Armani hesitates. "No good? I can get something else delivered."

"No, no," I say, waving him closer. "This is great. My stomach's just been...off."

"I figured. That's why I got you something light. Pasta primavera with lots of vegetables and grilled chicken on the side, for protein."

"That sounds perfect. Thank you."

"Should we picnic up here, or go down to the dining room?" he asks. "Or we could eat by the pool if you want. I don't have to be back at work in a hurry."

"Here is good."

Armani sets up our lunch on the coffee table, then insists I use a few throw pillows to sit on, even though the rug is cushy enough.

He's about to sit down on the rug when he says, "Forgot the drinks. Be right back. Is sparkling water okay?"

I nod, and a minute later he's back with two bottles of Perrier and two glasses of ice. Settling beside me, he seems surprised that I haven't touched my food yet.

"Eat, eat, eat," he commands. "Before it gets cold. You didn't have to wait on me."

Laughing, I twirl my fork in the pasta, making sure to stab a fat slice of zucchini while I'm at it. As I chew, Armani pours my water and then kisses the top of my head.

When he digs into his panzanella, I watch him out of the corner of my eye. There's got to be a catch to all of this. What is it?

Armani catches me staring and arches a brow. "Is something wrong?"

"Just wondering what I'm going to owe you for all your recent kindness," I say levelly.

My husband has an expert level poker face, but he doesn't realize how well I've learned to read him. One useful thing about growing up in an abusive home is, you learn how to read the body language of the people who have the power to hurt you. Which is why my intuition is so good at picking up on subtle things that other people might miss.

His slight pause before looking slightly wounded is exactly the cue I'm looking for.

"You're carrying our child," he says carefully. "What could you possibly owe me? I'm the one who owes you."

I don't believe him, but I don't have it in me to argue. My mind keeps telling me to savor this time with him. Take whatever he's offering and enjoy it while I can.

"You're right. Thank you for lunch," I say.

Relaxing, he makes light conversation about work and some of the new accounts he's working on pulling together —out-of-state distributors for Bellanti wine that he wants me to take a look at. The topic shifts to a rare variety of grape that Frankie has been pushing Dante to import from Italy. She hopes to test some vines on a patch of land being specifically cultivated for the finicky variety. If it's a success, the Bellantis will be the only growers outside of Italy to produce it. Talk about exclusive.

"So would this be a brand-new wine, or would you use the grapes for blending?" I ask.

"We'll press a few batches with this grape alone, see how we like it, and then decide."

We talk wine some more, and then I catch him up on the work in sales that I've just started getting back into. Armani so rarely makes day-to-day conversation like this with me that I'm completely caught up in it. The normalcy gives me a much-needed reprieve from the Russian threat still looming over our heads.

"How is it?" he asks, nodding at my spaghetti.

"Delicious. Here, have some," I say, scooping a portion from my to-go container into his. "And thanks for taking your lunch break with me."

Armani nods. "Of course."

Our eyes meet. A shock of heat instantly flares between my legs. I look away, grabbing my water and taking a few sips while silently scolding myself for being so susceptible to his charms. Except maybe...maybe I should stop defaulting to defensive mode. Maybe I should trust my heart this time.

When I'm with Armani like this, just the two of us, he makes me feel like we could really work together. This connection, this attraction, the fact that being with him is so easy. All of it makes me want to surrender to him, and to have him surrender to me.

He returns to his food, and I do the same, but the surge of warmth and emotion inside is urging me to say something. To tell him how I feel. Tell him to screw the six-month agreement; I want us to pull together and try to be a real family.

"You know that I only want to keep you safe and happy, right?"

His question comes out of nowhere, and it throws me. Where is this going?

"Ye...es?" I say hesitantly.

Setting his fork down, he turns toward me.

"Good. Look, I know we've been through hell these last few months, and it's not over yet. But I also want you to know that we're united. We're a team."

"I feel the same," I say quietly, dropping my gaze. This is all too much.

"Look at me."

His rough, demanding voice washes over me, sending a shiver of want down my spine. I raise my chin to look up at him and he cups my face, running his thumb lightly over my cheek. His touch is so sweet, I can't help but lean my face into his palm. All the emotions I've tried to keep under control suddenly flood to the surface.

He draws me closer, his gaze flicking to my mouth. Lips tingling in anticipation of his kiss, I slide a hand over his firm bicep.

"We still have a lot of work to do," he says against my lips.

"Yes," I whisper.

And then he kisses me, full and all-consuming. Moving baby items out of the way with a sweep of his arm, he lays me down on the soft rug. Instantly, my legs go up around his hips and I lean back to drink in his kiss as he feasts on my lips.

The scent of his cologne radiates off his neck. It's so intoxicating, I can't help putting my lips there so I can taste him. Armani groans deep in his throat.

"Do you want to take me to bed?" I purr.

"I always want to take you to bed."

"Then what are we waiting for?"

I push him aside and sit up, but he stops me with a hand on my chest. Assuming he wants to do it right here in the future nursery, I reach for his belt, but he catches my hands and kisses my knuckles.

"I need to ask you a favor, Candi."

Smirking, I say, "Sounds promising. What can I do for you?"

"It's not sexual."

He's gone serious, and I can feel my lust deflating already. I knew this was coming.

"What is it?" I ask, fully on my guard now.

He kisses my hands again. "I need your help with Juliana."

It takes a second for my brain to process what he said. "Juliana? What do you mean?"

"I need to talk to her. But the only way I can do that is if we bring her here."

"How's that supposed to work?" I frown. "You're saying you want me to somehow...trick her into coming to the house?"

Armani sighs. "Not exactly. Our best bet is the element of surprise. She can't know we're planning to take her away, otherwise Sergio Bruno and the Bratva will have time to form a counterattack. Not to mention, we'd never be able to successfully capture her."

"*Capture* her?" I scoff, ripping my hands away from him. "You mean *kidnap*? I don't think so. You don't want to talk to her, you want to interrogate her."

Shaking his head, he says, "What I want is to keep her safe. Whether she's my sister or not. But I can't guarantee her safety as long as she's under the watchful eye of her uncle and his guards—she's basically their prisoner. We need to help her. Help get her out of there."

Glaring daggers at him, I say, "Right. So she can become *your* prisoner. Sounds real safe. My answer is no. Not a chance."

My stomach turns as the pieces all fall into place. The nursery, the shopping. The sweet words. The snuggling. His truce with Mr. Sprinkles.

"None of this was real, was it?" I say slowly. "You were manipulating me all along."

18

CANDI

My husband's face goes stony. "Candi—"

"No. I'm done listening to you, Armani."

"You're overreacting. You need to calm down," he says, which pisses me off even more. "I'm just trying to—"

"Fuck off."

Getting up off the floor, I grab a bag of knit blankets and toys and dump it over his head. Then I turn my back on him and storm out the door.

I make it about halfway down the hall before Armani grabs my elbow and spins me around. Straightening my spine, I brace myself for a standoff. He's about to find out that it's a lot more difficult to intimidate me into doing his bidding when I'm this freaking furious.

"Let's just sit down for a minute and talk about this like adults," he says in a soft, hushed tone, leading me into our rooms.

I pull out of his grasp the second the door shuts behind us and then drop onto the sofa in the sitting room, arms already crossed over my chest.

"How *dare you* play on my emotions like this," I hiss.

"Candi—"

"Whatever you have to say to me right now, I really don't want to hear it," I interrupt. "You're not going to convince me to get on board with your little kidnapping plan."

More than being angry, I'm humiliated. I should have known better—I *did* know better—but I still let myself believe that we might actually be on our way to becoming a family.

Armani rubs his face as he paces in front of me. "You realize she's biding her time in a death sentence, don't you?"

"You'll say anything to get me to do what you want. But guess what? She's a lot safer with her guards than in your torture dungeon with no one around to hear her screams."

Armani tries a new tactic. "You're my wife. You're supposed to support me."

A cold laugh escapes me. "There's a whole lot of things you were supposed to do as my husband, but you never gave a shit about any of it. So no. You can't guilt trip me into this."

"Can you set aside your hurt feelings for one goddamn *minute*?" he rails. "What I'm asking you to do has bigger consequences than your broken heart!"

My breath stops. My muscles go completely still. I don't think I've ever hated Armani as much as I do in this moment.

I'm pregnant with his child, yet he still subjects me to his cruel moods at every turn, his sarcasm and insults and all the other shit he puts me through. And then when he tosses out the tiniest of kindnesses, I basically swoon, all while knowing full fucking well that he doesn't mean any of it. What's worse is that he never apologizes for the mess he leaves behind for everyone else to pick up. I'm not even sure he realizes that what he's doing is wrong. In his mind, it's all to serve the greater good. The greater good that only benefits him.

But things are different now. I have a baby on the way. I can't afford to bear the brunt of his bullshit anymore. And I can't allow an innocent child to spend his or her entire life waiting on breadcrumbs from their ice-cold father. I need to protect my baby no matter what.

"I'm done with you." The words grind out of my mouth.

He stops mid-pace and whips his head toward me, brows raised, as if I've truly shocked him with my bitterness.

"You're not done with me, wife. Not even close. But that's a topic for another time. Right now, this situation with Juliana is urgent. Look at me, Cassandra."

He can order me around all he wants, use the name I hate, try to implement his emotional blackmail and whatever other Machiavellian methods he's got in his back pocket, but he'll get nowhere with me. Not anymore.

Rising from the couch, I say, "I'm not lifting a finger to help you kidnap my best friend. I'm done letting you take advantage of me. And I'm done giving any part of myself to you, including my attention. As far as I'm concerned, this six months can't be over soon enough."

I lift my chin, daring him with my gaze to come at me again with his excuses and lies.

"Do you want her to die?"

There it is. More manipulation. He doesn't care if Juliana lives or not, of that much I am dead certain. But he knows that I care about her, and that there was a time I'd do anything for her. Sadly, things have changed. I have a baby to think about now, and sticking my neck out for my best friend—who is also incredibly manipulative, so I guess I have a type?—isn't a priority to me anymore. It can't be.

"Why is she so important to you now?" I prod. "You didn't care this much when I told you she's your sister, but suddenly you want to go after her, guns blazing. Why?"

He shakes his head. "Not guns blazing. That's the opposite of what I want to do, which is why I need your help. Look, you know Juliana better than any of us. You're the only one who can get inside her head. Believe what you want about me, but I don't want to see her harmed."

Every instinct inside of me is screaming at me not to help him. And why should Juliana be in any more danger now than she's ever been in before? She knows how to take care of herself. I've no doubt about that. Hell, she made it this far sandwiched between the Italian and Russian mobs. And Armani can try all he wants to get to her, but wherever she is, I'm sure Orloff has her very securely stashed away behind locked doors. The Bellantis don't stand a chance against an entire Bruno security team and a bunch of Bratva hitmen.

"A week ago you didn't care what happened to her, Armani. I know you're not doing this because you're afraid Bruno will hurt her. You only want to stop the Russian alliance."

His expression goes neutral. The Resting Bellanti Face is back. But he doesn't have to respond for me to know the truth: it doesn't concern him in the least that Juliana might be his blood relative. His only interest in the matter is in stopping Sergio Bruno's power grab.

Juliana is nothing more to Armani than I am. We're pawns, pieces to be played and used in these mob men's war games. If she had died in the bakery fire, she would have merely been a casualty of war to him.

"Can you at least tell me where she might be? Relatives or friends she'd stay with, known safe houses, family properties?"

I narrow my eyes at him. "Up until a couple days ago, I didn't even know she was *alive*. I can't get a hold of her, either, so how the hell would I know where they might have taken her? I have no clue where she is. But even if I did, I wouldn't tell you."

He stares at me, assessing me in that cold, calculating way that he does. I can practically see the wheels in his mind turning as he analyzes my body language, the tone of my voice, and every word to see if I'm being deceitful in some way.

"You haven't heard from her at all? Not even a text?"

"No. You know I haven't!"

He knows damn well, too, because we've talked about it over the past few days, and I've expressed how anxious I've been not being able to hear her voice and reassure myself that she's really okay.

A muscle twitches in his jaw. He's losing patience with me now, but I don't have the capacity to care. Sliding a hand over my abdomen, some of my anger begins to cool. I press there gently, comfortingly, as if to shield my growing baby from the turmoil all around them. Armani's gaze tracks to my hand, then back up to my eyes.

"It's important to keep my stress levels low, and that's not going to happen if we keep arguing," I tell him. "So, for the last time, I've had zero communication with Juliana since the fire, and my best guess as to her whereabouts is either the Bruno compound or one of Orloff's places, wherever those might be. I really don't know."

"Fine. I'll find her myself. And when I do, you'll help me bring her here."

I shake my head before he finishes his sentence.

"I meant what I said. I will not be involved in any further trauma toward her. She already survived a fire and there's no way I'm going to take part in a kidnapping. You're on your own."

Armani narrows his eyes. "I could turn you in to Sergio Bruno this instant."

"And risk your unborn child's life? Really? How twisted are you?"

That gives him pause, and I stand there waiting for him to come at me with some other empty threat. But he doesn't.

"I can't believe I actually thought a cold-blooded killer like you could be capable of caring about anyone besides yourself," I say harshly. "Shame on you. And shame on me for being fooled by a goddamn Bellanti."

Trembling with rage and indignation, I leave the room, slamming the door behind me as hard as I can. Then I go downstairs and grab my keys. I'm going to Frankie's. Her house will be safe. It's just up the street, on the very next property adjacent to the Bellantis', and I know she won't turn me away. Armani's precious security detail can follow me there and run their fucking surveillance on me all the livelong day for all I care.

As I pull my car onto the main road, I try to take deep, calming breaths. I know I can't keep getting this worked up. It's not good for the baby. But the more I think about separating from Armani and living somewhere far away from him, the better I start to feel.

Maybe I'm looking forward to this divorce after all.

19

CANDI

AFTER GETTING some work done at Frankie's on a borrowed laptop, I submit a handful of new purchase orders to the winery's online system and then join Frankie for a little play time with Lili Grace before she conks out in her mama's arms. We watch some home renovation show while Lili is napping, and then we have a lovely family dinner with Dante, who doesn't make a peep about me helping his brother kidnap anybody.

It's all so domestic and soothing. I'm envious. I can't imagine having a life like this with Armani. Or actually, I guess I can. I'm just not sure it could ever be possible.

Or if it's even something I still want.

"Heard anything from Armani yet?" Frankie asks me after dinner.

I'd given her the barest outline of what was going on between him and me, but I'd framed our argument in the context of the new baby. I hadn't mentioned Armani's vile kidnapping plot.

"No. Not even a text."

"Jackass," Frankie huffs.

"I agree."

He hadn't come looking for me either, not that I expected him to. I'm sure his security team has been reporting my location to him at regular intervals.

"Do you want to spend the night? My mom is out of town with Livvie, so you can take the guest room. Lili wakes up a lot at night, but you'd be at the other end of the house so you shouldn't hear anything."

"Thank you so much for the invite, but I think I should get home," I say. "Who knows? Maybe Armani will finally be ready to talk to me like an adult."

"Maybe." She gives me a sympathetic smile. "But if he's not, just give him time. You know how pigheaded these boys can be. He'll come around."

"Yeah. Maybe."

She gives me a hug and I drive down the road and back to the Bellanti estate. The house is dead quiet when I get there. I find Armani's bedroom empty, so I grab my toiletries and some pajamas and spend the night in one of the guest rooms down the hall, curled up with my e-reader.

When I wake up in the morning, I go back into our bedroom to get fresh clothes. It's hard to tell if the bed has been slept in. Knowing my husband, he probably slept on the couch in his office or downstairs in the first-floor library.

After a shower and breakfast, I debate going to my office over at the winery to do more work. Instead, I end up in the baby's room. There's still a mess from the bag I upended over Armani's head yesterday, but otherwise it's just as I left it. For some reason, it makes my chest hurt knowing that he didn't come back in here to clean up the mess. That he didn't wake up this morning with the urge to select a paint color from one of the swatches and paint the whole nursery, just to surprise me. Or put together the crib that's in its box in the corner.

Why do I keep letting him disappoint me? Why does my heart keep hoping? I need to just expect nothing from him going forward, that way I can stop getting my soul crushed. Easier said than done, though. Mostly because I've seen how wonderful Armani can be. I've experienced it firsthand. I've witnessed his vulnerable moments, his worry and his care. I know he's better than he acts like he is. He just doesn't know it yet.

Still, it's not my job to try to change him. He needs to find the way himself. But—

"Enough of this," I chastise myself quietly. I can't keep letting my thoughts spin in circles all day.

Besides, I don't need Armani to set up the whole nursery. There's plenty I can do myself.

First things first, I call Donovan to ask where I might find a few basic tools. He ends up bringing me a toolbox with more than enough stuff inside: a hammer, a screw gun, a picture hanging kit, a level, measuring tapes, pencils, and hardware in all different sizes. He also offers to help me with my project, but I insist that I want to do it myself since it's for the baby.

Once he's gone, I turn my attention to the curtains.

The windows in this room were bare before, so I have to put the curtain rods up first. I measure once, twice, three times, make marks with the pencil, drill some pilot holes, and finally get the brackets up and level. Somehow, an hour passes. I'm frustrated and sweaty by the time I'm done attaching the rods and hanging the curtain panels, but I'm also very proud of myself.

I go back to the pile of bags from various boutiques, looking for the wood bead curtain tiebacks I found, but then I find the box with the baby mobile and sink into one of the armchairs to open it. Beneath layers of pale blue tissue paper, beautiful forest colors emerge. Grasping the loop at the top, I gently pull the handmade mobile out of the box.

A rush of awe fills me as I hold it up. Forest creatures made of felted wool hang from the strings. There's a deer, a raccoon, a rabbit, a bird, and three little pine trees. I don't know why I was so drawn to this piece, but I fell in love with it the moment I saw it on the display.

The crib isn't built yet, so there isn't a place to hang it over, but then I decide to suspend it from the end of the curtain rod so it can give the room some whimsy. Once it's up, I stand with my hands on my hips, looking back and forth between the mobile and the paint swatches. And that's what decides it for me. The cool-toned, calm sage green is a perfect match for the mobile. Ding ding, we have a winner.

Next, I unbox the pieces of the crib, separating each of the components into piles on the floor. Once everything is laid out, I start to read the instructions. Admittedly, it's going to be a big job trying to put this thing together. But that means it'll be even more rewarding when I get it done. I don't need Armani's help. Not with this crib and not with anything else.

My phone buzzes inside my pocket with a call. Is it him? My stomach instantly knots.

But when I take out the phone, it just says No Caller ID. I hesitate and then pick up.

"Hello?"

"Candi. It's me. I'm calling from a burner phone. Orloff has mine."

I gasp, the phone slipping from my fingers, but I catch it before it hits the floor.

"Juliana! Oh, thank God."

It's a good thing I'm sitting down, because the shock of hearing her voice makes my entire body weak. Tears sting my eyes as my heart thrums with sweet relief.

"I'm so glad you're alive," I murmur, my voice catching.

There's a beat of silence and I can sense her analyzing my reaction, my every word.

"No thanks to your husband. Did you know he was going to burn the bakery down?"

The accusation in her voice makes my cheeks go hot, even though what she's saying isn't remotely true. "No. How could you ask me that? I was there with you, remember? Why would I go if I'd known? Besides, I would have warned you, I would have tried to stop it—"

"I just thought it was mighty convenient how you ended up in exactly the right place at exactly the right time to get rescued."

"I almost died that day," I tell her, my voice going sharp. "And you obviously made it out alive yourself, but I'm not accusing you of luring me there to bump me off."

"Touché, and fair point," she concedes. "Look, things are happening, Candi. Things that your husband and his little minions set into motion. I'm not safe where I am."

Does she mean she's not safe from her uncle, or from Orloff?

"Isn't your fiancé able to protect you?" I ask, trying to fish for more information.

"I'm starting to wonder if he thinks that's in his best interest," she says quietly. "Or if he wants me out of the way more than he wants to go through with this wedding."

"Oh, Jules. I'm sorry. Is there any way you could—"

"Shh," she snaps. "I don't need your pity. Just listen to me."

The desperation in her voice is unmistakable. I'm not sure I've ever heard her like this. The fear in her tone gives me a sinking feeling.

"Tell me what's going on," I say softly.

"My uncle has allies—lots of them—but they're not happy right now. They're having a shit fit about all the violence with the Bellantis, plus the old Brunos in Italy thinks my uncle is getting too big for his britches. Not to mention, the fire made things a thousand times worse with the Russians. They're blaming *us* for the hit that your husband put out on Orloff, I guess because we've had this long-standing feud with the Bellantis for so long and haven't 'dealt with it.' I just don't think it's a good idea to be pissing off so many mobsters."

"No. You're right. I get it."

"So I'm thinking the best course of action is to just eliminate of *all* the Bellantis and end the squabbling once and for all."

As her words hit me full force, the floor falls out from under me. My ears are ringing, my adrenaline rushing. No. This can't be happening.

"Is that's what's going to happen next?" I babble anxiously. "Are they coming for us?"

Is *she* coming for us?

She makes a noncommittal sound, and I don't know what the hell she means by it. The back of my neck prickles. I need to talk to Armani. Now.

"Juliana—"

"You owe me, Candi. If it wasn't for that goddamn fire, I'd be picking out floral arrangements right now. You need to find me a place to hide before the mob decides I'm worth more to them dead."

"Orloff wouldn't let that happen."

A bitter laugh slices through the phone. "You have no idea what he's capable of. Do you think he actually cares about me? He's *using* me. They're all using me; the same way Armani is using you."

Letting out a breath, I try not to be offended. She's not wrong. Not at all.

"What do you want me to do?"

"I told you. Find me a place I can hide out for a few days." Her voice drops even lower, and then her words get muffled, as if she's moved into a closet to talk to me. "If I get caught trying to sneak out, I'll tell Orloff that my uncle was getting restless, and I was worried about my safety. He already knows I don't trust my uncle's security guards."

"Is Orloff there with you now?"

"No, but his men are here, and I don't trust them, either. I don't trust anyone right now but you. That's why you have to come get me," she whispers.

"Okay. I think I know somewhere you can stay," I

whisper back. "Where should I pick you up? I can probably sneak out tonight, but—"

"No. Tomorrow. Write this down."

She gives me detailed instructions and then hangs up without saying goodbye.

I stare at the phone in my hand, paralyzed by panic. What if this plan doesn't work? What if I get caught? What if something happens to Juliana before I can get to her?

What if the Brunos' allies are about to murder the entire Bellanti family?

No. I can't let that happen. I *won't* let it happen.

Because if they're coming for the Bellantis, that means they're coming for my baby.

Surely there must be some way to talk this out, to negotiate a compromise or a deal that everybody can live with, without anyone getting hurt.

And if I have to be the sacrificial lamb and throw myself in the middle of things, then so be it. I can be the peacekeeper. Hell, I did it my entire life growing up.

But first, I'm going to rescue my best friend from the mafia.

20

CANDI

I SPEND another night in the guest room down the hall from Armani, even though I want more than anything to face him and find out if he's ready to apologize. Not that I expect him to suddenly do a complete one-eighty, but I at least want to give him the chance to look me in the eye and say he's sorry. Unfortunately, I have to stay away from him.

I don't trust myself around my husband right now.

If he gets one look at me, he'll know I'm up to something. In which case, I'll be interrogated until I break down. I can't let him get suspicious about what I have planned. It would make it impossible for me to slip away.

I'm so anxious, I'm not sure how I manage to get to sleep...but I do.

The second my alarm goes off the next morning, I quickly shower and dress, then bolt down a poached egg and toast—skipping breakfast might raise alarms and get reported to Armani—before heading to the big garage where the vehicles are kept. Normally, I'd call Donovan and have him bring my car around, but I don't want to have to lie to him.

Even so, I know the guards will tell Armani I left the property, so I have a shopping bag in hand with a ready excuse: I'm returning a few of the new baby things that didn't match the nursery. If Armani watches the GPS tracker for my vehicle, which I'm sure he will, he'll see me visiting Frankie first and then going to the boutique to make the return.

Nothing out of the ordinary.

Praying that I don't run into any of the Bellantis on my way out, I brace myself to get stopped by security as I drive out of the garage or followed when I pull onto the main road. But nobody chases after me. I get to Frankie and Dante's house in less than five minutes.

There's only one car in the driveway, and it's Frankie's. I let out a breath of relief. I had figured Dante would be at work, and Frankie would be up with the baby. This is perfect.

She answers right away when I knock on the door and looks genuinely happy to see me.

"Hi again. Wasn't expecting you back so soon. Did Armani apologize yet?"

"No. He didn't," I say with a sigh.

Lili Grace rests in the crook of Frankie's arm. My hand slides to my abdomen instinctively as I start to worry about the baby all over again.

What if something goes wrong today and the baby gets hurt?

"Ugh." She shakes her head. "I'm sorry. Do you want to sit and talk for a bit? It's just me and Lili."

"I'd love that. If it's not too much trouble."

Waving me inside, she says, "Not at all. Do you want some tea? I just made a pot of chamomile lavender. It's supposed to be calming. Sounds like we both need a cup."

"Yes, please. I'm sorry to intrude on you, I just...don't know how much more of this I can take."

Frankie leads me to the living room, sits me down, and hands me the baby. Surprised, but very pleased, I take the tiny bundle and hold Lili close to my chest.

"You're a natural," she says with a wink. "Figured you could use the practice."

"Thank you."

She nods. "Let me get you that tea."

She disappears to the kitchen and comes back with an extra mug. Then she pours us each a cup, adding a spoon of honey to hers and then mine when I nod my approval.

"So," she says. "Armani's being a jerk to you, you've got the pressure of knowing a baby is on the way, and you're dealing with a bunch of fun pregnancy hormones on top of all that, so everything feels like the end of the world even if it's not. Boy, does that sound familiar."

"Does it? Tell me more."

I adjust my arm so the weight of the baby is supported by the sofa's armrest and then carefully sip my tea with my free hand.

"Dante and I were having a lot of problems when I moved to Florida last year. My plan was to hide out at my mom's and basically try to build a new life without him. I didn't know I was pregnant at the time, but once I did, I was even more determined to make it on my own. But it didn't take long for him to come after me. Men always want what they can't have."

"Wow. I didn't know all that back story. Are you suggesting that I run away, too?"

She laughs and sets her mug down. "Honestly, it couldn't hurt. Although I doubt you'll get far with all the security lurking around these days. Not that we don't need it, just to be safe."

"Yeah," I say with a deep sigh.

Then I look up at her innocently.

Here goes nothing.

"I just wish there was somewhere I could go be by myself for a few days. Like a mini retreat. I could reset and clear my head. And give Armani some space to think things over, too."

She nods sympathetically, looks off into the distance, and then—I see it. The moment her eyes light up with a brilliant solution.

Hopefully, the exact same solution that I came here today to coax her into offering me.

"You could stay at the B&B!" she says excitedly.

"Really?"

"It's perfect! The renovation's not completely finished, but the bathrooms and kitchen are fully functional, and two of the new guest rooms are like, 90% ready. And Mom and Livvie are at Charlie's in Nob Hill until next week, so you'll have the place completely to yourself."

"Oh my God, that would be incredible," I say, only feeling slightly guilty for my manipulation. "Are you sure it's okay?"

"Definitely. In fact, I'd feel better knowing the house isn't empty while they're gone. Let me go get you the keys."

This worked out better than I'd even dreamed. She didn't even make me ask, which was the original plan. The B&B is the perfect hiding spot for Juliana while we figure out her next steps. It's only for a few days, so we'll be long gone before Frankie's mom and sister get back.

Frankie returns a minute later with a set of keys, and I trade her for the baby. Checking my phone, I realize it's almost time to go pick up Juliana. A rush of adrenaline hits me.

Giving Frankie a hug, I thank her again before begging off with some errands to run.

Elated that phase one of my plan worked without a hitch, I drive downtown to the baby boutique. Parking at the curb in front of a row of shops, I go into the boutique with my shopping bag and return the items I brought—because my cover story has to be verifiable and rock solid. Afterward, I get back in my car and start to drive toward the Bellanti estate.

But I don't go straight there. Instead, I take a detour to a small café, which isn't suspicious at all, since it's almost noon and I barely ate anything at breakfast. And of course a pregnant woman with a growing baby would need no excuse to stop for a bit of refreshment.

This is the part of the plan that hinges entirely on Juliana.

I pull into a spot in the rear lot, parking as close as I can to the back entrance of the café. Then I walk inside, doing my best to act natural and trust in Juliana's ability to slip away from her captors. My instructions were to find a spot next to the wall covered in succulents, and luckily there are a few empty tables to choose from.

After ordering tea and a scone from the waiter, I scroll mindlessly on my phone to make myself look busy while subtly scanning the café for any sign of her. Five minutes pass. Then ten. My tea goes cool. And then it's noon on the dot, just like we agreed, and still no Juliana. Fuck.

I have no idea if the plan has been aborted on her end, or if she's gotten caught on her way here, or worse—and I can't reach out because her burner phone has a blocked number, and she told me not to try to contact her on it. Eighteen minutes pass and my heart begins to pound wildly. The back of my neck prickles with awareness and all the hairs on my forearms stand up.

Something is wrong.

Getting the strongest urge to get the hell out of there, I force myself to sit a few minutes more. Are Bruno's men already here, lying in wait for me to leave so they can snatch me? Did Juliana sell me out? What if this whole thing was a setup, and she's not even coming?"

Jolting to my feet, I knock right into the waiter, who was just approaching my table.

"Shit!" I blurt out. "Sorry, I'm so sorry. I was just—"

Suddenly, I'm aware of someone coming up behind me, too close for comfort.

"Hey, I know I'm late, but something came up and we have to run," a voice says.

Juliana!

I spin around to find her digging out money for the waiter, waving at the food and drink I've left untouched on

176

the table. She's in sunglasses and a hat, but it's not much of a disguise.

"This should cover it," she says, handing a twenty over. "Keep the change. Thanks!"

Hurrying through the café, I squeeze her hand. "I thought something happened to you."

"I had a little trouble getting out."

"Were you followed?"

Her quick glance makes my stomach flip. "I don't know. Where'd you park?"

"Right by the door, like you said."

"Good. Get in the car and back out of the spot. Then I'll jump in the back seat and we can floor it."

I do exactly as she asks, and we make it onto the street as smooth as can be. Once we're a few blocks away from the café, she leans forward between the two front seats and opens her purse to show me the gun inside.

"Jesus! You didn't say you were bringing that!" I hiss.

"It's just in case," she says. "I've got it, okay? I've got us. We'll be fine."

Letting out a breath, I nod. When I glance at her in the rearview mirror, our eyes meet, and I feel that connection we've always had. The one that made us sisters by choice.

"You should duck down," I tell her. "In case there are people out looking for you already. And one of my hoodies is back there. You can put it over your head when we get closer."

"Closer to where? Where are we going?" she asks.

"Someplace safe," I tell her cryptically.

The whole drive there, I can hear my heart pounding in my ears. With every passing second, my anxiety doubles.

Right now, Juliana and I are on the run from Bellanti security, Bruno's men, and the Russian mob. This could go wrong in so many ways.

But we're not stopped, and no blacked-out SUV pulls up next to us with a machine gun poking out the window. I don't think we're being tailed, either. Every time I check my mirrors, the road behind us is clear.

Thinking about the gun Juliana brought, I realize how in fear of her life she really is. Something went south with Maxim Orloff. Why isn't he the one hiding her and protecting her? I guess that's a question for later.

Pulling onto the property of what was formerly known as the Abbott Winery, I drive us to the back yard of the soon-to-be bed-and-breakfast. There's no sign of anyone around, just like Frankie said. The tension drains out of me, my shoulders sagging. We made it.

Juliana's head pops up from the back seat. "Where are we? We're still in Napa."

I turn around. "This is the Abbott Winery. Or it was. The Bellantis own it now."

Her eyes go wide. "Fuck, Candi. We have to go. Now! This is the last place I should be."

"Which is *exactly* why nobody would ever think to look for you here," I tell her. "Including the Bellantis themselves. This house is their new B&B that isn't open yet, so it'll just be us here. I'll stay with you for the next few days, and we can get things figured out."

She frowns. "What about your husband?"

"I doubt he'll care that I'm gone," I say bitterly.

I want to tell her about the baby so badly, but the timing isn't right.

"Stay here while I get the door unlocked, okay? I need to make sure the key works."

"Okay," Juliana says.

I guess she's done arguing about the venue. Which is good, because I don't have an alternative.

The yard is populated by sprawling, old growth oak trees, which gives us an extra layer of privacy. Once I get the door open, I wave Juliana inside. Then I lock the door behind us, deadbolting it as well. It's eerily quiet.

Juliana waits, clutching her purse to her chest, her lips pressed into a hard line. It's so strange to see her not looking totally poised, in control, at the ready with a quip or a sarcastic remark. She's *scared*. I don't think I've ever seen her like this before.

"This way," I say calmly, though I definitely don't feel calm.

Evidence of ongoing construction, plaster dust, and plastic sheeting line the hallway, but then we enter the side of the house that's been completed. I show Juliana the kitchen, the upstairs bathroom, and the guest bedrooms. She walks back to the first bedroom and sits on the edge of the bed, runs her hands over her face, and then lies back on the mattress. She must be exhausted.

"Thank you, Candi. Thank you, thank you. I can finally breathe."

She draws her hands from her face and lets her arms flop at her sides.

"You're welcome." Leaning against the doorway, I hesitate and then add, "Listen, there's something I've been wanting to tell you. I only just found out about it after the fire, but—"

"Oh, please, do tell."

All the hairs on the back of my neck stand up. Juliana bolts upright at the male voice sounding from the hallway behind me. I spin just as she scrambles to her feet. From the corner of my eye, I see her fumbling in her bag for her gun.

But there's already one drawn, and it's aimed right at her.

Armani brushes past me as he walks into the room, his finger on the trigger.

21

ARMANI

"I TOLD you to come over—I didn't say bring a gun!" Candi yells.

Ignoring her, I incline my head at her friend.

"Put the purse on the bed and step away from it," I order.

Candi moves to my side, still frantic. "Please. Put the gun down, Armani."

But I don't move a muscle. The woman, Juliana, quickly assesses the situation and then sets her bag—with the gun still inside—on the bed, as I instructed. Smart girl.

Palms in the air, and never taking her eyes off me, she steps to the middle of the room. Only then do I move to retrieve her weapon, tucking it into the holster at the small of my back.

"I can't believe you're doing this," Candi says, sounding like I've betrayed her.

Maybe it feels like a betrayal to her, but Juliana Guerra is the key link between the Brunos and the Russian mafia—and the alliance that could destroy all of our lives. I don't trust her, and neither should my wife. I don't care how long they've been friends.

I'd immediately gone on high alert when my wife texted me earlier, inviting me to meet her at the B&B on the Abbott property to talk to Juliana. Of course, Candi immediately followed that up with a plea that I not hurt her friend or cause any "major drama." The last message she sent had said that she was trusting me to do the right thing.

That's all good and well, but Candi has proven time and again that she's simply too kindhearted and, frankly, naïve to make the right decisions when it comes to her interactions with the mafia. In my line of business, true friendship is never guaranteed. And nobody gets the benefit of the doubt. Especially not someone who's already agreed to marry into the Bratva for the sole purpose of taking my family down.

"Stop acting like she's not dangerous when it's her fault you got dragged into this war in the first place," I tell Candi harshly.

My gun is still trained on Juliana, who regards me with a look of disgust.

Notwithstanding, I'm struck by how much she looks like my mother, even more so than in the recent photo that Candi showed me on her phone. Even the tone of her voice is familiar—it's uncanny and unsettling. The shape of her mouth reminds me of Marco's, and the prominent line of her jaw is pure Dante. It's true, she resembles my family. It can only mean one thing.

That Sergio Bruno did a bang-up job picking her out for this. Either that, or his plastic surgeon deserves a goddamn award for the amount of work they did on her. Sure, there's still a slight chance she could really be a Bellanti. But I'm not stupid, and I'm not falling for shit without irrefutable proof.

"Sit down," I command, gesturing to a chair in the corner.

"Nice to meet you, too." Guerra's voice is crisp and sarcastic as she sits.

Quite the attitude on this one, which aligns with the personality that Candi described.

My wife looks between me and Juliana as if she's not sure what to do. Juliana wastes no time breaking the silence.

"I can't believe you told him to come over here, Candi. You *set me up*. How could you?"

Candi shakes her head. There's anguish on her face as she hurries to her friend.

"I didn't. I did not set you up, Juliana. I swear. I was just hoping you two could talk."

Juliana scoffs and leans her head back against the chair.

"*Talk?* My God, when are you going to wake up? He's a fucking *murderer*."

Candi has no reply to that. Because obviously, the statement is true.

Both women look over at me, as if waiting for me to jump in and defend myself. I don't bother. It's not important what they think about me. The only thing that matters right now is that I have Maxim Orloff's fiancée in my possession, all thanks to Candi's well-meaning rescue attempt. I'm impressed, even if she didn't do it for the right reasons.

"Where did you grow up?" I ask Juliana.

Her lip pulls into a disbelieving sneer at the question.

I'm sure she was expecting me to start grilling her about her connection to the Bratva, and what her uncle's war plans are.

"I grew up all over," she says dismissively.

I train my gun lower, where her leg is. The unspoken threat is clear. Talk, or pay.

"All over where?" I prod.

With a sigh, she says, "I was born in Napa. I home-schooled starting at age five, then got sent to live with relatives in Paris when I was six. I attended the Marymount School there. At age eight, I transferred to Renaissance International School in Italy and boarded there until I was twelve, then went to Switzerland to yet another boarding school for four more years."

She recites all this in a bored monotone, as if she's recounted her CV so many times she could do it in her sleep.

"A real global citizen," I say dryly. "Why did your parents send you to so many places?"

Dead-eyed, she says, "They didn't. They were killed when I was four. My uncle took me in, but I couldn't stay. He had an empire to run, and his home wasn't safe for a small child."

"Your uncle Sergio."

"Yes."

"That's interesting. Because Sergio Bruno only has one sibling. And she's still alive."

In fact, she's the mother of Marco's wife, Karina.

"Sergio isn't a blood relative," Juliana clarifies, her tone irritated. "He was just close to my parents. He's like my godfather."

Something is niggling at me—the notion that Sergio's house wasn't safe for a child. Why was young Juliana supposedly in danger there, yet Karina grew up in that exact same house without anybody raising an issue? It doesn't make sense. My bullshit detector is starting to beep.

"Okay. So your quasi-godfather, with your best interests at heart, sent you packing. Got it. Continue."

With a roll of her eyes, Juliana says, "My last stint abroad was in the UK. That's where I did my uni prep at Roedean and completed my A-levels, followed by my enrollment at the University of San Francisco to complete my major in business administration. I've been in the Napa area since then. Does that about cover it?"

I frown. Something else isn't adding up.

"Why UCSF? It's not exactly the most prestigious university in the country, and they're known for medicine, not business. After all that elite education, you could have gone anywhere."

"It was close to home," Juliana says, venom in her voice.

"So even with all that moving around, you still considered Napa home," I say.

"I guess?" she says with a shrug. "Although honestly, nowhere is home. I've never belonged anywhere. Maybe I just got tired of all the relocating."

Under the bravado, I catch a tinge of sadness. Most people wouldn't even notice, but I've spent decades fine-tuning my senses to pick up on the moods and vulnerabilities of others.

So Juliana Guerra, after being rejected by her "uncle" and sent halfway across the world at the age of six, has led a life of loneliness and isolation? Interesting. I wonder why she was sent away. And who was bankrolling all those years of private schools and boarding costs.

"You remember the name of the street you lived on when you were a child?" I ask.

"Old Sonoma Road, south of Westwood Hills Park," she says icily. "But the house there is long gone. Because your fucking father burned it. *To the ground*. With my parents inside."

Again, that same monotone, automatic response. Almost as if she's been coached.

"My condolences," I say coolly. "Are there records of this fire? Maybe an article in the Napa Valley Register?"

"No. Because your father bribed the police and the media with hush money."

"Plausible, I suppose. What makes you so sure it was Enzo Bellanti who did it?" I ask.

"Or one of his soldiers. Whatever. Either way, he was responsible!"

"Your uncle tell you that? Huh? Is that the only shred of evidence you have?"

She doesn't answer, just glares at me with hatred.

"You know, I'm wondering now...have you ever seen the remains of this house?"

"Yes. My uncle took me to see it, and I've driven by many times over the years. It's nothing but a dirt lot. The fire destroyed everything, down to the last stick of furniture."

How convenient. Who knows if there was ever a house there to begin with? Or if Sergio Bruno himself didn't set fire to the house that was there?

"So I'm guessing that means you don't have any photos

of your parents?" I prod. "No baby pictures, either? They all got burned in the fire?"

"Yes. What the fuck does this have to do with anything?"

"Maybe nothing," I say with a shrug.

I glance over at Candi. She's still standing in the same position, her whole body tense, as she observes my exchange with Juliana. But there's something more guarded in her expression now. Maybe she's taken aback by her friend's attitude. Maybe she's never seen Juliana so hostile and combative before. This woman might be a far cry from the Juliana she knows.

"Do you enjoy swimming?" I ask, returning to my interrogation, choosing to let Juliana's avoidance of my question about the street name slide.

She lets out a harsh, humorless laugh. "Is this a first date?"

I'm losing my patience. I take two steps forward, holding the gun steady. "I asked you a question, now it's your turn to answer. Do you enjoy swimming. Yes or no."

"I don't know how to fucking swim, okay? I have a weird phobia about water—bodies of water—but I can doggy paddle my way around a pool just fine. Okay?" She gives me a very judgmental stare. "You know, you have a reputation for being one hell of an interrogator, but so far you suck."

Candi moves a little closer to her friend. "Juliana, don't. Please. Don't antagonize him."

Juliana fixes Candi with a hard look. "Why? Worried he'll shoot me? I can't believe I thought you were my friend, *Cassandra*. If he kills me, it'll be on you."

Her open hostility toward my wife sets me off. I'm in front of the chair in a blink, fixing Juliana with my dead-eyed, dangerous interrogation gaze.

"You are the key to what could become one of the most savage, bloodthirsty, and violent criminal organizations this country has ever seen," I grind out. "So you will excuse my wife for doing what she thought was best in dealing with you. You are nothing more than a viper, and I swear to God if you strike at her, I will kill you."

Juliana watches me, but I can't tell if she believes me or not, or if she's even intimidated in the slightest. Because it seems that this woman, like me, is an expert at hiding her emotions. Her face is expressionless, a perfect poker face. I never realized until this very moment how absolutely infuriating that is. Normally, I can read people with ease, but somehow she's blocking me at every turn. Another Bellanti trait.

No. I'm not buying it. Not without real evidence.

"I would never hurt Candi. Never," she hisses.

The women look at each other and suddenly my wife is hugging her friend. Her back is to me, as if she's shielding Juliana from any further interrogation, but I can tell that Juliana is not hugging her back.

"How heartwarming," I say dryly. "But I'm not done."

In fact, I'm nowhere near done, but I'm willing to give my wife this allowance. I know this isn't easy on her. I'm sure it tore her up inside to text me this morning.

Regardless, I'm done playing the "what if" game.

Holstering my gun, I withdraw a small black zippered case from inside my blazer. Then I unzip it and approach Juliana.

"Roll up your sleeve."

Candi looks over her shoulder at me and then stumbles back, her eyes wide. "What are you doing?"

"Are you drugging me now?" Juliana sasses. "Is that some kind of truth serum?"

"No. Just taking a sample of your DNA."

She recoils as I pull out the syringe. "Then swab my cheek, asshole."

"Oh, no. I want the good stuff. A blood sample will leave no doubt."

Juliana squirms in her chair but finally sits resolute. I instruct Candi to roll up her friend's sleeve and then pass over the elastic tourniquet so Candi can tie off Juliana's upper arm and get one of her veins to pop. All the while, Juliana clenches her hands into fists, eyes glittering as if she'd love nothing more than to kill me.

The feeling is mutual, but I'm collecting her DNA first —because if it turns out that she really is my sister, I'll have to change tactics.

Kneeling at the side of the chair, I puncture Juliana's cephalic vein with cool efficiency, fill a vial, and withdraw the needle.

"Sorry, I don't have any Band-Aids," I tell her as I slip the vial into the black case. "Best to put some pressure on it."

She doesn't respond.

"You'll stay here with Candi until I get the results," I add.

"The results of what?" Juliana asks.

I glance over at Candi, who looks away. Ah. So she

hasn't told her friend what she suspects about her genealogy. Probably hasn't had the chance yet.

Ignoring Juliana's question, I add, "The house is heavily guarded, so it'd be in your best interest not to step outside. I'll take your phone now."

Candi crosses her arms. "She'll stay here if you ask her to. No demands."

There's a beat of silence. Does she really expect me to back down?

Fine. What do I care? It's merely a formality.

Pulling my gun out again, I politely ask, "Juliana Guerra, won't you please make yourself comfortable in this house while I attend to some pressing matters?"

Juliana rolls her eyes. "I don't actually have a choice, so fine."

"The phone now," I say.

"It's in my bag. Take it. It's a burner, anyway," she says with a huff.

I go over to the bed and pull the phone out of her purse. Then I hold my hand out for Candi's phone as well. I can't have her handing it over to Juliana to call for help. Luckily, there's no landline hooked up at the house, so I won't have to cut any wires on my way out.

Walking toward the door, I look back at my wife one last time. She stands resolutely next to her friend, her arm draped over Juliana's shoulder. I'm impressed by what Candi got done today. I don't think she realizes how beautifully she played both sides. Not only that, but she benefited all of us. I got to Juliana without having to resort to violence, and soon enough we'll all know if she's a Bellanti. Win-win.

"I'll see you at home," I tell her. "But you are not to leave the grounds."

Candi lifts her chin but doesn't respond to me.

I feel the weight of both of their gazes on my back as I leave.

22

ARMANI

THE FIRST THING I do when I leave the B&B is get in my SUV, take a pleasant little drive, and hand off a set of four different blood samples to an associate of mine who works in a diagnostics lab downtown. He's not a mafioso himself, but he owes me a favor. A big enough favor that he can be counted on when I need him for situations like this one. He's both efficient and discreet.

Back at the Bellanti offices, I lock myself into my executive suite and brood. There's no way I can concentrate on work right now. And not just because I'm waiting on the results of that blood sample, either.

It's Candi.

What she's done today is causing me some serious internal conflict.

Before her "rescue" of Juliana Guerra, I'd never quite been able to shake my conviction that Candi was trying to sabotage my family. Even after I confirmed my suspicions that she was a Bruno mole and confronted her—effectively ending her participation in Bruno's spying schemes—I still considered her an enemy. Not because she was still actively passing off intel to Sergio Bruno, but by virtue of the fact that she wasn't doing anything to help my family win this war. In fact, I was certain that my wife secretly took pleasure in watching me struggle to counter each brutal Bruno attack, and in watching the Bellanti empire suffer.

All of my assumptions changed the second I got her text this afternoon.

How can I continue doubting Candi's loyalty when she hand-delivered Juliana to my doorstep, knowing full well that she was potentially sacrificing the closest, most valuable friendship she's ever had? In doing so, my wife may have single-handedly stopped the most dangerous mafia alliance of all our lifetimes. Not to mention giving me a golden opportunity to get the DNA that will finally prove once and for all if this stranger really is my lost sister.

Now I can't stop thinking back on all the interactions I've had with Candi over the last few months and casting them in a whole new light. It's starting to dawn on me that when it comes to my wife, I may have been overly defensive, overly paranoid. I automatically framed her as an adversary instead of giving her a chance to prove herself as an ally. Do I honestly still believe she's working against me and my family?

No. I don't.

Which means...maybe she's been a better partner this whole time than I ever gave her credit for. Maybe she was being truthful in those moments when she revealed her feelings for me. And maybe her small gestures of kindness and acts of devotion were real, too.

In the moment, I'd thought it was all an act. Nothing more than manipulation, just another part of the game.

But now I feel like I was wrong.

My biggest mistake of all? Accusing her of getting pregnant to trap me. Damn my bitter, curmudgeonly soul, my knee-jerk reactions, my default to thinking the worst of people. She's carrying my child, and the only support I've shown her has been in service of getting something else out of her. I've spent our entire relationship convinced that she was the master manipulator, but it's been me all along. To my own detriment. And to hers.

I need to see her.

Taking out my phone, I'm about to call her when I remember that she doesn't have her phone. Because I took it from her. Of course I did. *Fuck.*

Maybe she's back home by now. If not, I'll go back to the Abbott property and ask security if she's left the B&B yet, or if she's still holed up in there with Juliana.

But when I step inside our bedroom, I find Candi curled up on the sofa in the sitting area, sobbing into a wad of tissues. I'm at her side in seconds, kneeling in front of her.

"What happened?" I ask softly, though it's obvious who the likely offender is.

"She...hates...me."

"I'm sure she doesn't hate you, even if she said she does."

I rub my thumb in soothing circles over her bare ankle, waiting for her to say more.

"But I betrayed her!" she finally chokes out. "I don't blame her for hating me now. I'd feel the same."

"You did what you thought was best," I tell her. "I think you did what was best, too."

"I feel like my heart is breaking," she says, her voice jagged with emotion.

"She'll come around," I say without believing it myself. I saw the fire in Juliana. I'd bet that woman can hold a grudge for a lifetime.

"Maybe," Candi says sorrowfully, but I don't think she believes it either. Turning her teary gaze on me, she asks, "What happens if it turns out she really is your sister?"

"I'll figure it out when we know more."

"How long 'til you get the results?"

"Couple days. Maybe tomorrow if we're lucky. I have a connection who works in a lab."

She nods.

Rising slowly, I hold out my hands to her. She hesitates for a moment and then takes my hands, letting me pull her up off the couch. When I wrap my arms around her she tenses briefly, then relaxes into my touch, head resting on my shoulder.

"Thank you for bringing her to me," I murmur into her hair.

"I shouldn't have done it. I betrayed her. I'm not a good friend. I'm a horrible person."

"No." I pull back. "You're not horrible. You did a really difficult thing, and you did it for *her*. Juliana wasn't safe where she was. Between Bruno and the Russians, she was in imminent danger. You got her someplace where they can't hurt her."

Candi nods slowly. "I...I guess I did."

"Nobody here is going to lay a finger on your friend," I

go on. "She's got more security assigned to her than the President. So yes, she might be pissed at you right now, but she's safe. That's the most important thing. She'll come around once she realizes what you did for her."

"Promise you'll protect her. That's all I ask."

"I promise I will."

Still holding her tightly, I dip my head down to cruise her neck with my lips, barely skimming her flesh as I work my way to the edge of her collarbone. She lets out a deep sigh, dropping her shoulder to give me better access. I kiss, and suck, and gently bite. When she shivers against me, the feel of her body trembling goes straight to my cock.

Tilting her chin up with my thumb and forefinger, I claim her mouth, tongue stroking aggressively against hers, leaving no question in her mind as to what I'm after. She surrenders completely, letting out soft little moans as I walk her backwards into the bedroom.

I kick the door shut, and she pulls away to gaze up at me searchingly. Her pupils are blown with desire, her chest heaving with breathless gasps, her lips cherry red and swollen from kissing. All the physical signs are there, and they all say *fuck me*.

But I'm feeling gentlemanly, so I ask first.

"What do you want me to do to you?"

"Make love to me," she whispers.

Something in my chest tightens at her words, but I don't have time to give it more attention because I'm already tugging her pants off, lifting her onto the bed, kissing her deeply as she leans back on her arms and I climb on top of her.

"Shirt off," I say, less commanding than I usually am.

She needs reassurance right now, and I know how to dial it down when necessary.

She sits up just long enough to whisk her shirt over her head. One flick of my fingers has her bra undone and sliding down her arms. I groan low in my throat at the sight of her breasts, plump and firm and ready for me to lavish my attention on.

I take her nipple in my mouth, sucking hard, my hands massaging her back as I suck. Moaning sweetly, she digs her nails into my scalp, sending pleasurable sparks of pain and heat through me. I work her nipples one at a time, using my teeth, my fingers, my tongue, relentlessly teasing until she's twisting and panting beneath me. Finally letting up, I shift lower on the bed and start kissing my way down her body. When I put my mouth over the satin panties between her legs, I look up to catch the hunger in her gaze.

Her lashes flutter as I move my tongue, licking her long and slow over the silky fabric. My body is strung tight with the instinctual urge to fuck and the sweet essence of her on my tongue. Her taste is driving me insane.

She's soaked, which I find out the second I slip a finger under the satin and trace the seam of her lips. Her hips begin to move as she presses against my finger, seeking more. God, she's hot for me. The thought has my cock straining painfully at my zipper. She's always been a greedy girl. The harder and more demanding I am, the more she wants it.

She's perfect for me in every way.

"You want more?" I ask.

"Yes," she pants.

She thrusts her pussy against my hand again, begging for me to touch her where she aches the most.

"I'll give you more when you're honest with me," I say.

Caressing her lips with my thumb, but never quite dipping inside her, I move back over her trembling body and kiss her.

"What do you want to know?" she asks, her voice breathy but guarded.

Before I ask, I pinch her clit, drawing a sharp hiss from her.

Without letting go, I whisper, "Tell me how you feel about me."

I pinch again, and a sharp, halting little moan escapes her.

"What do you mean?"

"Tell me." Pinch. "How you feel." Pinch. "About me."

Her breathing is ragged now, all of her muscles tense with barely constrained desire.

"I hate you," she says, pushing against me again.

"You're a bad liar," I tell her, laughing cruelly. "Try again."

Desperate now, she grabs my wrist and tries to guide my hand, but I easily resist.

"No. Not until you tell me."

She moans in frustration. "You're infuriating. And cold. And manipulative. Mercenary."

"And?" I prod.

"And sometimes, I can almost actually stand you. Happy?" she says petulantly.

Smirking, I give into her, sliding my longest finger inside her as I reposition my thumb over her clit. But I don't do anything else. I give her just enough so she can feel me there, right on the cusp of getting her off, without giving her any real, deep stimulation.

"Armani, come on!"

"Tell me. I know there's more."

Kissing her neck, I bite right above her collarbone. She jerks under me with a gasp, but I don't let go, her tender flesh so vulnerable between my teeth.

"Tell. Me."

She knows exactly what I want, and she's going to say it, even if I have to drag it out of her. Thrusting another finger into her, I sweep my thumb over her clit. Candi instantly cries out and tries to clamp her legs around me, but I withdraw my hand and shift my hips away. Her eyes flash as she whips me a desperate look.

"Say it," I demand.

"Say what?"

Look at her. Cheeks flushed, eyes ablaze. So stubborn. So furious with me for doing this to her. But so fucking horny at the same time, and nothing will convince me otherwise.

"Say. It. This is the last time I'll ask, and then I'm walking out."

I start to withdraw my hand, and that's what finally breaks her.

"Fine! You want me to tell you that I love you? Is that what you want to hear?"

A smile pulls at my lips. "Good girl."

My face is inches from hers as I work my pants off with my free hand and then pull her panties to one side.

"Now say it again."

Candi gasps as I rub the fat tip of my cock against her soaked center.

"I love you," she moans. "I...love you."

So throaty. So raw.

I can't hold back. With a groan, I drive straight into her, balls deep, connecting us undeniably. Her cry is loud, affirmative, ecstatic. I slide halfway out and then thrust again, watching the tears spring to her eyes.

"Mine," I whisper. "Mine."

She's mine in every way. The perfect woman, the perfect wife.

"Now I want to hear you come," I tell her.

I roll onto my back, taking her with me, giving her the freedom to ride me at her own pace, her own depth. She looks down at me as she grinds her hips, her fingers fumbling to release the buttons of my shirt until finally, my chest is bare. Leaning over me so her pebbled nipples brush my pecs, she latches her mouth onto mine, cooing softly in her throat as she sucks my tongue.

Bringing a hand between us, I work her clit, drawing deeper and deeper moans out of her while she rocks back and forth on my steel cock. Her thrusts get faster, harder, her tits bouncing against my chest with the force of her movements. With every hot, wet slip of her pussy up and down my shaft, I have to focus more and more on my self-control. I'm primed to explode.

"Armani," she cries, breaking our kiss, and the sound of my name wrenching out of her throat is almost enough to send me over the edge.

But I don't need to hold back anymore as Candi comes hard and tight on my dick, the contractions so deep that I can feel her muscles squeezing me. Grabbing her face and pulling her lips back down to mine, I groan into her mouth as I release everything I've got into her.

We ride out our orgasms together, perfectly in tandem, and when I open my eyes and find her looking right back at me, it only makes the euphoria more intense. My climax peaks and then, just as I expect it to taper off, it expands, stretches longer, impossibly sweeter, leaving me gasping and shuddering.

I've never shared anything like this with a woman before. The feeling of her shattering around me in blissful waves as I come apart beautifully inside her, the two of us connecting on a level I never would have thought possible. And that's when it hits me.

I think I love this woman.

Fuck. I do. I love her. I just can't tell her.

Because love? It's a liability.

And right now, it's exactly the kind of liability that could get me killed.

23

CANDI

AFTER ANOTHER ROUND, slower and more languorous than the first, we both lie back in bed. I'm completely spent, my body awash in a warm, blissful haze. I don't know what's come over Armani, but I'm afraid that if I ask, it will ruin whatever this is. So I don't ask.

Instead, I keep my head on his chest and listen to the sound of his heartbeat in the afternoon stillness of our room.

My emotions are such a dumpster fire right now. I hate the way he rolled up at the B&B with his gun drawn on Juliana. He should have just showed up with empty hands, an open mind, and a willingness to sit down and have a frank discussion with her, like I had envisioned.

But I also understand why he felt the need to be cautious. And honestly, he wasn't that out of line...because Juliana brought a gun, too. And how could he have known what he might be walking into? The Armani Bellanti I know would never show up to a meeting with one of his enemies unprepared, not without arming himself appropriately.

That doesn't mean it was the right move, though.

Do I regret asking him to meet us today? I don't know. I was terrified when I sent him those texts, and not because I was worried about what he might do to Juliana. No, I was far more concerned about what might happen to her if I didn't get her out of both her uncle's and the Bratva's reach, ASAP. It was a risk either way. On the scale of good and evil, however, I consider the Bellantis to be much more on the side of good. At worst, they're the lesser of two evils.

On top of that, I'm fully aware of how urgent it is to stop the alliance between the Bratva and the Brunos. It's terrifying to think what might happen with a union that powerful taking over the Mafia underground. So yes, it was imperative to get Juliana to a safe place. Or at least, a "safer" place. I genuinely hope that I made the right call.

If I'm honest with myself, I had ulterior motives as well. I wanted Juliana and Armani to meet face-to-face so that the issue of Juliana's genealogy could finally be resolved. I can't imagine how Jules will take the news if my hunch about her being a Bellanti turns out to be correct, but that's a bridge we'll have to figure out how to cross (or not) when the blood test comes back. Regardless, Armani did promise to keep Juliana safe. That's all that matters.

I just hope she can find it in her heart to forgive me after all's said and done.

A fresh wave of guilt hits me. Here I am, freshly fucked, nuzzled up against my husband, while my best friend is panicked and alone in a strange house, surrounded by her sworn enemies' guards. Despite the fearless, antagonistic attitude she displayed when Armani cornered her, she's probably terrified of what might happen to her now that she's in enemy hands.

After Armani had left us alone, Juliana really unleashed on me. She swore she'd never talk to me again and accused me of selling her out to a family of murderers for some good dick. She told me that I'd broken our friendship, that we were done, that she couldn't even stand to look at me. It crushed me. Not just because she was so angry or because I might be losing her forever. But because everything she was saying about me betraying her was 100% true.

I wonder if Orloff is looking for her yet. Surely the Brunos are, since Juliana's babysitters would have reported back to Sergio Bruno the second they realized she was gone. Would Sergio have gone straight to the Russians then, or would he try to keep her escape under wraps in order to avoid the Bratva's wrath? Either way, I think it would be smart to talk Armani into giving Juliana her phone back for a supervised call. She needs to speak to Orloff. If he finds out she's missing and he doesn't hear from her, it'll only be a matter of time before he starts burning Napa down to find her.

The thought sends a chill down my spine.

Maybe I shouldn't have brought Juliana here. I might have put all of us in the path of unspeakable danger.

"What are you thinking about?" Armani drawls sleepily next to me. "I can hear those wheels turning."

"Nothing, really."

"Liar. Don't forget how well I can read you, Candi. There's something on your mind."

I let out a deep sigh.

"There are a lot of somethings. I'm worried about the

baby. I'm worried about my best friend. I'm worried about this DNA test. I'm worried about..." *About you.* About *us.* But I don't say that out loud. "I'm worried about what the test results could mean for you and your family."

He runs his fingers lightly up and down my back. "Everything is going to be okay."

"Do you really believe that? Or are you just trying to make me feel better?"

Armani doesn't answer right away. After a few moments, I start to wonder if he's going to answer at all.

But then he says, "I really believe it. Our family is strong. Resilient. We've been through hell before, and we've survived. Whatever lies ahead, we'll meet it with everything we've got."

And in this moment, I believe him. My gut says he's right. It's as simple as that.

I look up at him as a mix of hope and fear washes through me. I wish I knew what he was planning. One minute he's telling me that the six-month expiration date of our marriage is almost up, and the next he's reassuring me about "our" family, as if I'm a part of it. But maybe that's just some seriously wishful thinking. Maybe I'm just lying to myself, pretending Armani could possibly be including me when he talks about the future.

"I'll call one of the guards and get an update on how your friend is doing," he says suddenly. "There's nothing stopping you from visiting her. Your phone stays with me, though."

My eyes sting with tears. "I don't think that's a good idea. You didn't hear the things she said to me. She told me I broke our friendship. She doesn't want anything to do with me. But yes, it would be good to get a status report from the guards."

Scrubbing a hand over his face, Armani gently moves me off his chest and gets out of bed. As he bends to collect his clothes and then starts getting dressed, I prop my chin on my fist and openly admire the view.

"Are you going back to work?" I ask.

He shakes his head. "I figured we could spend the rest of the afternoon working on the baby's room. Maybe decide on the paint options so I can get started on the walls."

"Oh. I actually decided already."

Eyeing me, he says, "The green."

"How did you know?"

"Easy. It's your favorite color."

"It is, but that's not why I chose it. I thought it matched perfectly with the mobile we got with the woodland motif."

"I'll take your word for it," he says, grabbing my clothes off the floor and tossing them to me. "Get dressed and we'll go downstairs and have lunch."

He's ordering me around, and yet...dammit, I like it. And I *am* starving. So I do as he says. I'm expecting him to order around the staff, but instead he takes me into the kitchen, pulls out a stool for me to sit on, and then puts together a few thick Italian sandwiches made with layers of cold cuts and olive salad. Before I can even ask, he brews some hot ginger tea for my stomach. Looks like my Model Husband is back. I do my best not to second-guess his motives.

We eat right there at the island, Armani sitting close enough that our elbows touch.

Afterward, we go upstairs to the future nursery. He

stands in the center of the room surveying the curtains I put up, the mobile hanging from the end of the rod, the variety of paint swatches we'd put on the wall. Then he nods and turns to me.

"Green is definitely the right choice. No question. Nice job on the curtains, by the way. And it looks like you started on the crib?"

I blush at his casual compliment. "Ah, the crib. Right. I didn't really make it past separating all the pieces, but yeah, I started."

"Why don't we finish it together?"

To my surprise, we actually make a good team. Some of the pieces are heavy—they're solid French oak, after all—so I get to stand there holding the corners flush while Armani handles the screws. Both of us work up a sweat; I'm glad I didn't try to do the assembly by myself. More than that, I'm glad that building the crib is something he and I did together for the baby. It feels meaningful, and nothing short of momentous.

The finished product is stunning. There's hand-carved woodwork on the headboard and rails, fluted legs, and an ingenious hidden storage drawer underneath. I can easily see this piece of furniture becoming a family heirloom. It makes me slightly less ashamed about the fact that it cost as much as a mortgage payment on a house.

Once we get it positioned against the wall, Armani gets the woodland mobile hung so the little animals dangle right above the crib. Then he rummages around in the shopping bags until he finds a crocheted blanket, which he drapes over the front rail of the crib. The finishing touch is a plush bunny rabbit. As I watch him gently set the rabbit against the headboard, his motions as tender as if he was handling a real baby, my eyes start to brim with tears.

"It looks great," Armani says, standing back with his hands on his hips.

All I can do is nod, a little sniffle escaping me. He looks over, sees how emotional I'm getting, and immediately comes over to pull me against his chest for a hug.

"Do you not like it? We can take it back and get something else," he says.

"No. It's beautiful," I whisper. "It's perfect."

"Don't worry. The rest of the room will come together in plenty of time before the little one arrives, I promise. We'll get everything settled and put into place."

Tucking my head under his chin, I close my eyes and pray that his words come true.

"Yes," I say. "Yes, we will."

24

CANDI

I'M up early the next morning, sipping tea down in the dining room by myself. The sun isn't quite up yet, but the horizon is just starting to turn golden orange and the sky is lightening to a soft blue. Even though I've managed to escape the kind of brutal, unrelenting nausea that Frankie talked about experiencing during her first trimester, I still wake up at the crack of dawn most days with my stomach in knots. A combination of baby hormones and stress, no doubt.

My emotions are in overdrive to boot, and the guilt is eating me alive. I've given it some more thought, and I've decided to go see Juliana and try to clear the air between us. Maybe if I bring her a peace offering—in the form of an impeccable cup of espresso and one of Chef Alain's signature breakfasts—she'll warm up enough to listen to what I have to say. I'm not expecting miracles, but I'm hoping we can at least come to a mutual understanding, if not a truce. I hate fighting with her.

It doesn't take much sweet talking to get Alain and his assistant Becca to agree to help me with Juliana's breakfast picnic. Despite the early hour, they're already hard at work preparing for the day's meals. Becca is busy washing and slicing organic produce from the local farmers' market while Alain kneads dough for bread. Alain has Becca assemble a citrus-heavy fruit salad while he finishes forming the loaves, and then he asks me what I'd like him to cook. Remembering the last time I had brunch with Juliana, I request the best avocado eggs benedict he can manage, which he levels up by switching out the English muffins for flaky puff pastries.

After packing a sturdy wicker basket with glass dishes full of fruit salad, the benedicts, and a separate container for the hollandaise, I fill a thermos with freshly brewed espresso. The coffee is my pièce de resistance. Jules is a total coffee snob, and she drinks pricy Italian espresso every day, so I know she won't be able to resist. Much like Juliana herself, the Bellantis do not fuck around when it comes to coffee beans. Maybe it's an Italian thing.

Donovan brings my car around for me and makes sure my picnic is secured (he even buckles the seat belt around the basket in the passenger seat), and then I'm off to the Abbott property. I park in front of the house this time, waving at the guards outside before unlocking the door with the key Frankie loaned me.

As I tiptoe through the house, I hear no sign of Juliana. It's so quiet you could literally hear a pin drop. She's usually an early riser, but maybe her captivity has her sleeping in. I hesitate for a moment, wondering if I should just leave the coffee and the basket in the kitchen for her to find later, but then I start to get anxious. What if she managed to climb out a window last night and escape, and the guards don't even know she's gone? I wouldn't put it past her.

As I make my way up the stairs I call her name, my heart pounding, but her grumpy response comes from the far end of the first floor. Thank God she's still here, safe and sound.

I locate her in the light-filled sunroom, sitting in a chair that faces the windows. This room used to be a dark, wood-paneled den, but it was completely redone at Charlie's insistence. Now it has a soaring cathedral ceiling with exposed beams, a rough-hewn stone fireplace, and an entire wall of picture windows overlooking the hilly green vineyard.

"Good morning," I say softly.

She barely gives me a glance over her shoulder as I walk in. It's obvious I'm not welcome, but too bad. She can hate me all she wants, but I need her to know that I'm here for her. Especially right now, when she's cornered and vulnerable and her future is so uncertain.

"Are you hungry? I brought you breakfast. Thought we could use some girl time."

I keep my voice light and cheery and even give the thermos a little wiggle, but Juliana doesn't acknowledge me. After setting the basket on a side table, I drop into the chair next to hers and crack the top of the thermos so the aroma fills the air. She doesn't even blink.

"I'll go get us some mugs from the kitchen. If you're not hungry yet, maybe we can watch a couple shows to pass the time? Catch up a little?"

She finally whips me a cold look. "Are you serious right now? You think I want to have girl time with you? Get out of here, Candi."

I don't take offense. In fact, I feel even worse for her. She's still in the same clothes she was wearing yesterday, and judging by how wrinkly they are, she slept in them. The bags under her eyes tell me she didn't have a very restful night, either. Her face is impeccable, however, because if there's one thing Jules never leaves home without, it's her fancy Chanel toiletry bag.

Ignoring the venom in her voice, I unpack the basket and set everything on the coffee table. Then I make a quick trip to the kitchen for silverware, napkins, and coffee cups. Luckily, since Mrs. Abbott and Livvie have been staying here, everything I need is at hand.

Juliana continues to ignore me as I fill a plate for her. She doesn't even pick up the espresso. I'm not giving up yet, though. I start to eat, waiting for her to thaw. The Juliana that I know won't be able to keep her mouth shut forever. Especially not when I've pissed her off so badly. She'll want to get two more cents in before I leave.

It's hard to eat when I'm battling both morning sickness and the disdain of my BFF, but I force myself to take small bites. As I watch the birds out the windows, a memory comes to mind.

"Hey, remember that time in college when we went to the dining hall on a Sunday, totally hungover, and stole the entire tray of bacon off the warmer while the cook wasn't looking?"

We'd reheated that bacon for all our meals for three

solid days until it got so hard and chewy that we couldn't eat it anymore. The food services staff never did find out who the thieves were, though amongst our friends, Juliana and I were legends.

She blinks but doesn't respond.

"I couldn't touch bacon for months after that," I go on. "Even the smell was enough to turn my stomach, we overdid it so bad. No regrets, though. Right?"

She huffs in annoyance.

Swallowing hard, it strikes me that if I can't fix this, my best friend will never know my baby. Juliana doesn't even know I'm pregnant yet. I want to tell her, but the timing is crap. I can't drop that kind of bombshell on her when she won't even look at me.

Pushing my plate aside, I pour myself some espresso and then glance over at her again.

"You should try the espresso. It's the good stuff. I think you're really going to—"

"Jesus, Candi, would you just stop it!" She swivels in her chair to glare at me. "Seriously. Just, stop. Bringing me food and all this cheery bullshit isn't going to fix what you did to me."

I stop mid-pour and set the thermos down.

"I was trying to keep you safe. You have to know that."

"Bullshit! You hand-delivered me to your husband knowing full well that he's the enemy," she snarls. "You really dove into this fake marriage and ran with it, didn't you? How much dick did it take before you decided to change sides?"

I jolt back, as if she's struck me.

"This isn't about taking sides, Juliana. It's about doing the right thing."

A bitter laugh escapes her. "Right. So you're saying that kidnapping your best friend is doing the right thing."

"Look, I understand where you're coming from, but you seem to have forgotten that you were the one who *asked me* to help you find somewhere to hide," I snap. "And I delivered."

"Somewhere *safe*, Candi. Not somewhere I'd be a prisoner. Your shitty fucking husband is probably going to kill me before anyone even realizes I'm here!"

"You *are* safe," I insist.

"Clearly we have two very different definitions of personal safety," she says icily.

"Armani won't hurt you," I say quietly.

But I'm not sure I believe that. Everything hinges on these DNA results we're waiting for. And even if Juliana is the Bellantis' sister, that doesn't mean Armani won't still want to drag her down to the Deep Cellar for a little brotherly interrogation session.

She's watching me as I run this all through my head.

"You look like you have something else you want to say, so spit it out," she hisses.

I take a deep breath and look her squarely in the eye. "I'm sorry you think I betrayed you, but I swear, that was never my intention. I was afraid for your life, Jules. I brought you somewhere I knew I could personally keep an eye on you, a place with plenty of guards who aren't working for your uncle or your fiancé. I really thought I was helping."

She bursts out of her chair and stalks to the window,

digging her fingers into her hair, then whirls to face me. She's positively shaking with the force of her anger.

"Do you have even the slightest inkling of what you've done? You are fucked. You haven't just made me your enemy, you've made the entire *Russian mob* your enemy. You're dead where you're standing."

My whole body goes cold, but my anger is boiling over.

"You told me you were afraid for your life!" I shout. "So I did what I had to do to get you out of a life-threatening situation! What would you have done in my position, Jules?"

She glowers at me. "I sure as hell wouldn't have done what you did. I would've grabbed my gun and all my emergency cash first, disguised myself the best I could, and then rented a car under a fake name, bought a bunch of burner phones—"

"Okay, okay, I get it! You're way better at this gangster stuff than me. Let's face it: you always have been," I say, earning a quick smirk from her. "But regardless of the fact that you hate me for bringing you here, there might be a silver lining for you. Because Armani thinks he has some answers about what happened to your parents."

Juliana freezes. That was probably the last thing she expected to come out of my mouth.

God, I wish I could tell her more—prepare her better for the possibility that she might, in fact, be a Bellanti—but I don't feel like it's my news to share right now. Not when we're literally a few hours away from getting those blood test results back and finding out for sure if my suspicions have been warranted.

Crossing her arms, she schools her expression back to neutral and looks out the window.

"My parents?" she scoffs. "What could he possibly know? Did Daddy Bellanti keep a diary of all his kills or something? Is Armani going to read me the entries out loud? Or did he have a hand in their murder himself?"

"No! He would have been a first grader at the time," I point out, exasperated. "And also, he's not that bad. He's also kind of...soon to be...the father of my baby."

My hand subconsciously drops down over my lower belly, and Juliana's jaw drops.

"Fucking *what* did you just say?" she gasps.

I can't tell if she actually didn't hear what I said, or if she's just so shocked by the news that she wants me to say it again.

Clearing my throat, I try again. "I said that I'm—that we're—preg—"

Her eyes dart to the doorway, and she immediately pulls her shoulders back, her whole body going tense. I spin to follow her line of vision.

Armani stands there with a sheet of paper crumpled in his fist.

I can tell by his expression that he must have the blood test results in his hand.

"What is it?" I ask, rising from my chair, my heart hammering. "What's it say?"

Looking Juliana square in the face, he crosses the room toward us, stopping in front of her chair. Then he runs a hand over his mouth, and I see he's got this look in his eyes that I can only describe as...shock. Or, no. It's more like...wonder.

And then he lets out a disbelieving laugh.

"Here. This is yours," he says, passing the paper to Juliana.

"What is this?" she asks.

"The results of the sibling DNA test." His voice is cool, collected, calm. As if he's trying to soothe a skittish horse.

"*Sibling*?" Juliana shakes her head as she scans the page. "I don't have any siblings."

Armani clears his throat and then says, "You do. You've got three brothers. Me, Dante—he's the oldest—and Marco. Marco's the baby."

Her head snaps up. "Bullshit."

"The blood doesn't lie," he says.

I can see the paper trembling in Juliana's hand. Armani leans over and taps something printed on the page.

"There. See? You matched with me, Dante, and Marco. All of us, full siblings. Same mother, same father. It's right there in black and white."

Juliana's face is a mask of disbelief and suspicion. "This isn't real." She whips her gaze back over to me. "This is fake, right? He made this all up. To—to fuck with me. To try to get me on their side. Right? Or he switched out the blood or something. How can—how can—"

She starts shaking, but she's still gripping the paper tightly. Her mouth opens and closes, but nothing comes out. Her whole world must be imploding.

"It's real," I tell her gently. "Nobody tampered with the test."

"But how...why..." She trails off as her chin starts to wobble. I can see her fighting back tears, fighting to process this.

"It isn't *possible*," she finally chokes out.

"The probability that we're a sibling match is 99.95 percent," Armani says.

He kneels in front of her chair and looks her in the eye.

"The truth is, your real name isn't Juliana Guerra," he says softly. "It's Liliana. Liliana Bellanti. You're my sister."

25

ARMANI

My brothers and their wives should arrive any moment. I called Dante and then Marco on the way from the B&B over to the Bellanti estate, and although I didn't reveal the results of the DNA test, I did let them know that the situation is urgent. There was just no way I was going to tell them that Juliana is our sister over the phone. They deserve to hear the news in person.

Neither of them questioned me, they simply agreed to meet me at the main house right away. Having provided me with blood samples themselves just a few days ago, I'm sure they know exactly what this meeting is about.

Meanwhile, Juliana seems to be in shock. She's been quiet and closed off since Candi and I escorted her from the B&B to my car. To an extent, I can empathize with how she's feeling. I'm still shell-shocked myself. The possibility that she was Liliana isn't something I ever really took seriously, despite Marco's insistence on the matter. Now, it's confirmed. Like I told Juliana, the blood doesn't lie.

This test changes everything.

In the living room at the front of the house, Juliana sits stiffly on the sofa with the expression of a caged animal. Candi is on the other end of the sofa beside her, and both of them are ignoring the steaming cups of tea that I had Becca bring out from the kitchen along with bottles of water and a pile of sandwiches that remain equally untouched. Juliana —no, Liliana—nearly jumps out of her skin at the sound of the heavy front door creaking open.

"Hello?" a voice calls out. It's Marco.

"We're in here," I call back.

Seconds later, he and Karina step into the living room. The first thing I notice is how tightly my brother is clinging to his wife's hand, the shifty look in his eyes. Is he nervous?

And then his gaze lands on Juliana, and he freezes. Seconds pass, and he just stands there, immobilized. I'm not sure if he's struggling to find the right words to say or if he's just been struck dumb by her resemblance to our late mother. Now that I'm no longer actively trying to come up with a million reasons why Juliana can't possibly be our sister, I see it too.

"Hey," Juliana says softly.

Still overwhelmed, Marco doesn't respond, but Karina does.

"Hi," she says. "This is Marco. I'm Karina, his wife. We were at a house showing on the other side of Napa, otherwise we would have been here faster. Nice to meet you."

Juliana studies Karina for a second and then silently nods.

"Why don't you two take a seat," I tell Karina, motioning for her to hustle Marco into a chair so he can try to get his shit together.

I'm anticipating more awkward silence, but then Dante and Frankie arrive, right on Marco and Karina's heels.

"Sorry we're late," Frankie says breathlessly. "Dante left work and came to get me, but then the baby needed to be changed right as we were walking out the door, and—well. We're here now, anyway."

Dante has baby Lili in his arms as Frankie babbles, and he gives Juliana a long, assessing stare—which she boldly returns—before turning to me. I subtly shake my head to deter him from asking any questions, and then he and Frankie and the baby get settled on the love seat.

Our family is arranged in a rough circle now. The tension in the air is thick.

"So. Now that we're all here, I won't draw things out," I begin. I clear my throat and then pause, making eye contact with my brothers before I speak again. "The DNA results came back, and...the test confirms that this woman is our biological sister, Liliana. Or, I guess, Juliana."

The uproar I'm expecting doesn't come. Karina pats Marco's hand reassuringly. Frankie covers her mouth as if she might cry. Other than that, everyone just sits there in stunned silence, staring at Juliana as if expecting her to give a speech or something.

I go on, "Juliana, you obviously met Marco and Karina already. It's not my place to get into detail about it at the moment, but Karina was raised in Sergio Bruno's house here in Napa. He's her uncle. Her mother's brother."

As I let my words sink in, Juliana's eyes widen. She clearly doesn't know much about Karina, even though they share the same "uncle."

"I thought you looked familiar," Juliana says wonderingly, addressing Karina. "You're the girl from the photos. I didn't have much contact with Unc—with Sergio, when I was growing up, but every now and then I'd get a package with a few photos, some generic holiday card, random cash. I figured you were a family member, just another kid in the background at Christmas and Easter. I didn't know you grew up in that house."

"It was no picnic," Karina says bitterly.

Juliana smiles sardonically. "Maybe we can talk about it sometime."

Karina offers a tight smile. "I never saw any pictures of you, and I never heard anyone mention your name. Also...I spent my childhood with my nose in a book, pining for friendships with other girls. So I'd definitely remember if we'd ever met. Sergio kept you well hidden."

"Yes. He did," Juliana says, her voice strained. "I grew up being told that there were mob men who'd kill me on sight if I tried to go home to Napa. Sergio had to plan each of my visits down to the last minute, and I could never stay more than a few days because of supposed enemy spies and surveillance and...God knows what else. But he was gaslighting me all along. He'd dodge my questions, saying the phones were tapped. Every time I'd ask when I could come home, he'd tell me it wasn't safe, maybe in a few more months, I was too precious to risk."

"I'm sorry," Karina says. "I know what he's like. I know exactly what he's like. Marco is the one who saved me. If not for him, I would've been in your exact same situation. Married off to a terrible man to settle mafia politics. But I got out of there. So did you."

Juliana's hands curl into fists on her lap. Her shoulders tremble with pent-up emotion.

I catch her eye and gently shift the conversation back on track. "As I'm sure you have gathered, this is your oldest brother Dante and his wife, Frankie."

Dante gives a curt nod, and Frankie scoots forward on the love seat with baby Lili on her lap and tells Juliana, "This is your niece, Liliana Grace. We named her after you. I know this is a lot to take in, but I'm glad you're here. Welcome home."

Juliana offers a tight-lipped smile and then looks away from the baby.

Now that we've all been formally introduced, silence falls again. Normally I'm at ease taking charge of these family meetings, but I'm lost. This revelation about Juliana is a shock to us all. It radically alters everything my brothers and I thought we knew about our family.

Marco finally speaks up. "Do you remember anything about our mother?"

Juliana shrugs. "I don't have much of a memory that doesn't involve my extended Bruno family. Everything before that is...fuzzy. I never thought that was abnormal. Nobody remembers much before the age of five or six, right? Except now I'm starting to question that."

"What did Sergio tell you about your parents?" he asks.

"That the Bellantis burned our house down, and my parents both died in the fire."

She lifts her chin, her posture shifting to one of defiance. But that chin lift, it triggers a memory. I see a flash of her as a young child in my mind. It's not a still image I'm remembering from a photograph, but something buried much deeper that's come to the surface. The four of us, playing tag outside, running through the vineyard, hiding in the vines, a warm breeze tossing our hair. Lili always wanted to be It, even though she was the slowest to find us all.

The accusatory edge to her voice is going to take some time to go away, I realize. It will, but first she has to accept that the story Sergio Bruno sold her was a complete fabrication.

"But even if that story about my parents dying in a fire is bullshit, I know Enzo Bellanti passed a few years ago, so I don't have a father anyway," Juliana says gruffly. She looks at me, Dante, Marco. "But your mother...our mother...is she...alive?"

The guarded but desperate hope in her voice crushes my soul.

"I'm sorry," I tell her. "She died in a boating accident two decades ago. The same day, we were told, that our sister died. But you're alive and well, and that's...a gift."

Juliana visibly slumps on the couch as she realizes she's still an orphan.

"Mom loved you more than anything," Marco blurts suddenly. "All of us."

But his words seem to do little to perk her up.

"You're positive the DNA test was accurate?" Dante interrupts. "Beyond any reasonable doubt?"

"She matched all three of us," I tell him. "The margin of error is less than 0.05 percent. That margin goes down even further considering that we all share virtually the same genes."

Marco sighs and looks up at the ceiling. "Jesus Christ! What the fuck did Dad do?"

Juliana leans forward on the couch, hugging herself tightly. She looks around the room assessing each person, and, if she's anything like me, calculating how dangerous we are.

"Okay, so what happens next? What are you going to do with me now?" she asks.

"What are we going to do with you now?" Frankie repeats incredulously. "You're our *family*. The only thing to do is to get you acclimated to your new...circumstances, I guess, and help you settle into things. I'm sure it won't be easy, and I know you've lost a lot of years, but when you're ready, we can all move forward. Together."

Juliana swallows hard.

"I just...I'm so confused," she says. "The day of the boat accident, somebody killed our mother, so that part is real, but...but what happened to me? Who took me? And why? How did Sergio end up fostering me? And why would he raise me as a Bruno? He told me for *my entire life* that my parents were dead because of your family. *My* family." She looks around again and takes a deep, shuddering breath. "What was her name? Our mom?"

"Gabriella," Dante says softly. "Gabriella Camille."

"What about Enzo? Our father. Was he...as bad as Sergio says?" she asks hesitantly.

Dante's brow furrows. "He was...a very focused man. Focused on power. On the Life. His *famiglia*. His actual family at home, though...not so much. None of us had a great relationship with him. I'm sure, over time, Marco and Armani and I can tell you everything."

"I'd like that," Juliana says, her voice barely a whisper. When she looks up again, her eyes are glittering with tears that she's too stubborn to let fall. "Everything I thought I knew about myself is a lie. I have no idea who I am. But that's something I need to figure out."

"You will, Jules," Candi says, speaking up for the first time. "Besides, you've always known exactly who you are, and it's got nothing to do with Sergio Bruno. You're strong, you're fearless, you're resilient and whip smart. You love intimidating men and...and blowing money on designer shoes and getting into mischief. That's all still *you*. Maybe you just need to take some time to sort out the real you from the version of yourself that felt beholden to him."

Juliana nods. "Yeah. Maybe you're right."

Some of the tension leaves the room. Even my brothers seem more relaxed now that Candi has, at least partially, diffused the existential crisis that Juliana is going through.

Marco and Karina ask Juliana a few more questions, and soon enough, a conversation starts. Everyone is still proceeding with caution, but they're getting closer, asking bigger questions. Jesus, it's going to take months if not years for us to get to know each other. Juliana was a child the last time she saw any of us. We've lived half a lifetime since then.

The talk starts to lull, and Juliana sighs to herself and then looks around at everyone. I don't need to be a professional interrogator to read the fury in her eyes.

"I'm not going back," she says. "Not to my unc—to Sergio, and not to my fiancé, either. At least, not until I figure out how I'm going to play this thing. I mean, I'm supposed to marry Orloff and play mafia wife, but I have no fucking clue what I want to do with my life now."

"You'll need to figure out your next move soon," I warn her. "I'm sure Bruno and Orloff are already looking for you. We can keep you safe here for a few days, but it's only a matter of time before they track you down. Better to preemptively take control of—"

"Control of the narrative," Juliana says, her words blending with mine. "You're right. I can't let them start coming up with their own theories. I have to spin this to my advantage. But I need to stay away from Orloff. He'll see right through me if I try to lie. He'll know something's off. And then I'll be dead."

"No. We won't let that happen," I tell her firmly.

"Good." She looks over at Candi. "Remember that girl time you offered me earlier? Does the offer still stand?"

Candi takes Juliana's hands and squeezes. "Of course. Anything you want."

"Excellent. Armani, may I have my phone back?"

She says my name as if it's unfamiliar and foreign on her tongue. Reaching into my pocket, I withdraw the burner phone and hand it to her. She unlocks it and doesn't bother to hide the screen from me as she pulls up Orloff's contact and calls him.

He picks up immediately. We can all hear his Russian-accented voice on speakerphone.

"Maxim, it's me," Juliana says quickly.

"What number is this?" he barks.

"Oh. It's just a temp. I had to get one of those crappy prepaid phones at a gas station, since you still have mine."

"A gas station? Where the fuck are you—"

"Before you say anything, I'm sorry," she says. "I know I should've told somebody I was leaving. But I'm totally fine. I've been with Candi since yesterday. You know, my best friend?"

Orloff spouts a string of Russian phrases which I'm pretty sure are expletives.

Juliana is unruffled.

"Don't you remember, babe? I asked you about taking a week away with my matron of honor, since we decided I wasn't going to have a bachelorette party. You didn't say no, so I went ahead and arranged us a spa retreat! Yes, it's a little pricy, but I really think it's worth it."

"You need to return to the safe house. It's too dangerous for you—"

"Oh, Max, come on. I'm safe! I promise. The spa is up in the mountains, and there's nobody here but a bunch of aestheticians and yoga instructors. We're having an absolute ball."

He starts to say something else, but Juliana cuts him off with a giggle and an excuse about how she's running late to her hot stone massage. Then she promises to check in soon and promptly hangs up on him. I have to admit, that was impressive. She didn't even break a sweat.

Not only that, but my sister just managed to buy all of us some time to plan our next move.

"That was pretty slick," Frankie says admiringly.

"Thanks." Juliana breathes a sigh of relief through her nose. "Well then, it's settled. I have almost a whole week to strategize. But first, I need to find someplace to stay."

Candi shakes her head. "No you don't. You're staying here."

"I can't—"

"You can," I interrupt. "Dante?"

He stands. "As the head of the family, my word is law. And I insist that you stay. There are plenty of rooms, plenty of staff to see to all your needs, and tons of security as well."

"In that case...I guess I'll stay," Juliana says, sounding relieved. "But just for the week. Or maybe less. The main thing is, I need to figure out what to do about this wedding. Because if I don't go through with it, it's not just me who's at risk anymore. It's all of you."

26

CANDI

"'No Caller ID' is calling me again," I tell Juliana, a tidal wave of anxiety hitting me.

We're on adjacent massage tables in a private room, wrapped in thick Turkish towels, the aromatherapy cranking hard. Both of us have been tapping at our phones while we wait for the massage therapists to come in, but this is the third time I've gotten one of these calls in the last five minutes. So much for rest and relaxation.

"Maxim," she says, reaching over to swipe my phone from me and staring down at the screen. "Fuck. I'm sending him to voicemail. There."

She hands my phone back, but it doesn't do much to quell my nerves.

Jules hasn't talked to Orloff at all since she told him we were away at her pre-wedding spa retreat together, knowing full well it wouldn't be the last she'd hear from her fiancé. He managed to get my cell number—I'm still not sure how he pulled that off—and the fact that he's keeping tabs on me as well only makes him scarier.

"Maybe you could just talk to him for a minute," I suggest. "That way he stops stalking you. You can say you've been getting gold leaf facials and reflexology massages and you're having a ball. I mean, it can't hurt to check in."

She makes a face. "No. The more I think about the shit-show that my entire life is, the more pissed off I get. And not just at Sergio. Maxim has been using me, too. I'm not talking to either one of them until I decide what to do about this wedding."

"Okay," I say placatingly, settling back onto the pillow.

We're at an exclusive, VIP-only luxury spa for a full day of head-to-toe treatments. Normally, it'd be impossible to get into a place like this on such short notice, but Armani took care of it...presumably with cash. He insisted on sending us here with a driver and six bodyguards, which I thought was excessive until Juliana asked for two more.

She and I had a light breakfast at Casa Bellanti and arrived here at nine a.m. These massages are our first treatment—although mine's a special prenatal massage. I'm not really sure what that means, but I hope it does something for all the stress I'm experiencing.

I don't like that Juliana's fiancé won't stop calling, and I like it even less that she ignores him each time. Talk about adding fuel to the fire. I'm surprised a bunch of Russian mobsters haven't burst in on us yet to take her into custody. Even texting the guy a dumb kissy-face emoji would go a long way toward keeping him pacified, but Jules refuses.

Maybe I should just steal her phone and do it myself.

My cell starts vibrating again. I don't even have to look to know it's Orloff again.

"You sure you don't want me to pick up and just...make up an excuse for you?" I ask. "It'd get him off your back for a bit, at least. I'll tell him your phone died because you forgot to charge it. Um, and that you're in the sauna so you can't talk."

As scary as it would be to speak to Orloff myself, it's the best solution I can think of. Not just because Juliana refuses to talk to him herself, but because even if she *did*, her temper might get the best of her, and I can only imagine what might come out of her mouth. When she's angry, she doesn't think before she speaks. I've seen the devastating consequences more than once.

We need to do whatever it takes to keep him—and Sergio Bruno, too—from getting suspicious about Juliana's loyalties. They can't find out that she knows about her true identity.

"You don't need to talk to him," Juliana says. "He'll just bully you into handing me the phone, and then I'd hang up on him, and then we're right back at square one."

Sighing, I set the phone on a teak table with a stack of towels on it and try to get some deep breathing exercises going. I can't lie; I'm relieved that Juliana said no. Her fiancé intimidated the hell out of me when I met him at the bakery.

Juliana takes my hand and squeezes. "Thanks for offering, though."

"You're welcome."

The tension between us is gone. She's still pretty shell-shocked as she processes the fact that she's a Bellanti, but it seems like I've been forgiven for tricking her into meeting with Armani. I guess if it weren't for my gut feeling about her uncanny resemblance to that old photo of Liliana, Jules never would have found out that most of her life was a lie.

It makes me sick to think about all the years she spent in boarding schools all over Europe, lonely and abandoned to strangers, clinging to the belief that Sergio Bruno was her protector, her godfather, her only family left, when all along he was keeping this dark, terrible secret from her. He knew she was a Bellanti this entire time. He had to be responsible for Gabriella Bellanti's death, too. I can't think of any other likely suspect. But what was his plan? Did he dispose of the mother so he could steal her child? And why? To raise her as a pawn?

So many questions have gone through my mind since finding out the truth about her, but I don't dare give voice to them. Not yet. Everything is too new and raw for her still. She needs time to adjust. Jules hasn't mentioned my pregnancy, either—that's how much of a tailspin she's in. Maybe she blocked it out or forgot, with all the earth-shattering revelations about her DNA.

Our massage therapists finally bustle in, and Juliana and I surrender to the pampering. At some point, I completely doze off. I wake to Juliana poking me in the shoulder.

"Don't wanna get up," I mumble.

"Come on. We're scheduled for facials next. You can sleep for that, too."

Two hours later, my face is glowing, my cheeks are pink, and my lips are baby soft and exfoliated. My body is loose, my brain relaxed. I haven't felt this calm in weeks, if not months.

"I'm going to sleep so good tonight."

Juliana links her arm through mine. "Me, too. Let's go find brunch. I'm starving."

I let her lead the way, trying to ignore the mini army of black-clad, hulking security guards following us. Admittedly, I do feel safe. But it's still unnerving.

We eat at the spa's outdoor café, at a table overlooking the ocean. Goddess salads, avocado toast on sprouted whole grain, sunshine tea, goji berry coffee cake. Delicious, all of it.

Our last stop is mani-pedis, and then it's time to leave. The guards escort us outside to the SUV that Donovan is driving. I'm about to slide into the back seat when my phone vibrates. Juliana's face drops when she hears the sound.

"It's him again," she says flatly.

"Maybe not." I pull the phone out of my pocket and wince. "Okay, it is him. It's a text that says, '*I am giving her two hours to call me, or else.*'"

Her lips press into a hard line. "I'll call him in one hour and fifty-nine minutes, then."

"Juliana—"

"How about you take me to the famous Bellanti tasting room? I'm dying for a drink."

I ask Donovan to take us to the tasting room, then text Armani to let him know where we're headed, even though I'm sure security is keeping him in the loop.

When we arrive at the tasting room, the place is empty save for a few Bellanti Vineyards employees. It's a cloudy day and a weekday to boot, which is why we have the place to ourselves. Taking advantage of the lull, I show Juliana around. Frankie is in the retail area with a clipboard in one hand, taking inventory of the wine that's currently out on display. Baby Lili is dozing next to her, in her car seat, which Frankie has placed on the floor at her feet. She sees me and Juliana and waves.

"Welcome in," Frankie says. "Just browsing?"

"For now," Juliana says, wandering off.

"Actually, there is something I'm looking for," I tell Frankie.

There's a particular wine I'd love for Juliana to try. It's a celebration wine, something normally reserved for weddings, births, or other joyful occasions. Today, I want to celebrate Juliana's return to her true family. And—by marriage, at least—mine as well.

I get Frankie's blessing, locate the prized wine, and then snag my friend so I can take her to the back room for some privacy.

"I have the best wine for you to try," I tell her excitedly. "It's not for sale yet, but we have some sample bottles that were just poured from the aging cask. It's Bellanti Brunello, made from Sangiovese grapes, with a technique that's a Bellanti family secret. Allegedly."

With a flourish, I pull out a stool for her at the ornate, Art Nouveau-style bar. Then, I display the bottle to Juliana as if I'm running a real tasting. The bottle has a hand-written white label, and nothing about it screams "fancy," but I know it's going to be incredible.

"Only four bottles were set aside for family use, or to gift to important guests if they popped in for a tasting. An official selection will be offered later in the year, and I have no doubt it will become a leading Bellanti bestseller," I explain.

"Wow. You sound like you'd make a killing in sales for this place," Juliana teases.

"Ha ha," I say. "This isn't just one of my usual sales pitches, though. I really believe in this wine. You will too, when you taste it."

Juliana looks around the room with its rough stone walls and matching floor, the ornate iron chandelier, the windows facing the vineyard. This is a nice, private room that doesn't get used much. It's usually reserved for either private parties, celebrity guests, or the Bellanti family.

"It's so pretty in here," she says.

"Yeah. Frankie had the Bellantis invest in a huge renovation last year. Worth it."

Using a corkscrew, I open the bottle. The cork comes out with a loud pop, and a powerful scent wafts from the opening. My stomach turns, revolting at the smell. My brain was expecting the sweetness of a rich, red wine made from heirloom Italian grapes, but instead, all I'm getting is something...sour, metallic, oily.

Must be pregnancy hormones, I think as I pour. The wine comes out in a thick stream. Much thicker than normal.

It clumps into the glass with a layer of lighter liquid on top. What is that? There shouldn't be sediment. And it shouldn't smell like this.

"Um, I need to ask Frankie something real quick," I tell Juliana. "I'll be right back."

Grabbing the glass and the bottle, I hurry back to the retail area.

"Frankie, can you take a look at this? The wine is off. It's...not right."

I hold up the glass. Her brows knit.

"Did you pour from an already opened bottle?" she asks.

"No, I just opened a new one."

Gingerly, she takes the glass and has a sniff. She recoils and covers her nose.

"It smells like blood."

Nausea hits me full force. "Are you sure?"

Taking the bottle over to a sink behind the bar, she dumps it. Small, coagulated clumps pour out. There's no question.

"Oh my God—"

"Call Armani," she says, her voice sharp. "Now."

Armani is at work, at the Bellanti offices on the other side of the property, but he answers in one ring. When I tell him what's going on, he says he'll be right over. I sink onto the floor beside Lili and put my head in my hands, trying not to be sick. And then Juliana comes out from the back room, rushing to my side when she sees me hunched over.

"What happened, Candi? Is everything okay?"

"I—"

But before I can explain, Armani bursts through the entry doors, followed by Dante and Marco. Dante takes one look at his wife and his face creases with concern.

"Where's the bottle? Show me the blood," he says.

Frankie gestures to the sink, and Armani goes behind the bar, grabs the bottle, and smells. His eyes flash as he whips Dante a look.

"It's the real thing. Go check the cask. I'll make the call."

Dante storms out while Armani calls the lead vintner in the cask room.

"Open cask 515, the Brunello." There must be some resistance because he tilts his head and then shouts, "I said open it. Now!"

A few tense minutes pass until Dante calls Armani to confirm what he already suspected: the cask is full of blood. Dante isn't sure if it's human or animal.

Either way, it's enough to push me over the edge. I run to the sink behind the bar and vomit, turning the taps on just in time to wash it down the drain.

Juliana pats my back while Frankie barks at Marco to get me a glass of water and a clean dish towel to wipe my face, and then Jules helps me over to a chair. The rest of the family gathers around. Everyone is tense.

"I'm done. It's time to get the fuck out of here and lay low," Marco says. "How the hell did these people get into the cask room? And whose blood is that, even? It's too much, Armani. We'll come up with a plan, but we need to do it from the safety of a private, well-secured location. We can't stay here."

"You're not going anywhere." Armani's voice is pure steel.

"The hell I'm not," Marco shoots back. "I'm not going to sit around here waiting for the Bratva to attack and putting my wife's life in danger. Not to mention our sister."

Baby Lili begins to fuss in Dante's arms. Frankie takes her from Dante and I don't miss the way she locks eyes with her husband.

Dante clears his throat. As the head of this family, he's the one in charge. Not Armani. And we all know it.

"I have a wife and a daughter to protect, as well," he says. "I agree with Marco on this. We're going to lay low, too. Juliana, the choice is yours. You're welcome to come with us."

"So you're all leaving town?" Armani scoffs. "Fine. Go. But if you think the Bratva and the Brunos aren't going to be following your every move, you've got another thing coming."

He shakes his head. I'm dying for him to look at me so I can get a sense of what he's thinking, of what our own course of action might be, but he won't make eye contact.

Which tells me that he's thinking the worst possible thing.

27

ARMANI

I MIGHT DIE TOMORROW. I've come to terms with it. There's no way around that simple fact.

The plan coming together in my mind will comprise the biggest risk I've ever taken, and also the option with the lowest chance of success. But it's the one with the greatest potential benefit, far and away, and that's what makes the risk worth it. I just need to pull this thing off.

My family's life and livelihood depends on it.

And if I die trying to save them? At least I'll go down fighting.

I pour myself a few more fingers of scotch and settle back into the leather chair. I've been in the war room all day, plotting and pondering, looking at this impossible situation from every conceivable angle. But there are no clear solutions. Just one hell of a gamble.

It's hard to believe that just days ago, I was actually starting to see a brighter future ahead. I'm going to be a father soon, the sister that my brothers and I thought we'd lost decades ago has miraculously reappeared alive and well, and as for Candi—I've realized that she's the only woman for me. Which has been a long and hard revelation to arrive at.

Any connection I've felt with her in the past has been swiftly pushed away, buried, denied. I told myself that my coldness was an act of self-defense, and that I didn't need anyone. That letting her in was dangerous, and keeping my distance was for the best. This is how I've operated my entire life. Family first, and no room for anybody else. Armor on at all times.

But the truth is, I've been a coward. I've been scared of Candi Gallagher ever since my brother hired her on as a freelance distributor for Bellanti Vineyards. I still remember the first time we met, when Dante made me attend her onboarding meeting with HR. I'd been expecting to shake our new distributor's hand, welcome her to the fold, and then promptly forget her.

Instead, I haven't stopped thinking about her since.

Candi and I had an instant connection, our eye contact sparking a jolt of electricity, both of us smiling like we were already sharing an inside joke. After that, it was all I could do to walk that fine line between cordiality and shameless flirting whenever I ran into her, but I always forced myself to keep a safe distance between us. Now, I can't believe I deprived myself of her for so long. She's the only woman in my adult life who's made me feel...accepted. Safe.

Home.

She's given me something I used to scoff at the mere idea of; something I never imagined I had any interest in. Something I never believed was even truly possible outside of historical romance poetry and Hallmark movies: unconditional love. And as much as I tried to shut her out, she's slowly but surely smoothed all the rough edges of my stone heart, honed it to a fine polish.

But some broken part of me is still holding back. Even though I know that if I die tomorrow, I'll never get the chance to say I love her.

Yes, I'm aware that I should just tell her now, while I still can. Blurt it out, get it over with, like ripping off a Band-Aid. Yet for some reason, whenever I even get close to spilling my guts, the words won't come out. My throat closes up, my chest goes tight. I shut down.

Because I can't make myself that vulnerable around her, or anyone. It's dangerous. Imprudent. Irrevocable. And I can't shake the conviction that admitting how I feel will make me weaker, somehow. Less invincible, less powerful, less in control.

If I say "I love you" out loud, I'll be giving Candi a form of power over me. It's more than that, though. Saying the words makes the emotions real, it puts them out in the world. If I don't acknowledge them, I can keep denying them. And I can't be hurt if she walks away.

Or if my enemies take her out.

How long can I keep running from her, though? How many times can I keep pushing her away before she turns her back on me for good? She doesn't deserve any of it. She deserves better. A decent man wouldn't keep hiding, but then...I'm not sure I'm a decent man.

I am, however, a man who lives by a code. A code that's tattooed right over my heart, in thick black ink. *Famiglia, onore, forza.* Family. Honor. Power. This is my code. All the things I live for, fight for. The things I'm willing to die for.

There's no way around this war but straight through it, and if I don't do something drastic to save my family, there's no telling how hard the Bratva will come down on us. How they managed to fill a wine cask with blood is a mystery I'm still trying to unravel. Our cask room is guarded with a full-time staff. No one is allowed in except employees and members of the immediate family. Yet, somehow, one of the Bratva thugs slipped in and emptied several gallons of what we suspect is cows' blood into the wine. Orloff's men probably cased the whole property while he was here for that wine tasting.

There's no telling what else the Russians are capable of after pulling off something so devious.

The sun went down a few minutes ago, and the light is starting to leave the sky. I walk out of the downstairs library and head upstairs, nodding at the guards as I go. I've increased security, once again, around the property and at Dante's house to ensure that Bruno and the Bratva can't launch any surprise attacks. Candi is still with Juliana at Frankie and Dante's place up the road, but I'm expecting my wife home soon. For now, I'm glad that she's not here, because I wouldn't be able to plot out my twisted plan if I had to look at her face.

After brushing my teeth and mouthwashing the taste of scotch from my tongue, I slip out of my clothes and step into the shower. I'm trying to clear my mind, but all I can think about is Candi and our unborn child. I have to keep them safe, at all costs.

No matter which way I've looked at it, I've only come up with two viable courses of action—and I don't like either of them. Option one: I give Juliana, my only sister, back to the Russians and the Brunos so she can proceed with her wedding and therefore solidify an alliance that will end with the destruction of my entire family. Option two: I keep my sister with us and bring a rain of fire and fury down upon us all. Either way, we all die.

Neither of those choices work for me.

Which is why I've come up with a third option. As I take my time in the shower, I think through my plan. There are parts of it that aren't quite coming together yet, since I can't predict how the Bratva will react, but I'm sure I'll be able to think on my feet once I'm in the thick of it. I always do. Still, there's a sinking feeling eating at my guts as I turn off the water and towel off.

Grabbing my cell phone, I check the time. Good. My lawyer should still be in his office. I dial his personal cell number and he picks up on the first ring. Considering the amount he's paid to be at my beck and call, I'd be surprised if he didn't. I brief him on the situation with as little detail as possible, then tell him I'll be sending an email over shortly, informing him that I need all of my instructions to be implemented before the end of the day.

After we hang up, I grab my laptop and sit on the couch in my sitting room, still in my towel. After composing a very precise email, I send it to my lawyer and CC my entire legal team, then close the laptop and stare out the window. It's almost full dark now, the sky a deep blue, shadows cast around the property. If I had the window open, I could probably hear crickets begin to sing, or birds calling to one another before settling in for the night. The house is hushed and quiet. How many times as a kid did I wish for the house to be this still? I always despised the noise of my brothers running around, my father's yelling, the clamor of the staff.

I never missed that commotion as an adult. Not once.

But I do right now.

In a few months' time, my baby's cries will fill these rooms. Their laughter and first words. The hushed pitter-pat of their shaky first steps.

No, I realize. Somewhere better than this house, some-where safer and more peaceful, where the Brunos and the Bratva won't ever be able to reach my child. Candi will have more than enough money to move into a new place, far from here, wherever she chooses.

Pulling a breath through my nose, a sense of calm comes over me now that everything is in place. I'm going to hold on to this feeling and fill myself with it tomorrow. I'll think of Candi's face. Of my child. And I'll be at peace.

The door opens, and I glance over from the sofa, ready to reprimand one of the new guards for not knocking first, but instead I see Candi stepping into the room.

"Armani? Why are you sitting around in a towel? Not that I'm complaining, it's just..." She looks concerned as she sets her bag on a side table. "Are you okay?"

If only she knew. "I'm fine. How's Juliana doing?"

"Still shaken, but she's settled into her room now. There are guards posted outside her window and at her bedroom door. That made her feel a little better."

"Good." I beckon her closer. "Come here."

She does, and I wrap my arm around her waist and press my forehead to her abdomen. Her hands slide into my hair as the warmth of her body radiates against my skin. I take a deep breath, just soaking up the moment.

Lifting the hem of her shirt, I kiss her soft skin, taking my time as I trail my lips over her belly and below her ribs. When I slide her leggings down, she widens her stance so I can kneel between her legs. I tug her panties to the side and lap at her pussy with my tongue, just enough to tease her. But she's already soaking wet and ready for me, and it's not long before she's digging her nails into my scalp, her soft moans stripping me of my self-control.

My cock is hard and aching as I pick her up and carry her to the bed. She looks up at me with open desire and I let my towel drop first, just to wind her up even more, before I finish undressing her. I could slip right into her like a hot knife through butter, but I want to make this last. So I do.

I start at her feet, then move slowly up her calves, using my hands and mouth to trace and kiss and worship every angle, every curve, every line of her frame. The ticklish backs of her knees, her silky inner thighs, her suckable hipbones. That smooth belly, her rib cage, the underside of her perfect breasts. Her body is a revelation.

For the first time I can remember, I don't have the urge to be dominant or controlling. I want only to memorize her scent, her taste, the feeling of her body beneath me. Most of all, I don't want her to forget me. I'm making a memory she can hold on to forever.

Candi arches against me as I gently knead her nipples, kissing my way back down to the V of her thighs so I can bury my face between her legs. I know I could easily fuck her into an orgasm in two minutes flat, but again, I take my time. Licking, sucking, nibbling. Thrusting my tongue inside her until she's so close I can literally taste it.

That's when I roll over onto my back and urge her to sit

on my face. I want her to ride my tongue, to grind her clit against my nose, to think of nothing but taking her pleasure from me. She's slow at first, hesitant. As if she's never done this before. Maybe she hasn't. For some reason, the thought that I'm the first man to give her oral this way turns me on even more.

I slide my hands up to her hips to guide her, coaxing her to move faster. Her pace starts to increase, and so do her moans. She's hot and slick against my tongue, and I revel in the sweet taste of her juices, encouraging her with lusty groans, making sure she knows how much this is getting me off. The sound of her breathless gasps tells me she's barely hanging on. But I know exactly how to push her off the edge.

Moving my hands to grip her ripe, round ass, I push and pull her over my lips and tongue, harder, faster. *Come for me,* I think. *Come for me now.* She starts to tremble as she grinds, as if she can hear my thoughts, and I can tell she's right on the cusp. Time to finish her off.

I slide one finger to her asshole, circling the puckered skin there just long enough to prepare her, and then plunge inside. She instantly shatters, crying my name. She's coming so hard, I can feel the walls of her pussy contracting around my tongue, her asshole tightening in tandem around my pumping finger. My groans are muffled, my breathing labored, my tongue aching, and my balls have to be bluer than they've ever been, but I don't stop until she's done riding out her climax.

Climbing off me, she curls up on her side and faces me with a dreamy little smirk on her face.

"That was..." But she doesn't finish the sentence. She just shakes her head.

"Amazing," I supply. She nods. "Incredible. Earth-shattering." She nods again. "Your husband is a sex god."

That gets a laugh out of her.

"Maybe," she says coyly.

I should be satisfied, but it's not enough. I haven't given her enough.

Running a finger over her swollen clit, I move her onto her back and then straddle her.

"That's good," she sighs, her eyes fluttering.

I switch to my thumb, rubbing her clit the way she likes as I line up the tip of my cock against her opening. She's soaking wet. I want her so bad, my mouth is practically watering.

"Tell me," I command. I want to hear her say that she wants me. Wants my cock.

But when her eyes open and she locks her gaze on mine, what she says instead is, "I love you, Armani."

A groan works from my throat and I slide into her without even thinking, desperate to connect to her on the deepest level possible. For a moment I stay there, right where I am, buried to the hilt, neither of us breaking eye contact.

"I..." I start to say, but I can't do it.

Because I know this is goodbye. I don't want to make it hurt any worse.

For her or for me.

"I know," she whispers, looping her arms around my neck to pull me down for a kiss.

Breathing her in, returning each gentle kiss, I start to

thrust. Not fast. Not hard. Slow, steady, deep, true. As if I can fuck my love into her. I hope she receives the message.

I hold myself back, keeping the rhythm gentle, letting her make a slow climb to her second orgasm. I kiss her cheeks, her forehead, her chin, her earlobes.

"You're beautiful," I whisper. "My beautiful wife."

"I'm going to come," she whispers back.

"Please come," I beg. For once, it's not a command. "Please, please come. Come for me."

I repeat it like a mantra, witnessing the exact moment the orgasm hits her, filing it away in my memory like a treasure.

When she's caught her breath again, I pull out of her and flip her onto her belly. I suck my middle finger and then trace a line down the crack of her ass with it, stopping when I reach her tight ring.

"Do you want more of this?" I ask, stroking softly there, making her shiver.

"Yes," she whimpers. "But I've never...done it this way."

"Do you trust me?"

"Yes," she says immediately.

"Then there's nothing to be afraid of. Get on your knees."

She obeys and I get the lube out of the nightstand. She looks over her shoulder at me and watches as I get my dick ready for her, every inch as slick as possible. Then I lube her ass, my movements precise but gentle, never rushed. Once she's dripping wet, I slide my finger into her hole halfway, preparing her for what's to come. At her sharp intake of breath, I stop.

"You okay?"

"Yes," she says, her voice strained. "More."

I push my finger the rest of the way in, feeling her clench.

"Shh," I say soothingly. "Try to relax."

She takes a deep breath and then releases just enough for me to rotate my finger.

"Ah," she gasps. "Do that again."

I let her call the shots, let her stay in control, giving her small tastes of pleasure until I can feel that she's ready.

I move close behind her and she makes a soft sound of agreement as I nudge against the tight rosette between her perfect ass cheeks. With all the care in the world, I slowly, carefully work my way inside. Never hurrying, taking breaks when she tenses up until I can feel her relaxing again, letting me in deeper. Surrendering herself to me, inch by agonizing inch.

A low moan that I've never heard before spills from her as I finally fill her ass completely. Both of us are breathing hard. Black edges my vision, my body on fire with the hot, compressive pleasure of her tightness around my cock. Fuck. I don't want to hurt her, and I need to make it last, so I make my thrusts as shallow as possible, taking my time as she adjusts.

Sliding my hand around her hips, I find her clit and roll it gently between my fingers as I increase my pace. Soon, she's thrusting back against me, seeking more. Wanting more.

Wanting it all.

So I give it to her.

"Yes," she whimpers. "Oh my God. Yes, yes, yes."

I lose myself in the feel of her, the dance of our bodies,

the sound of her moans. When she orgasms, she screams my name, her face buried in the pillow. The hot, tight squeeze of her ass pushes me over the edge before I can slide out, forcing me to spill my seed inside her.

The climax hits me like an earthquake, a tidal wave, a nuclear explosion. I can't move. I can barely see or breathe. My heart expands, warm and elated, even as something inside me dies.

Because this is the last time.

And all I can do is hold her tight afterward, promising myself not to think about anything besides the feel of her in my arms.

CANDI

There was such a sense of finality in the way Armani touched me last night. He was slow, purposeful, gentle. Utterly focused on my pleasure, barely interested in his own. I was so caught up in the moment that my intuition didn't start tingling until I woke up this morning and realized: he didn't fuck me last night. He made love to me.

Like it was the last time.

Like it was goodbye.

Now, I can't shake the fear that he's about to do something very dangerous.

If not for Juliana asking me to meet her at Frankie's house ASAP, I would have stayed by Armani's side today. But he'd insisted that I go see Jules, said he had a bunch of important work meetings to deal with anyway, and swore he'd see me later tonight. The thing is, I don't believe him. Not for a second. I'm not even sure he's going into the Bellanti offices at all. I wish I could send a security team to follow him today and make sure he doesn't do anything stupid.

When I get to Frankie's, Juliana meets me at the door and silently leads me to the sitting room with an urgency that does nothing to ease my mind.

"Sit down," she commands once we're in the room.

I drop into a chair, a sense of dread washing over me. "What is it? What's wrong?"

She shakes her head. "Everything."

"Okay, fair, but what's so urgent? You're scaring me right now."

Taking a drink of her coffee first, she turns the mug in her hands nervously and then looks back up at me and blurts, "I have to go back."

My limbs go cold. "What? No. You can't. Jules—"

"There's no other way to stop what's coming."

Desperate, I get up and kneel in front of her chair, taking her hand and pressing it to my heart. "Please. I need you here, Juliana. And in a few months, you're going to be an auntie, and this baby needs you, too. We all need you. We're your *family*."

She smiles, just a little.

"I still can't believe you're going to be a mom," she whispers. "And believe me, there's nothing I want more than to be a part of your baby's life...but if I don't do this, none of us will survive to see his or her first birthday."

"There must be some other way. Maybe we can broker another truce, or—"

"How well did that work out last time?" she points out. "It won't stick. Sergio completely disregarded the contract he signed before, and if he's forced to sign something again, he'll break the terms again. Nothing is going to deter him from executing his plan to take out the Bellantis. He thinks it's the only way the Brunos in Italy won't have him killed. And he's probably right."

My stomach sinks. "I'm not agreeing with you. But what are you thinking?"

"I have a part to play. Unless we want all the Bellanti casks to be filled with blood, or worse, I need to go back to Maxim and pretend I don't know anything about my true identity. I'll just slap on a smile, go along with Sergio's plans for this wedding, and figure it out from there."

I rock back to sit cross-legged on the carpet. I feel sick. As much as I hate what Juliana is saying, I can't come up with an alternative course of action that seems like it would actually work better than what she's suggesting.

Not only that, but I know my friend all too well, and when she's set her mind to something, there's no stopping her. She's going to do this with or without my blessing.

"We should talk to Armani first," I tell her.

"Pfft. Are you kidding? The guy's in overprotective big brother mode and he'll never let me leave this property if he knows what I'm planning. I need to do this without his knowledge. Once things have settled down, I'll reach out and explain it to him. I'm sure he'll be pissed, but too bad. I can't just sit back and let the Brunos tear apart my family for the second time."

"I don't like this. You're throwing yourself to the wolves."

"There's no other way," she says. "I've made peace with it. Once I'm officially Maxim's wife, I'll try to sway him to leave the Bellantis alone. Maybe even convince him to turn the Russians against the Brunos. Sergio's not the only one who can break an agreement."

The plan is iffy, at best. We both know it.

We lapse into silence, both of us lost in our own heads. I feel her anxiety taking up the most space in the room. Like a true Bellanti, she's not afraid to sacrifice herself for the greater good of her family. Even if she only reunited with that family less than 48 hours ago. Amazing.

Finally, I let out a long breath.

"Okay, so let's say you do go back. How do you plan to pull that off without getting yourself killed?"

"Oh, don't worry. I've been up all night thinking about that. I figure the best move is to play Bridezilla. Throw a hissy fit about how they ruined my 'relaxing spa week' with the blood-in-the-wine stunt. Maxim won't even think twice about why I've been avoiding him."

"You really think that's going to work?"

"Of course. Maxim and his men don't know me. They think I'm just another spoiled mafia princess, so that's what I'll give them. I'll pitch a fit that my R&R time was ruined, complain about how the stress is making my skin break out right before the wedding, cry because I've gained two pounds. It's all about me, you know? Maybe I'll break a vase."

"I guess that...*could* work," I admit.

"I'm also going to bitch about the fact that all the hours I've spent grooming you as a spy are now in the garbage—because your husband has locked you up for safety after the blood incident, hence making you unavailable to me. So now, not only have I lost my spy, but I've also lost my matron of honor."

"You don't want me to come to the wedding?"

"It's not safe, Candi. Especially not with the baby. But

we can figure it out later." She shrugs. "I can always say that you managed to convince Armani to let you attend."

"Okay. So...when are you planning to go back to Orloff?"

"When my alleged spa week is over—another few days, I guess. That's when Maxim will be expecting me to turn up."

I still think we should involve Armani, and regardless of what Juliana wants, I'm going to let him know about her plan. I don't care how mad she'll be when she finds out I told him. Maybe he'll be able to think of a way out of this.

"What about after the wedding?" I ask softly. "What will you do? Are you going to tell him you're a Bellanti? What if he takes you to Russia and you get stuck there?"

She shakes her head, her eyes glittering with unshed tears. She quickly swallows and runs a hand over her eyes. "I'll figure it out. Just like I always do."

Those nine words seem to sum up our conversation, and she goes tight-lipped after that. Her gaze drifts out the window and I recognize that she's turned inward and needs to be alone. I hug her and tell her to call me later. Truthfully, I need time to think about this myself.

And Armani's going to help me think it through.

On my drive back to the Bellanti estate, I call his work number, but his assistant says he's not in the office.

"Did he come in this morning?" I ask.

"No. Mr. Bellanti took the day off."

Shit.

I try his cell, twice, but he doesn't pick up. After I park in front of the house, I rush through the door and upstairs to the bedroom. The guard standing in the

259

hallway gives me a nod. It's a good sign. Armani must be inside.

When I open the door and step into the sitting room, I hear a shuffling sound from the bedroom. I'm nearly overcome with relief.

"Thank God you're here," I say, crossing the room to the bedroom doorway. "I just talked to Juliana and—"

A packed suitcase sits on the end of the bed. Next to it, garment bags are neatly laid out, along with...my laptop bag. Another bag holds my cosmetics case and a variety of toiletries stick out from the top. Armani breezes out of the closet with an armload of shoeboxes. My shoeboxes.

Nausea roils in my gut. Are we fleeing the Brunos? Going on another "honeymoon"?

"What is this?" I ask. "Where are we going?"

"*We* are not going anywhere. Our arrangement is over, effective immediately. My lawyer will meet with you tomorrow. A condo has been leased for you here in Napa, but you're welcome to find a place of your own choosing, which your support payments will cover in full."

Dumbstruck, I can only stare at him. There are still months left of our "arrangement." Why is he kicking me out now? What the hell changed?

"I don't understand," I murmur, so shocked that I'm having trouble processing.

"It's over. Done. I can't make it any clearer than that." His voice is bitter. "We had an arrangement, and I'm ending it early. You need to be out today."

Swaying on my feet slightly, I press my hand against the wall to hold myself steady.

"No. You don't want this. You're just...pushing me away

in self-defense. You're panicking over everything that's happened. You don't really want me gone."

He nails me with a glare. "I do, Cassandra. There's no question."

"But...what about our baby? We're still working on the nursery, we're—"

"The baby will be well taken care of and provided for, for the rest of their life. And so will you. Stop trying to guilt trip me. You're leaving. End of discussion."

Pushing away from the wall, I walk toward him. He puts a palm out to stop me.

"You're not going to change my mind. My decision is final. What's done is done."

He says it with no emotion, as if he's not talking about us at all, but a simple business transaction. A month ago, a week ago, I might even believe that he still felt that way about our relationship. But not anymore.

That's how I suddenly know with 100% certainty that my suspicions are correct. That he really is planning something dangerous. This is his attempt to get me out of the way.

To save me.

I stand straighter. "I know you love me. Even though you can't let yourself say it. And you love this baby, too. Don't push us away."

"I'm keeping the cat," he says coolly. "They don't allow pets at the condo. Mr. Sprinkles will be well cared for until you make other arrangements."

He's keeping my cat. The absurdity of it is almost enough to make me laugh, but it's too late because I'm already crying.

"Armani, please. Don't do this."

I try to touch him, but he shoves my hands aside. I try again and he grabs me by the upper arms to keep my hands pinned to my sides.

"If this is really over, why won't you let me touch you?"

"Because I don't want you!"

"I don't believe that," I tell him. "You *do* want me. And I want you, too. I want to be with you. I want to stay. Whatever is going on, whatever you're about to do, I want to be at your side for it."

"It doesn't matter what you believe or what you think you know. All you need to be concerned about right now is taking care of our child."

The lump in my throat gets bigger. "Just tell me, then. What are you planning?"

The question hangs between us before he finally looks away and brushes past me.

"Goodbye, Candi."

29

ARMANI

THIS IS ARMANI BELLANTI. I'd like to talk. Tell me when and where to meet you.

I sent the text message to Maxim Orloff late last night, and he'd responded almost immediately with an address and a time.

Now, driving myself to the meetup point, I'm having a hard time focusing on what's ahead. Because my mind keeps straying to what's behind me.

A wife, a baby on the way. Brothers and a younger sister —a sister only discovered and welcomed back into the fold a few days ago—as well as sisters-in-law and a niece.

But if I die today, I'll die knowing I sacrificed myself for my family. And the Bellantis will thrive. Without me, my brothers will finally be able to quit the mafia for good.

Yes, my brothers (and Juliana) will have to sell off the winery, the house and the acreage, the horses, the Abbott B&B and the vineyards, all of it. But then they'll split the proceeds and get to leave the country to go live quiet, normal, comfortable lives. Candi and our child will inherit my share, so they'll be just as comfortable.

I've already handled the legal channels with my lawyer. My will has been changed. Business documents updated. Everything signed in my hand. The legacy I've structured will stand up in any court of law, even if my brothers try to contest it. Not that they would. I've made things extremely fair, and the logistics are very precise. It won't be a headache for anyone. I consider that going out on a high note.

The address Orloff provided is outside of town at the old industrial park. The buildings here are run-down and dilapidated. Businesses started moving out a few decades ago when a larger, nicer industrial area was developed in Napa. Now, the place is abandoned.

I'm looking for an entrance along the rusty, barbed wire-topped fence when my phone rings. I have every intention of ignoring whoever it is, but the name that pops up on my car's info screen is Clayton. The man I sent on a mission to dig up the truth about my mother's death.

I might die today. I can't ignore this call.

"Is this urgent? I'm on my way to a meeting," I say, pulling over.

"I'll make it quick, but you'll want to hear this," he says. "You sitting down?"

My pulse picks up, the hair on the back of my neck prickling.

"As a matter of fact, I am."

"So here's the deal." After pausing for dramatic effect, he drops the bomb: "Sergio Bruno ordered the hit on your mother."

The world tilts on its axis. My ears start to ring. My brothers and I have spent our entire lives navigating the cold, gaping darkness where our mother and sister should have been.

And now I know exactly who's responsible.

"You're sure it's Sergio? You have proof?"

"Literally in my hand. I've got a copy of a recorded conversation from twenty years ago that's so incriminating, it'll turn a jury against Bruno in two minutes flat," he says. "I've also got the testimony of not one, but *two* former associates who cut ties with Bruno *because of this hit*."

"Damn, Clayton. How'd you get them to talk? I know you didn't crack any skulls during visiting hours at a prison."

"I may have let our new friends think I was a cop. A friendly cop. They were keen to talk to me. Said they'll go on the record if I can guarantee that throwing Bruno under the bus will lessen their own time behind bars. So if you know a good lawyer who can help broker them a deal, that'd be grand. I hate making promises I can't keep."

"I know someone. Won't be a problem."

"Brilliant. You're going to like this next part a lot less. Your sister being on the boat that day wasn't some unforeseen complication that forced Bruno to take her in and hide her to cover his tracks. He planned the entire thing *around the kidnapping*. Fucker plotted it for years. He's a fucking ghoul. He wanted her all along. I got the details about the day, but...it's rough."

I can tell by his hesitation that whatever else he knows could destroy me. That once he tells me, there's no going back. This information will be seared into my mind forever. But I've never been one to shy away from the hard truths.

"I want the details," I say, closing my eyes. "Don't hold anything back."

He clears his throat and quietly says, "The day of the hit...Bruno's soldiers boarded the boat first, took care of your mother, grabbed Liliana, and then planted the bomb to destroy any evidence. Your mother was....she was shot. I'm sorry. I was told it was quick. Painless. Your sister was in her arms. She died looking at the ocean. She had a smile on her face. Fuck, I'm sorry, man. I don't know if it makes any difference, but I'd want to know if it were my mother."

The breath goes out of me, my chest hitching. But I also feel a strange lightness in my chest, a weight lifting off my shoulders. I finally have answers about what happened that day. And yes, there is some small measure of comfort in what I know now. Mom didn't suffer. But my sister did. No wonder she blocked out her childhood memories. That day scarred her.

"Thank you," I say, my voice choked up.

This changes everything. Absolutely everything.

Sergio Bruno is going to pay.

As for the meeting with Orloff...I need a new plan, and fast. Thankfully I'm a man who thinks quickly on his feet. The pieces are already coming together.

"Listen, I need to get to this meeting now," I say. "You did good work, man. I owe you. My whole family owes you. I'm going to loop in my lawyer about those inmates, too. I'll have him call you shortly."

I hang up with Clayton, make a quick call to my lawyer, and then drive up to an old security gate that couldn't even keep out a couple kids with cans of spray paint. I can see their amateur graffiti all over the abandoned warehouses.

None of this seems real. It doesn't feel real. Or maybe I'm just shellshocked, still reeling from the information that Clayton just handed me. But I'm on a mission, and nothing is going to stop me.

As I roll through the broken gate, my tires crunch over gravel, broken glass, and random debris scattered over what used to be a parking lot. I leave my car behind a long, low warehouse, brick with broken windows like gaping teeth. A wave of apprehension hits me.

The sensation of being watched is potent as I walk away from my vehicle. Raising my hands in the air to show submission, I head toward the specified warehouse, where a metal door slowly opens. One by one, men appear on the roof and through window casings with various weapons aimed my way. I can feel my probability of survival lessening with each footstep.

"Orloff is expecting me," I say as a man lumbers toward me from the open doorway.

He's huge, dead-eyed, with tattoos covering his skull. I'm not one to be intimidated by looks, but this guy literally radiates death. I'd bet anything he's a Bratva executioner.

"Dobriy den," I say, wishing him a good day with the only Russian greeting I know.

"Put hands over head," he replies.

Well, at least he speaks English.

I do and he pats me down for weapons, which I'm not stupid enough to be carrying, and then rips my shirt open, sending the buttons pinging everywhere like tiny bullets. After he scans my chest, he pushes the shirt down over my shoulders, still scanning me.

"I'm not wearing a wire," I tell him honestly.

The man narrows his eyes and I shrug my shirt back on. There's no sense in trying to close it because all the buttons are gone, so I let it hang. Seeming satisfied, he takes my arm and marches me inside the warehouse. Daylight doesn't reach in here and it's devoid of any electric lighting. Apparently, the Russians are happy to skulk around in the dark.

"Bring him!" Orloff's voice bellows from above.

Glancing up, I spy a catwalk that leads to an upper office. My captor violently drags me up some rickety steps and down a narrow walkway. Then we pass through a caged door. Inside, Orloff sits behind a battered metal desk with his hands folded in front of him.

"Armani Bellanti," he announces jovially, a disturbingly charming grin on his face. "The next time I planned to see you was with my hands wrapped around your throat, yet here you are. Welcome. Apologies for the condition of the place—I haven't had a chance to call a decorator."

With that, he starts laughing. The sound makes my blood run cold. Then he seems to repeat his joke in Russian, because my captor begins laughing as well.

I wait until their chuckles taper off and then say, "Let's get down to business, Orloff. We need to talk."

Spreading his hands, Orloff says, "Or I could just kill you and save my ears from the sound of your voice. It would be much more efficient, no?"

The back of my neck tingles as I hear the footsteps of more Bratva soldiers filing into the room. Glancing over my shoulder, I find six more men lined up behind me. They're almost as huge as my captor, bald or buzzcut, faces marred with tattoos. Dead eyes, every single one.

Turning back to Orloff, I say, "Here's the deal. The

woman you're about to marry is my sister. My biological sister. She's a Bellanti. I'm assuming Bruno didn't tell you, but maybe you're already in on it. Either way, my family just found out. Juliana didn't know either. Bottom line is, this marriage is no longer the deal closer you were looking for."

I wait for his reaction. Orloff's face reveals nothing.

"What do you hope to gain with such a lie, Mr. Bellanti?"

"It's not a lie. I have the DNA results right here."

I slowly reach a hand into my shirt pocket, sliding the folded paper out. When I hand it over, Orloff takes it without looking at it.

"Your fiancée, Juliana Guerra? Her real name is Liliana Ariel Bellanti," I tell him.

"And how did this convenient little mix up come to pass?" Orloff asks, clearly not believing a word I'm saying.

"We thought my sister was dead. She and my mother perished in a boating accident, decades ago. Or so we were told. A bomb destroyed the vessel. Both of them allegedly drowned. My sister's body was never recovered, but it was chalked up to strong tides and how small she was. We never imagined she'd been taken, hidden from us all these years. But...she was."

He motions impatiently for me to continue.

"As for the bombing, we had no idea who was behind it. The police were useless; they closed the case eventually. Nobody got caught. It was a thorn in my father's side until the day he died. My brothers and I rarely spoke of it. But new information has just come into our hands.

"An associate of ours recently met with some of Bruno's

269

former operatives, and my family is now in possession of evidence that proves Sergio not only ordered the hit on my mother twenty years ago, but arranged the bombing in order to kidnap my sister. Those operatives are meeting with a lawyer right now. They plan to share this information with the authorities."

Orloff's jaw works to the side as he finally unfolds the paper and skims the DNA report, but his expression doesn't change. Yet I catch the way his fingers subtly tighten on the paper, his fingernails going pale with the pressure. He's angry, but he's hiding it. Angry at Sergio for lying to him, or for what happened to Juliana, I don't know. Maybe both.

"I'm not sure if the Bratva has a code," I go on, "but among the Italian families, killing women and children constitutes an unforgivable crime, and *stealing a child* as Sergio did is the utmost sin. The alliance you're hoping to make will crash and burn once the Italians learn of Bruno's betrayal. He'll be murdered by his former allies before he can even stand trial."

Suddenly, Orloff gets up to lean over the desk and look me straight in the eye. He's built like an MMA fighter, lean and strong, with the kind of carefully cultivated muscle that makes him quick and lethal. He radiates violence, but I can tell he's also in complete control of himself. It gives me a flicker of hope that I just might be able to reason with him.

If a decade of interrogation hasn't prepared me for this encounter, nothing has.

"Did you think revealing this information to me would save you?" he says. "This is why you're here, yes? To beg me to spare your family?"

"I'm not here to beg for anything. I'm here to save your ass. A gesture as befits one honorable man to another."

"An honorable man. You are using my own words against me. I like it."

"Look, I didn't come here to lie to you—in fact, I originally planned to offer you my family's winery. Because I know a successful, legal business enterprise in America would greatly benefit your operations here. And I thought the only way my family and I could save ourselves was to sell everything we have, take the money, and disappear. But that's not on the table anymore. Because Bruno has signed his own death warrant. It's over for him."

He shrugs. "According to you, Mr. Bellanti. But you cannot predict the future."

"In this instance, I can," I say. "When the Italians find out that Bruno betrayed my father while they were allies, when they hear about the bomb Bruno planted on that boat, how he killed my mother, kidnapped my sister, then kept her identity a secret for twenty years, all for the purpose of employing her as a pawn—Bruno will be *done*. So if you join forces with him, there won't be a single Italian family willing to partner with you. And, worse than that, you'll bring a whole new war upon the Bratva."

"Ah, but what if no one ever finds out? These people who know of Bruno's indiscretions...they could all die tragically," he says, insinuating the worst. "And suddenly."

He's right, of course—if the Bratva kills my whole family, and the two former Bruno associates in jail, it's possible that Bruno's ordering of my mother's execution— and Juliana's kidnapping—could remain a secret forever.

But that's not going to happen, thanks to the letters that

my lawyer is sending to every family who has ever allied with the Bellantis or the Brunos. Complete with copies of Juliana's DNA test, and digital copies of the phone call recording that Clayton just acquired. The news of Bruno's treachery will spread like wildfire. He's dead in the water.

After telling all of this to Orloff, I ask, "Do you really think I came here armed with this information and no plan to use it?"

He laughs. "Threatening blackmail. A quick way for a man to get killed."

"This isn't a threat. It's a series of events that are already in motion, even if you kill me right now. Bruno's crimes *will* be made known, whether you're linked to him or not. Informing you in advance is a courtesy I'm extending because I'm an honorable man, and I believe that you are, too. But maybe you still want to take your chances. I can't stop you. The choice is yours."

"I'm done listening to you, Mr. Bellanti," Orloff says.

I shrug, as if I have no skin in the game.

"That's too bad, because I have some advice for you. Call off the alliance with Bruno. Keep the Bratva from getting pulled into a mob war with the Italians. Then ask your friend Armani Bellanti to arrange a meeting for you with Nicolo Riggante, as a courtesy. This will give you the opportunity to forge a better alliance, one that presents no danger to the Bratva and which your bosses won't be unhappy with. Hell, you might even get a promotion."

I saw the way his brows shot up in recognition when I mentioned Riggante's name, but now Orloff shakes his head as if he can't believe I dared to offer him my advice.

Without warning, he whips a gun out of his jacket and I

find myself staring down the barrel of a Makarov pistol, a favorite of the KGB.

"Did you actually think I would fall for this?"

"Fall for what? I've provided you with information that will enable you to cut ties with Bruno, thereby preventing future strife with the Italians who will soon wage their own war on him for breaking our code. All you have to do is walk away, Orloff. It's that simple."

He cocks the gun.

I don't break eye contact. I don't blink. I'm barely even breathing.

"Alexei!" Orloff's voice booms through the building in a cold, hollow echo.

The door opens and another man hurries inside. They speak in Russian, they laugh, and then my arms are grabbed from behind. The man spins me to face the door.

"Goodbye, Mr. Bellanti," Orloff says. "Alexei will take care of you now."

A gun is jammed into my spine.

I'm done. A dead man. This is it.

But at least I tried.

I gave this meeting with Orloff all I had in a last-ditch attempt to secure my family's safety. But even though I failed, the fight isn't over. My lawyer will execute my plans to take down Sergio Bruno and ensure that all the Bellantis are taken care of. Once Bruno is destroyed, my brothers can finally leave the mob. With their wives and children at their sides, they'll be able to live the lives they've always dreamed of.

As Alexei marches me through the darkened ware-house, I think about my baby being born into such a strong, loving, and tight-knit family, and my heart begins to ease. Dante and Marco will be great substitute fathers. I couldn't have chosen better men for the job.

I'm shoved roughly to my knees, and that's when I realize I've been taken outside.

"Hands behind your back. Count to ten."

Silently, I do. Ten. Nine. Eight.

The gun cocks.

Seven, six, five.

The sound of boots on gravel.

Four.

The air is still. Quiet. I'm on high alert as my whole body strains with tension and rushing adrenaline, as I wait for the impact of a bullet to the back of my head.

Three...

The space behind me feels empty. The oppressiveness of men there is gone.

Two...

The click of a door against a metal frame.

One.

My shoulders tense even tighter as I brace myself. Heart pounding, lungs aching, I hunch into myself for protection, but the blast doesn't come.

There's nothing.

I wait another few seconds. Take a deep, shuddering breath. Slowly get to my feet.

And then I shakily walk to my car, still waiting for the shot to ring out.

It doesn't.

Not when I open the driver side door or when I slip inside. Not when I look back at the building, then start to think the SUV's going to blow up the second I turn the ignition. But that doesn't happen either.

I shift the car into drive and gently tap the gas pedal. Nothing. I'm...free to go.

I don't stop to second-guess why Maxim Orloff is letting me drive away.

I just get the hell out of there.

30

ARMANI

As I DRIVE through the ornate iron gates of Bellanti
Vineyards and head toward the house, resplendent in all its
stately, century-old glory, I realize I've never been happier
to be home.

It's easy to take a place for granted when you see it day
in and day out, but after my meeting with Orloff, it's impossible not to appreciate the beauty of the rolling green acres
of grapevines, the sprawling California live oaks, the stone
outbuildings, our fine ancestral manse. Even the air smells
sweeter, the birdsong sounds more musical.

The house is quiet when I enter, and I'm about to call
Candi's name until I remember that she won't be here.
Because I sent her away, hours ago. My steps falter.

She's probably long gone by now, and I don't have the
first idea where she'd run to. Under normal circumstances,
she'd probably go to Juliana's, but Juliana is at Frankie and
Dante's place. Unless...maybe Candi is there, too.

But even if she is, it's highly unlikely she'll talk to me if I
show up. After every shitty thing I've put her through over

the last few months, every mood swing, every rejection, I wouldn't blame her for slamming the door in my face. I threw her out, told her I didn't want her, that I was divorcing her, and now I expect her to take me back? I'm delusional.

It's almost funny. For the first time since I've known Candi, I don't have a game to play. No ulterior motive. I'm finally free to let my guard down and be with her in a genuine way.

But it's too late.

And it's all my fault.

I suppose it's exactly what I deserve.

A few of my guards follow me up the stairs, but I'm barely aware of their presence.

There's still work to be done. Since I managed to walk out of the meeting with Orloff alive, I need to get on the phone with my lawyer again and debrief him, then find out what his plan is to broker a deal with Bruno's former operatives. But I have no doubt he'll succeed. Sergio Bruno's days as a free man are numbered. His days alive may be numbered even fewer.

I'd expect to feel pleasure knowing these things, but I don't. No amount of retribution or revenge can make up for the loss of my mother, the years without Liliana. All I can do now is move forward. Try to make up for the lost time with my sister and welcome her back into the fold with wide open arms. The thought of that is what finally brings a smile to my face.

When I reach my rooms, I fling open the door and stride into the sitting room, readying myself to call my legal team, but I nearly trip over an empty suitcase lying open on the floor. Stepping cautiously over it, I see more emptied bags piled up as I look through the bedroom doorway. The closet doors are wide open and I can see Candi's clothes hung back up on their hangers, her shoeboxes back on their shelves.

She's unpacked. Why?

I hear a sound from the bathroom—the medicine cabinet banging shut—and hurry that way, but Candi flings the door open and steps out before I get there. Our eyes meet and hold.

"Hi," I say dumbly.

She looks me over, clearly taken aback by my ripped shirt hanging open. Concern washes over her face, but it's immediately replaced by fury.

"How dare you, you asshole!" she yells.

She advances at me, fists swinging. I don't move. I let her have at me. Her small fists pummel my chest with all the effect of a couple of wiffle balls. Still, I wince at the contact, just to make her feel better. No sense riling her up even more.

"Candi. Hey. Please calm down."

"I'm not going to fucking calm down! Frankie told me you tried to pawn me off on her and Dante to start some new life in Italy. What the hell were you thinking?"

Gently grabbing her wrists, I put a stop her energetic but futile assault. "Not just Italy. The *south* of Italy, in the most beautiful—"

"You're a fucking idiot!"

Isn't that the truth?

"It doesn't matter anymore," I tell her. "That whole plan is getting called off. Okay?"

Candi seems nowhere near ready to stop beating me, so I pull her into my arms. She fights me, squirming and trying to push away, but I hold her tight. So tight. I bury my face in her hair and breathe her in until she finally goes still against me.

"Do you hate me?" I ask.

"Of course I do," she says breathlessly. "But...I'm not going anywhere. I don't care what Orloff said or whatever stupid shit you're up to trying to play the hero. I love you, and regardless of what happens with Sergio now or how bad things are going to get, we're in this together."

Closing my eyes, I soak in the feel of her against me.

"I know."

"You're my family," she goes on. "I'm not going to just go off and live my life without you. This baby is not going to live without you."

Threading my fingers in her hair, I hold her tighter. "I hope they won't have to."

"Good. Because this baby needs a father! A decent one! You should know that better than anyone."

I know that, too.

We hold each other tightly and it feels like I'm embracing her for the first time, as if we're starting over. I can't believe I never realized how perfectly she fits against me, the comfort that her body brings.

Her arms finally loosen from around my neck, and she pushes me back.

"What did you do?" she asks, searching my gaze.

I don't even bother trying to lie to her. I'm done with that now.

Taking her hands gently, I tell her all about the

evidence Clayton dug up that incriminates Sergio Bruno in my mother's murder and Juliana's kidnapping. About the consequences Bruno will be facing from the Italians soon, not to mention the justice system. I tell her about how my mom died, gently brushing away the tears that spill down Candi's face as I do. I hold nothing back. Finally, I tell her about the meeting with Orloff, and how I revealed Juliana's true identity and advised him to walk away from the alliance with Bruno before it's too late.

"I have no idea if he believed me or if he thought everything I said was a lie," I admit. "Honestly, I expected him to shoot me in the back afterward, but he let me go. I'm not sure yet what that means."

Candi's eyes widen. "It means your plan worked."

"No. He was skeptical the whole time—"

"Armani, I'm telling you, it *worked*. I talked to Juliana a few minutes ago. Orloff called off the wedding. He's not going to be Bruno's ally."

Goosebumps rise on my arms.

"This isn't a ploy? You're sure he was serious?"

"It sounded like he was serious. He was pretty nice about it, I guess. Apologized for the breakup and told Juliana it was just a business thing, and to go have a nice life without him. Does that mean...that it's over? The alliance, the war, the...all of it?"

"I think it is. We're free to just...live. All of us." I reach down and cup my palm gently over her belly. "Baby too."

"So what happens now?" she asks.

I can't help it. I laugh.

"Anything we want," I tell her. "No more war. No more mob. No more looking over our shoulders. And the best part is, we won't have to raise our child in a mafia family the way my brothers and I were raised. The way Juliana was raised. We get to start a new chapter. Together. If you'll have me."

"Of course I'll have you. And you'll have me. Always." She throws her arms around me, her tears warm against my neck. "I love you."

I close my eyes. My heart feels like it's expanding in my chest. This is everything I want. This woman, this baby, this life.

"I love you," I tell her.

Fuck. I finally said it out loud. And somehow, it was the easiest thing in the world.

"Do you, now?" she asks teasingly, as if my declaration isn't news to her at all.

Cupping her face gently, I kiss her. Softly, purposefully. With every last ounce of conviction inside me.

"More than you'll ever know, Candi."

She smiles against my lips. "Then I guess you're going to have to tell me that every day until I *do* know."

"Every day, for the rest of our lives. That's a promise."

EPILOGUE

ARMANI

THE BED-AND-BREAKFAST IS DECKED out in full holiday regalia. After going back and forth about what to call the place, Frankie's mother Miriam suggested, simply, The Inn. My family instantly and unanimously agreed. I think it suits the establishment perfectly.

Sparkling string lights highlight the ornate architecture of the Victorian farmhouse's freshly restored exterior, and glow from the trees and shrubs on the lawn. Inside, you immediately breathe in the fragrant boughs of fir and pine, the live wreaths studded with pinecones, the clove-studded oranges. There are multiple Christmas trees positioned throughout the house, each decorated with its own different color-coordinated ornaments and glittering garlands, and there are also brass menorahs and electric candles that flicker cozily in each window. The weather report said we might even get a light dusting of snow tonight.

I have to admit, the overall effect is nothing short of magical.

There's a bittersweetness in the air, though, since this

might be the last time we're all together as a family for a while, at least here in Napa. Because after the New Year, most of us will be scattering to the winds.

Frankie's got her heart set on a house in Tuscany where she can cultivate a small vineyard of her very own, so she and Dante are taking baby Lili on a trip abroad for the next few months so they can look at properties and get a feel for the area. Meanwhile, Marco and Karina will be going to Monaco, so Marco can build a top-of-the-line garage and establish a new homebase for his racing career. As for Candi and myself, we're still making plans to explore the world, though we'll have to time our travels around the birth of our baby.

Charlie and Clayton, for their part, are more than happy to celebrate their newfound freedom by simply staying at home in Nob Hill with their new baby—toddler is probably more accurate; his name is Gregory and he was adopted from Ukraine—and Livvie, who just started a program in Equine Studies at Santa Rosa College. Meanwhile, Miriam Abbott is still planning to manage (and live at) the B&B. It's a relief to know the Inn is in good hands.

But that's all in the future. For now, we look like a billboard for a Hallmark channel movie, and I couldn't be more pleased. I honestly can't remember a holiday when my family has been together quite like this. We're gathered around the massive dining table, which has been moved into the sitting room at the rear of the house. The vaulted ceiling makes our conversations echo, filling the space with the sound of happy chatter, and there's a cozy fire roaring in the stone fireplace, with Mrs. Abbott's huge English Mastiff,

Miggy, snoozing on the rug nearby. The ambiance is perfect.

At the other end of the table, I can see Candi talking animatedly with her mother and Mrs. Abbott. Probably something to do with The Inn's upcoming grand opening.

In a shocking turn of events, Mrs. Gallagher—soon to be Ms. Cassandra Sullivan once again—filed for divorce from Candi's father and showed up on our doorstep a few weeks ago with plans to move into a women's shelter and a lengthy, heartfelt apology for Candi. We set her up at the B&B temporarily, but she'd quickly formed a friendship with Mrs. Abbott, and the two have been inseparable ever since. Candi's mother is now formally in training as The Inn's assistant manager, and in the meantime she's shadowing Mrs. Abbott and helping her with just about everything that needs to be done before the place officially opens to guests.

To my left, Frankie is deep in conversation with Charlie and Clayton about the latest real estate listings she's compiled, located in and around Tuscany. At their feet, Lili is "helping" Gregory build a castle out of wooden blocks on the floor. Even though she's mostly just making a mess, Gregory is getting a kick out of her antics. She only recently took her first wobbly steps, and I can only imagine all the trouble they'll get into once they're both fully mobile.

As for Marco and Karina, they're off in the kitchen "checking on the turkey," which probably means "having sex in the pantry" if I know anything about my little brother.

And then there's Dante, standing by the fire next to Livvie and her very new boyfriend Tom, another equine studies major at the college. The kids stopped in to say hello, but they're on their way to Tom's parents' house in Healdsburg—another quaint town known for its wine—for the next few days. Tom's parents aren't in the wine business, but they do own a farm, where they breed horses. Which I know because Dante had me run a full background check on the boy. He's clean. Absolutely no mafia ties of any kind.

From the looks of it, Tom is utterly smitten with Livvie, his blush visible even across the room. He also looks utterly terrified of Dante, who looms over him, interrogating the poor kid with the kind of uber judgmental and incredibly intimidating expression that clearly says, "If you hurt my sister-in-law, I will break all of your fingers."

The only person who's missing from the festivities is Juliana. Though I'm sure she'll be here any minute. She group-texted us all earlier to say she might be running a little late.

Thank God she didn't have to marry Orloff. She's no longer a pawn, and she'll never be one again. She's free to live her life now, just like the rest of us. We've all invited her to join us on our various trips and travels, but so far she hasn't committed. She's been talking about doing her own thing for a few months, then meeting up with me and Candi afterward so she won't miss the birth of her new niece or nephew.

The clock on the mantle strikes six, and everyone says their goodbyes to Livvie and Tom as Mrs. Abbott and the former Mrs. Gallagher bring out the bread and hors d'oeuvres. We're still hopeful that Juliana will be here soon, but for now, we can get started.

"Tom didn't seem so bad," I say to Dante as I butter a hot roll for Candi.

"He's fine," Dante says. "But Livvie can do better. And the kid needs a haircut."

"Oh, stop!" Frankie says, slapping his arm playfully. "I think he's very sweet. Plus, I've never met anybody else who likes horses as much as my sister does."

"He's adorable," Charlie chimes in. "Bit of a nerd, but maybe that's not a bad thing."

"Livvie can stand to be with someone who's studious and focused," Mrs. Abbott agrees. "She's had enough upset in her love life already. I'm happy she's taking it slow with this one."

"They've only been dating a few months. We'll see how long he lasts," Marco says cynically. He's the only person more protective of Livvie than Dante is.

Candi leans her head on my shoulder and whispers, "When should we tell everyone our baby names?"

"Let's wait until dessert is on the table. It'll make a sweet surprise even sweeter."

She giggles. "I love it. I never knew you were so sentimental, Mr. Bellanti."

"There's a lot you don't know about me," I tell her, teasing my hand up her thigh under the table. "But I'd be happy to show you more of myself later."

"In the bedroom?"

"Anywhere you wish."

Soon, the main courses are brought out. We start passing the steaming dishes around the table, loading up our plates. Until suddenly, the sound of the heavy front door slamming has everybody looking toward the hallway.

"I knew it! Livvie changed her mind about spending the weekend with Tom," Dante says with a smirk. "Let's get an extra place setting for her."

But it's not Livvie who strides into the room.

It's Juliana.

My sister is glowing, her dark hair swept up into a glossy ponytail, her ruby red lips matching her knee-length wool coat, her high heels clicking assertively on the hardwood floor.

"You made it just in time!" Candi says, waving Juliana over.

"I said I would be here," Juliana responds coolly.

Her spot at the table is already set and waiting, right next to Candi's. I start to pull out Juliana's chair for her, but my sister waves me off as she studies everyone. With a little chuckle, she steals my glass of wine—a Bellanti red—and takes a long sip, then hands it back to me. We all watch her expectantly.

"Mrs. Abbott, Mrs. Gallagher," she says. "If I might have just a moment with the Bellantis. The adult Bellantis. Privately."

The moms in the room nod, scoop up Lili and Gregory, and bustle off to the kitchen, insisting they were just about to take the pies out of the oven anyway. Clayton starts to rise, but Juliana motions for him to sit back down. I guess he's a Bellanti in her eyes as well.

"Sergio Bruno is dead," Juliana announces, without preamble.

Gasps go around the room. Dante and I exchange a look. I think the only thing either of us is shocked about is the fact that it took this long to happen.

"When? And how?" I ask. "The last I heard, he hadn't left his house in months. I guess it wasn't enough to keep him safe."

"A member of his staff found him in the bathtub this morning. Drowned. The police are calling it an accident," she says. "Funny enough, they found a teddy bear and a toy boat in the tub with him. Odd, isn't it?"

The symbolism of the boat and the teddy bear does not escape Marco, Dante, or myself. Or anyone else in the room. Accident, my ass. This was an honor killing. An execution. Punishment for Sergio's trespasses against the woman he killed and the child he kidnapped.

"Was it the Russians or the Italians?" Dante asks. "Or is that to be determined?"

"Italians. It was another Bruno," Juliana says. "Those are the only people Sergio has been allowing onto the property. It was done by one of his own."

"I can believe it," Karina says quietly. "My uncle didn't exactly inspire loyalty."

"Oh! Speaking of loyalty..." Juliana says. "Be right back."

We can all hear her footsteps echoing down the hall, and she returns moments later with a bottle of vodka in her hands. The label is red and black. It reads Maximum Vodka.

"*Za zdorovy!*" she announces, passing it to Dante. "Cheers."

"What is this for?" he asks.

"Just a little gift from Maxim Orloff. He's gone into the beverage business as well. Apparently he's having a lot of fun with it."

"Is it poisoned?" Frankie asks suspiciously.

Juliana laughs. "Of course not. He sent it to me as a thank you. I thought we could all share it. Maybe have a round of martinis after dinner."

"Wait. A thank you for what?" I ask, alarm bells going off in my head.

"Oh, I forgot to tell you," Juliana says. "I fixed his little green card problem. I felt like I needed to ensure he remains an ally to us. You know how it is with international relations."

Green card problem? Is her wedding to Orloff back on?

Candi glances at me nervously. She must be thinking the same thing.

"And how did you do that?" I ask, almost afraid to hear the answer.

"I found him a new fiancée! Through a matchmaking agency run by an old friend of mine. There's actually quite a market for powerful men looking for specific types of wives. You'd be surprised."

"I've never heard of it," I say. Something about the whole thing feels off to me.

"That's because it's *very* exclusive," Juliana says. "Which is how I was able to find the perfect match. The family Orloff will be marrying into has all the wealth, stature, and respectable business ties a Russian mobster could ever dream of—she's a Vanderchild, of the banking Vanderchilds. Orloff is very pleased with the arrangement. I wish I could say more, but I signed an NDA. So. Shall we raise a toast to our continued successes, in love and war?"

With that, Juliana steals my wine again and sits in her chair, holding up her glass.

For a moment, we all just sit there in stunned silence.

And then everyone starts talking all at once, laughing and chattering, raising glasses of water and wine and cranberry juice (that would be my very pregnant wife, of course).

Candi's mom and Mrs. Abbott come back into the room with the kids then, someone turns on a Christmas music radio station, and suddenly we're all joining hands around the table.

"Who'll say grace?" Mrs. Abbott asks.

"I will," I say, surprising everybody.

Heads bow, and I begin.

"God, we thank you for...for this moment. This time. The guidance and protection we've been granted, especially these last few months. You've kept us safe and healthy and humble, and that's no easy task when it comes to an Italian family."

Quiet laughter goes around the table.

"We are grateful for all the abundance in our lives—not just material things, but the intangibles that matter to us most," I go on. "Love. Strength. Security. It is a privilege to have these things, and we are blessed to be able to share them with each other. In the name of *famiglia*, *onore*, *forza*. Family, honor, and power. Amen."

"Amen."

Under the table, Candi reaches for my hand and gives it a squeeze. Then she carefully places it over her round belly, pressing it against the firm curve.

That's when I feel it. A kick. A strong, joyful kick. One that speaks to the promise of new life, that makes my chest expand with the enduring love I feel for my beautiful wife and the baby we'll soon bring into this world.

It's nothing short of a miracle.

Stay tuned for an all new spinoff featuring Juliana Bellanti, Forbidden Offer...

Coming up next, Stella Gray returns to the Zoric world with The Client.

She was a gift I didn't want.
But now I want to keep her forever.

Sign up for our newsletter to never miss a release.

PAIGE PRESS

Paige Press isn't just Laurelin Paige anymore...

Laurelin Paige has expanded her publishing company to bring readers even more hot romances.

Sign up for our newsletter to get the latest news about our releases and receive a free book from one of our amazing authors:

Laurelin Paige
Stella Gray
CD Reiss
Jenna Scott
Raven Jayne
JD Hawkins
Poppy Dunne
Lia Hunt
Sadie Black

ALSO BY STELLA GRAY

The Zoric Series

Arranged Series

The Deal

The Secret

The Choice

The Arranged Series: Books 1-3

Convenience Series

The Sham

The Contract

The Ruin

The Convenience Series: Books 1-3

Charade Series

The Lie

The Act

The Truth

The Charade Series: Books 1-3

The Bellanti Brothers

Dante

Broken Bride

Broken Vow

Broken Trust

Marco

Forbidden Bride

Forbidden War

Forbidden Love

Armani

Captive Bride

Captive Rival

Captive Heart

ABOUT THE AUTHOR

Stella Gray is an emerging author of contemporary romance. When she is not writing, Stella loves to read, hike, knit and cuddle with her greyhound.

Made in United States
North Haven, CT
19 January 2024

47665370R00189